AN ANSWER FOR PIERRE

This is the story of a man who, in the turmoil of our time, seeks to renew his spiritual moorings. Jacob Harald cannot accept the idea (so widespread at the close of the millennium) that objectively seen, nothing is either good or evil, and that to call things right or wrong is just a matter of social custom or individual preference. When he is confronted with fathomless corruption, he is driven to search for an ethical standard beyond the human. He looks to the new science for help, to a new concept of the sacred. Can it be that a powerful ethical imperative rises from the very depth of the cosmos? We see Jacob's struggle against a background of human relationships: his marriage, the alienation of his children, and his harrowing friendship with the enigmatic Pierre, who sends him on the most desperate quest of his life.

*   *   *

Gretl Keren Fischer (née Kraus) was born in Olomouc, Czechoslovakia (now Czech Republic). She spent twelve years, including World War II, in London, England, and came to Canada in 1951. She studied English Literature, earning degrees at the University of British Columbia and at Carleton University, where she taught for many years, and in 1972 received her Ph.D. from McGill. Sporadically, she has published short stories, poems, and literary criticism.

An Answer for Pierre

by

Gretl Keren Fischer

Borealis Press Ltd.
Ottawa, Canada
1999

mine alone. I also thank all those who contributed to the physical production of this book.

To my publishers, Professor Glenn Clever and Professor Frank Tierney, I here express, with a very special Thank You, my gratitude for their confidence in my book and for their help.

Contents

At The Lake

I

There are certain questions a modern mind generally prefers to leave unanswered; and Eve Harald had a distinct feeling that just now, her husband had asked one of them. It was followed, inevitably, by a pause; not a pregnant pause full of competing thoughts but a rather empty, helpless moment of indecision.

They were sitting in deep, comfortably upholstered cedar chairs at the edge of the lake, and for a time they had been quietly watching the miraculous play against the dark. Chilled into cold luminosity, light from the hidden star seemed afloat on the water—a gently shifting trail of liquid moon glistening toward them. In a strange amalgam of contentment and longing, it evoked the summer nights of their youth. To capture this luminous tranquillity and make it stay, and yet to feel restlessness like an anticipation, like a promise. . . .

Eve Harald would have liked to remain silent. I want to absorb this, she thought. She didn't know how, but she wanted it to become part of herself and to be part of *it*—this indefinable splendour; and she had a great desire to reach out, somehow, to do something wonderful in this transparent night. Usually, such thoughts led to their long kisses, to their bodies thrilling against each other. But tonight this was not possible. They were not alone. And now her husband had broken the silence and had asked one of those awkward questions.

A clear voice came to them from across the lake. It called once, a second time, and then again. "I wonder whether this could be a heron," she said. There was no reply. None of them knew. They were city people who had come to stay at one of the cottages over the long Thanksgiving weekend. They knew very little about the birds of the place, or its geology, or the slow murder in the underbrush and the precarious life in the lake. They were simply grateful to be here. A good part of the day they had spent gazing at the wilderness, just revelling in the colour—the intensity of it—and breathing, breathing much more deeply than they ever did in town.

Jacob Harald had recently retired from a university where he had been a professor of English, and he hoped to spend his summers and the long weekends working the cottage garden with his wife and exploring topics that interested him, but which he could only now study with sufficient leisure. He wanted to read as much as possible. Now, at last, he was able to read freely, blissfully unhampered by obligations to make notes for future lectures or learned articles. He had worked out a systematic plan to study the archaeology of the East Mediterranean littoral, and later, provided their modest reserves (invested mostly in government savings bonds) would yield sufficient interest, he hoped they might travel to the Middle East and visit unhurriedly some of the famous archaeological sites. It was something he and his wife dreamed about.

The strange, cold voice from across the water called again. "Such a poor bird," said Pierre. "He sounds—" and there was a disconcerting pity in his voice, "so alone." No one replied.

Jacob Harald felt the embarrassment of people who are suddenly taken into someone's innermost confidence, unprepared to share his grief; and his wife, though she groped for a soothing phrase, felt herself go blank. She had nothing to say. Then she looked at her husband. Evidently, he was still waiting for a reaction to his question.

"Yes, I agree with you," she said to him. "It *is* of paramount importance; but let's be honest: does anybody we know think about it seriously? I mean, it's such an uncomfortable subject."

"I, for one, don't know anyone else who would consider it a topic for conversation," Pierre said; and he added with unexpected levity, "Nevertheless, deep down in a very dark nook of the mind, there is the question of immortality, and it is permanently hooked into everybody's fibre—as if one had swallowed a question mark." At this all three of them laughed.

"And what about you?" asked Eve, looking straight into Pierre's deep-set eyes, assessing with earnest clinical detachment the state of nerves behind that pale, lean face with its sharp nose. "Do you personally consider it a topic for conversation?"

He smiled, his habitual sarcasm ready to pounce. "It's of no consequence to me. Whether people talk or think about it, after all, doesn't change the facts. Maybe we should use our energies where we can have some influence. Everything else is a waste of time. Probably."

Jacob Harald shook his head: "I know you too well. You don't really mean this, do you?"

But Pierre remained unmoved: "I sell washing machines, remember? My concern is whether that little single mother ought to choose a top-of-the-line model with fluorescent light, a deluxe bleach dispenser, and a cycle with ten choices, or whether the least expensive model will be just as useful to her and save her money. I worry about that, even though my boss would like to sell her the most expensive machine and have done with it. Never mind if it takes her I don't know how many years to pay for it. Those are the things that concern me. That's something I know about. What good would it do if I brooded over questions of immortality? I know nothing about it. You are a professor; and your opinions in this are no better than mine. So—?" He spoke with a bitterness more harsh than his friends were used to, although they had plenty of experience with his ill-humour, his erratic moods, his occasional outbursts. Eve came to the rescue. "All of which does not change the fact that it's of paramount importance."

"Is it? Is it?" Pierre taunted her with his tone more than with his words.

Enough, Jacob Harald thought, and he got up. "It's getting quite cool now. I think we'd better turn in." Eve and Pierre rose at once. As they walked towards the cottage, Jacob said, "The important thing is that we keep on asking, that we are not shamed into silence."

A faint lamp above the veranda welcomed them back to questions of strictly human dimensions.

*   *   *

Next morning they wakened to bright sunlight and the mellowness of Indian summer. Mr. McIntyre, their neighbour, passed the cottage with his Labrador mongrel. He was returning from the corner store two miles down the road and taking a shortcut, which brought him within shouting range. "This's got to be the warmest Thanksgiving Day folks around here remember!" he called out by way of a greeting as he caught sight of Eve, who was standing at the sink by the kitchen window. She smiled and nodded: "Isn't it glorious?" He brandished a pint of cream: "Unexpected guest! Good job that Chinese fellow keeps his store open on Thanksgiving."

"Enjoy!" Eve called back as Mr. McIntyre disappeared among the trees; and she returned to her carrots. She loved getting fresh, young carrots ready for the cole slaw.

In the Rideau Lake system, the waters were still and so mild that the Mazzini children, who lived near the point, went swimming, and in the distance one could hear their laughter and shouts and shrieks as they dove from the rocky juts and splashed around the wharf.

At the Harald cottage, everybody helped to create the Thanksgiving dinner. It was vegetarian, simply prepared but festive. There was an abundance of dishes, some made from heirloom recipes and some newly discovered ones with exotic names like Armenian tourlou or minted raita. They were made from wholesome ingredients that had been selected with expert care and garnished with fresh, home-grown herbs; and their honest, natural colours were as inviting as the fine aroma that scented the air even beyond the garden gate, where a family of sleepy raccoons took note. Little jokes and friendly commands passed between the three people as they worked in magnificent harmony.

At noon, the dinner was served in the kitchen of the old cottage, and as they settled down to eat the good food and looked about the well-scrubbed place, the Haralds felt immense contentment. Never, never would they get tired of admiring the rough cedar walls, the large, horizontal logs bonded one upon the other by layers of white chinking, which could be seen both indoors and outside. They would never want to part with this old kitchen table of sturdy maple wood that had come with the cottage. And they loved the place almost as if it were an animate creature. And Jacob, who enjoyed a nicely set table, noticed with pleasure that Eve had brought out the bright, coarsely woven mats, his favourites from Quebec, and that she had filled the little majolica vase (a souvenir that reminded him of a long-ago, wonderful day in Florence) with blue and yellow flowers. They were late wildflowers she had found on their weedy lawn.

As bowls and platters were passed from one to the other and they made light conversation with Pierre, the Haralds exchanged glances, and each of those glances cried, "In all of this I love you."

* * *

When the leftover food was cleared away and the few, quick chores were done, a deliciously idle afternoon stretched before them. They walked along the lake, not speaking much. The apple trees in the cottagers' gardens were speckled with crimson and yellow and purple. The brilliant days declining before the frost had left the butternuts like a lacework of black-veined gold, and on the surrounding hills, where fiery sumac and evergreens crowded birches and maples and beech, the forest stood glowing.

Their path led into sunlit woods, and a sweet fragrance and moist, fecund warmth rose from soil and bark. From time to time, they stopped and looked up: intricate patterns of leaves—translucent in auburn or flame or scarlet against a cloudless, forget-me-not-blue sky. And once, in a shady spot, Eve discovered a little tree frog under a leaf. They thought they had never seen anything zoological so intensely green, such an inexpressibly beautiful, pulsating jewel. Eve wanted to float through the air in great big leaps like the lemurs of Madagascar she had loved in a documentary, primeval man dancing through a forest of paradise. She wished she could sing, own a voice that could soar jubilantly. She wanted to embrace everything. And she spread her arms toward the sun on the high branches.

The path was narrow, and Pierre was walking ahead of them as they stepped into a clearing on the bluff. From here, one could see a small, pine-covered island beyond the promontory. Two canoes were gliding toward it, leaving smoothly expanding ridges on the surface of the lake. It was at this moment that Pierre turned and faced his friends. They smiled encouragingly, expecting him to express his delight at the view; but his face was impenetrable, and suddenly he asked: "Why did God forsake the Jews in Auschwitz?!"

For a moment, Jacob and Eve stood motionless. The obscenity of the word hung in the air like a stench. Then Jacob said, in a voice more severe than he intended, "For me, such a question cannot exist. It has no meaning."

An insect in shimmering armour settled fleetingly where the sun was warm on an outcrop of granite.

Pierre's face remained perfectly impassive. He shrugged his shoulders and slowly walked away, back into the forest, lightly touching the branches of bushes and conifers as he went.

II

For several nights after that, Jacob Harald found himself without sleep. This is not to say that he was entirely without rest. He was a busy man whose retirement had freed him to toil three times a week at a local soup kitchen, where he obeyed grudgingly the ever-efficient instructions of Mrs. Weymouth, the lady in charge of the volunteers. The kitchen committee needed, desperately, a pair of hands to help with the potatoes and sandwiches, and Jacob Harald got a certain satisfaction out of doing humble jobs for the unemployed men and the mothers on welfare who came for their midday meal with their babies and peripatetic infants. He also served as secretary on a senior citizens' committee that was supposed to advise City Hall on housing and social services, and he was treasurer of an organization that supported the symphony orchestra. When these voluntary punishments did not enslave him, he read books on archaeology, or he was walking with Eve or swimming at the local public pool. So, at night, when he put his head on the pillow, he was tired enough to drift at once into a sullen sleep. But every night, just before dawn, he suddenly wakened, and then he lay sleepless until morning.

Eve seemed to know by osmosis how plagued he was. She would open her eyes for a moment: "Can't you sleep, my darling?" but never stayed for a reply. Jacob looked at her peaceful unconsciousness. His envy was tender, as if she were a sleeping child. "Where are your wrinkles now?" he murmured, his eyes groping through the dark to find her utterly youthful face.

Sometimes he thought making love could release him into sleep, and they made love; and when Eve's body received him and, at last, when he could feel her grateful fingers in his hair, there was a lightness, and his worries drained away. But still, sleep eluded him for the rest of the night.

When the Haralds returned to the cottage at the lake for the weekend, Jacob was sure the country air would make a difference, and he tested his vigour exerting himself unsparingly, sweeping the floor and turning the sod for a bed where he wanted to plant raspberry canes in the spring. Yet, even here: it was five o'clock in the morning, and again he could not sleep.

Eve's hair—loose, flowing over the pillow, and her slender hand lightly touching her cheek . . . so gracefully. Now she curled like a little animal, eternally young. He felt the warm haze radiating from her, and he wanted to gather her up so that she would be absorbed by him and in turn absorb him in her peace that was a kind of inward gladness. And then again, he was conscious of his stomach or his nerves or his bowels or his chest, questioning where the sleeplessness had its source but not why it was dominating him, undeniably there, something that prevented him from touching her.

*   *   *

Sleepless nights, one after the other, endless debilitating repetition. . . . How can I make this night different? *Mah nishtana ha-leila ha-zeh mikol halaillos? Why is this night different from all other nights?* My thoughts are sliding into another groove. Hebrew words recited as a child at the family table on the night of the Passover Seder, at the moment when slavery and deliverance are solemnly remembered. . . . It *is* possible to free oneself. I have to remember this. And the knowledge that freedom is attainable anchors deep in the red sea of my arteries. . . .

Where the hairline meets her temple and the hair sweeps away, gentle and proud . . . the spot where I kissed her for the first time . . . on that dim landing between two deserted flights of stairs leading from the lecture room . . . in the Vancouver twilight . . . . My thoughts were strictly on my supper: what to buy—pickled herring or a little steak. And walking ahead of me, she suddenly stopped, convinced (as she later confessed) that I was scheming to kiss her, sure that I was only waiting for her to give a signal, show a willingness; and so, to my surprise, she suddenly turned toward me as I came to a halt, and offered her face, pressing her cheek against my chest . . . offered her mouth. Of course, the way things were, I had to think of my position, the complex difficulties lying in wait. . . . What could I do? I kissed only that special place—the gentle and proud sweep of hair from her temple. . . . I want to kiss it now. I am thirsty for it. But is Mohammed not reputed to have cut off with his sword a corner of his coat so that the cat that was resting on it might not be roused from her sleep when he walked away? And am *I* to disturb the slumber of Eve? Involuntarily Jacob gave a sigh, and this time she rallied.

"Old worry-guts," she said, smiling at him as she propped herself up, ready to deal with the matter at hand in an energetic manner. "Are you still thinking about Pierre? Is that what still bothers you?"

"I don't know."

"Look, it's not the first time he made a scene."

In Jacob's reply brooded a great, uncharted sadness: "He didn't make a scene."

"Exactly," Eve said. "So he wasn't very talkative after our walk. So he preferred to go home by bus. What's so terrible about that? He wanted to be home early. And we did have an awful lot of kitchen stuff in the car. You really can't blame him for wanting to be more comfortable. All those leftover casseroles. Maybe he was afraid I would press him again to keep some of them if he let us drive him to his door. You know how he is. . . . A well-to-do person would accept and enjoy."

Jacob Harald was astonished at his grating uneasiness when he finally was able to formulate it. "Pierre asked us a question," he said. "And he didn't get an answer. Not a very good one, at any rate."

* * *

The very fact that she did not have to inquire which of the many questions that had come up troubled her husband's mind was enough to make Eve recognize the depth to which she, too, felt involved in their failure. "What on earth could you have told him?" she asked.

Jacob said, "I don't know what I should have told him. I wish I knew."

"We'll ask him over next week, and you can make it up to him," she suggested. "We'll discuss it with him."

"No, not next week. It's too pushy. Maybe he doesn't want to come again so soon." In pleading for time, Jacob knew he was less concerned with Pierre's feelings (for Pierre was lonely enough to jump at any invitation) than with his own inadequacy. He had to come to grips with his own thoughts, with snatches of information, glimpses of inspiration that had floated through his consciousness over the years, with mountains of reading matter that had crossed his desk. "Not yet, not next week."

He turned and at last dozed off while Eve carefully adjusted the duvet along his back.

* * *

Jacob and Eve were convinced that their thinking was in great harmony, although neither of them quite knew what right they had to this assumption. There was no recent proof. Way back, before their marriage, they had discussed religion and all sorts of philosophies; but since then, they each had been cutting trails into a jungle of ideas, sometimes casting their curiosity into far-flung territories and remote periods of history, and sampling the luxuriant flora (some of which, admittedly, displayed rather beastly characteristics) from lectures and novels and plays and poetry; and nowadays they rarely discussed religion precisely because of that underlying instinct that they shared a secure home base.

It was then somewhat of a surprise to Eve when Jacob, after lunch, asked her whether she knew what Pierre's concept of God might have been when he assaulted them with his disturbing question. Would she be likely to discuss with Pierre topics that she was not in the habit of pursuing even with her husband? "Very naive," she said. "Extremely naive, I suppose. Otherwise, how could he believe in a God who *abandons* people?"

"But isn't Pierre a fairly educated man?"

"As if that had anything to do with it."

"I suppose it hasn't. Very often it hasn't." Jacob thought of his fellow congregants at the synagogue he and Eve attended infrequently. Most of the people there were very well educated: professionals and business people. What was their concept of God? Did they have a concept at all? If pressed, most of them would probably acknowledge that they were agnostics; but Rabbi Kohlblatt knew better than to press them for their opinion.

Jacob Harald had been far less prudent, at least once, a long time ago, and he had paid with sheer, stinging embarrassment. He had tried to instigate a discussion that should have gone to the root of their religious conviction. Why did educated modern man still belong to synagogues, churches, mosques, when, clearly, much of the content of the sacred books contradicted the teachings of science? And what, ultimately, was the faith of this congregation? Should they not try to clarify in their minds what precisely they meant when they repeated the words of the ancient liturgy?

The evening was a disaster. The discussion never got off the ground. One man said, "I was raised a Jew. I want my children to be raised as Jews." A lady, who was director of adult education, said, "We have to affirm our identity." But when they were asked to try and formulate their faith, they all shied away, resentful. A professor! Who else will bring up difficult topics for which people who have done a day's hard work are too tired?! Yes, they wanted to be intellectually stimulated; but within reason. Many were plainly bored. "What do I know of theology?' one of them asked. "That's for the Rabbi to worry about." They preferred to relegate theological questions to the back of the mind where such matters could be stored away safely. Jacob Harald had never again attempted to discuss with them problems of faith.

* * *

Today he suddenly felt a pang of recognition: discussions are too dangerous—always ready to flush to the surface all sorts of slimy doubts. To be forced into a discussion—it's like being forced into sin. And could he not, after all, admire that bravery in traditional believers who, in so many words, told him, "Get off my back; I refuse to discuss?" Challenged by modern science and the horrendous experience of their generation, they were clinging to their faith in an all-powerful, merciful, supernatural Being—desperately, stubbornly, heroically ignoring the difficulty that modern thought was dishing up for them. Surely, there was a kind of holiness in such faith. Of the others, well. . . . Many of them were drifting away from religion altogether. And most of the rest sought refuge in the agnostic "we don't know." There was comfort in just letting it be.

In his present mood, it was pity more than anything else. Poor little specks of consciousness unable to believe and afraid not to believe, and flustering about in their infinitesimal corner raising their little dust in such scurry and hurry and crying deep down for the parent against the vastness beyond and putting it all together in this "we don't know"! The persistent echo of the primal scream —where is the warmth and moist and safety in this cold harsh brightness? I want the womb, the Parent! And where is this to be found? We don't know . . . we don't know. . . . Maybe growing up means trying to understand one's parents in a new way.

And among all this drifting and clinging, where did Pierre

fit in? What was going on in that traumatized mind? Was his terrible question born from the anguish of a believer? Was it the cynicism of an atheist? Whatever it had been, Jacob Harald was conscious of having come in contact with a despair so profound that he ached when he thought of it.

He sat down at his desk in a corner of the living room. "I wish we could explain to Pierre that the word 'God' can be removed from mythology and still retain its power. If he could understand that there is a concept of God that is in accord with modern science, do you think this could have a—a healing effect?"

Eve was lounging with a novel. She had put up her feet, and clearly she wanted to go on reading. "For Pierre to understand what you are talking about, he would have to do some studying. He would have to get into a lot of books. Nowadays he doesn't seem to have much inclination to do that. You should talk to him. I mean really talk." She returned to her story.

Jacob let his eyes roam over the shelves along the wall. He noted with satisfaction how many of his favourite books he had transferred to the cottage. He pulled a volume off the shelf, *The Upanishads:*

> The Inner Soul of all things, the One Controller, Who makes his one form manifold—

From an unfathomed barbaric past came glimpses of luminous intellect. It had kindled an idea that was permeating the Orient; but in western lands, too, it was lapping its way through the millennia—sometimes like a hidden flame, its light almost forgotten; sometimes like a forest fire that springs up here and there, uncontrolled, untamable. It was a fire that did not consume but gave strength to the mind that fed it.

He opened *The Bible.* A bookmark brought him to words he loved: Ezekiel's vision of the *merkabah*, God's Chariot. He pored over this passage with unrelenting patience as he had done from time to time since his undergraduate days. A friend who was in rabbinical school had pointed it out to him with a remark that was haunting him still: "Do you know that the sages of antiquity were actually afraid of this vision?" They were so shocked by its audacity, he explained, that they forbade all discussion of it, except with someone who had found out on his own what this was all about.

*   *   *

Jacob felt drawn to this difficult, elusive passage with its fragmented grammar and mystical symbolism. Ezekiel tells of a chariot in the shape of a fiery cloud. Issuing from it are fiery creatures, each proceeding in its own direction and yet all of them linked together; and the spirit that is animating the creatures is animating also the wheels of the chariot. And the creatures issue from the cloud and run back to it as in a flash of lightning. What was it in this vision that put such fear in the minds of wise old men?

The strand of meaning that Jacob extracted from it was irresistible. He tried to translate it into modern terms. We might say: the world and all its creatures are but individualized strains of energy emanating from a great, energetic Source. They each go their own way, and yet all are linked and form one indivisible whole filled with the enlivening power of the Source whence they are born and to which they return. Jacob felt strangely elated because this idea, so ancient and so modern, had a place so close to the heart of his own tradition.

It was an idea that had never been extinct. Its glow was discernible in the musings of the ancient world, neo-Platonic, Stoic. In the Middle Ages, when a rejuvenated Judaic culture burned under a Spanish sun, it wakened with new inspiration.

Among the paperbacks on the shelf, Jacob found one that

contained translated excerpts from *The Zohar, The Book of Splendor.* And here again, out of thirteenth-century Spain, the idea sprang forth in its compelling power. This was how the author of *The Zohar* had imagined Bereshit, Genesis, the Beginning: "The expansive force proceeding from the hidden recesses of the secret supernal ether opened a path and produced from itself a mysterious point. . . .When it expanded, it emerged into being." Again—a force issuing from the Divine Source welled into the realm of our experience, became visible, became the world. A beautiful fantasy, like so much else in cabalistic literature? Jacob Harald saw in it an awesome example of human intuition.

* * *

More books, more notes and mounting excitement. The idea that had started in the imagination of mystical visionaries was absorbed and transformed in the logic of great philosophers. Here it was: the stirring proposition of Spinoza, in which he declared that whatever exists is a manifestation of one single Substance, eternal, infinite, the One worthy of adoration. But the fear was here, too, a persisting, stifling, terrible, ancient fear of the thought that our world could have issued from God and was part of Him. Poor Baruch Spinoza, hounded from the synagogues, shunned and disowned by the Jewish community of seventeenth-century Amsterdam. Why was it so important to them that God should be thought of as supernatural (whatever the word "supernatural" might signify)? Why so much rejection of the idea that nature is part of one all-encompassing Divine Substance? Why this fear—even now, even today? Is it because nature seems unclean to your myopic minds? Can't you see it whole? To you, the horse's dung is dirt, but to a sparrow it is a feast! A dim inkling told Jacob that his rhetoric was splendidly simplistic. But like Michelangelo's serpent that on the ceiling of the Sistine Chapel coils around the Tree of Knowledge, his thoughts wound themselves about the gigantic WHY. He railed at the Jews of old Amsterdam and all the timid souls for whom a world view in which God and nature were in any way equated was a sin, a heresy, an abomination: Poor Fools! Can't you see that, far from weakening your faith, in this equation you can find proof of God's living existence? WHY do you scurry away?

He knew the old fear was persisting. He had come to know it. Personally. Once he had been invited to address a large group of orthodox ladies. He was talking to them about the Canadian Jewish poet A. M. Klein, and they were all smiles and attention. The room was alive with questions. Obviously he was delivering quite a capital lecture. He was at his best and enjoying his power. But as soon as he began to explain how Klein was attracted to Spinozan thought, abrupt changes were chilling the room. The women began to turn away from him, to whisper among themselves, to shut out what he was saying. They didn't want to hear. They didn't want to know. Jacob recognized his terrible *faux pas*, quickly adjusted the script, concentrated on poems that extolled Jewish tradition. The whispering died down. They were attentive again. Polite. But it was too late. He had lost his audience.

Yes, the ancient fear was alive still; but so was the fire of the thought. The great Romantics of the eighteenth and nineteenth centuries had embraced Spinozan ideas with fervour and with joy, and his influence permeated countless works of modern literature. Slowly, slowly, there emerged also in modern science a cognition of the great unity. Slowly a road opened toward a knowledge where religion, philosophy, and science could meet.

*   *   *

Jacob began to pull book after book from the shelf. Some were science textbooks in which, as the years went by, he took more and more pleasure. Others were science books for the layman, a jumble of surveys and summaries. How it all evolved! How it all began to fit together!

Eve looked up and saw him leafing through the literature with that peculiar urgency, scribbling down page numbers, making notes. She smiled at him: "This is your China. Your Samarkand."

"Isn't it yours, too?"

"Yes. *Our* Samarkand." She submerged again. Always when there was something to it and she came to the end, a near frenzy made her go on reading as fast as she could, and at the same time she dreaded the moment when it would be finished. Jacob watched her for an instant. She couldn't share his excitement right now. No use trying, he thought. But he didn't really mind. They were travelling separately, but they were travelling together. In her enchantment, she half rose, and sitting on her haunches, was hovering over her book as if she wanted to hurl herself into the turmoil of its final chapter.

*   *   *

Jacob meanwhile had found what he was looking for. He had scanned pages on the works of physicists from Max Planck to J.S. Bell, had snaked his way through the labyrinth of their interpreters: Capra, Davies, Hofstadter, Pagels, Zukav, and how many others, a wild assembly of theories.

But here it was: Spinoza was right! His mystical dream of the oneness of all things—today it stood confirmed, proved, and explained in the mathematics and laboratory experiments of modern physicists. Today, any knowledgeable schoolboy had it pat. All that is matter, all that visible, touchable stuff in the universe, ultimately consists of the same basic subatomic particles.

The grass and the crocodile and the stars, garden fence and ocean, a piece of flint, a mountain goat, or a human being, all are aggregations of the same elusive array: protons, neutrons, quarks vibrating at the speed of some million-billion-billionth of a second, swirling clouds of electrons, all of them seething eddies of energy, insubstantial, minute patterns of strength. Jacob wanted to splash it across the sky, maybe put it on one of those banners that stream from aeroplanes above the crowds and advertise beer and hockey: the brotherhood of all things is no longer just an idealistic fantasy, a poetic figure of speech! It's a deeply understood fact, discovered through the exploration of quantum physics!

And the better he began to understand the physics of the twentieth century, the clearer it became: all matter consists of atoms, and the atoms consist of even smaller particles. But these subatomic particles do not truly exist as separate entities. If we saw one, it wouldn't be a clear-cut object like an apple or a brick or even a stitch in an embroidered pattern. These "particles" are merely areas of concentrated energy, infinitesimal units (quanta, that is, measures) without sharply defined demarcation to separate them from the surrounding expanse of cosmic force. The ideas had an astringency that made him feel as if he had rubbed his skin with alcohol or snow. When energy is condensed, it "crystallizes," forms new particles of matter. Today this is no longer just a theory. That matter is born from energy is routinely proven in laboratory experiments. True, the particle mixture thus newly created by human beings is violently unstable and, after a most fleeting appearance, is annihilated. But it is a dawn, a new understanding of our ancestry, our origin.

Is it here, then, in cosmic energy that the Divine can be found? Is this the One worthy of adoration?

* * *

In his youth, Jacob's interest in physics had been marginal, just strong enough to get him through exams. Now, more and more, he felt that here lay the germ of all philosophy.

More books, notes, a feverish search for half-remembered articles on Einstein, Clifford, Wheeler, Kaluza, Klein. These had pointed to a stunning conclusion: Space (or rather space-time, for the two are no longer considered separate concepts) is able to bend, undulate, ripple, curl; and mathematical exploration suggests that on an ultra-microscopic scale (of at least twenty powers of ten smaller than the atomic nucleus), there is a violent curving of space, a foam of spacial motion.

Whenever Jacob read these pages, he was gripped with new excitement. Hold on, he thought, hold on! I want to understand!

But real understanding was impossible. It would always remain impossible for him. He had no illusions about this. Without adequate background and without being able to penetrate the poetry of advanced mathematics, he would never have a true appreciation of the geometries of space; his mind would never be tracing the strange dimensions of emptiness. Modern physics would remain a mysterious, enticing structure, beautiful, terrifying, astonishing like a dream, and inaccessible except in the restricting translation of ordinary language. It was a limitation he had to accept.

This much he had gleaned: the words "vacuum," "space," "emptiness" have changed their meaning. They no longer suggest utter absence of everything. Space-time is power. There is motion in the vacuum; or rather, the vacuum is in motion and generating energy. He dismissed the inevitable question of the layperson: but what is it that moves?! Our senses cannot grasp and our instruments cannot analyze the essential nature of that which constitutes space-time. Yet, the logic of mathematics and observation has nevertheless led to the suggestion that it is the power of space-time which brings all energy and all matter into being.

*   *   *

Like a student before exams caught up in some pet sentence of his professor, Jacob returned again and again to one page. Here, the physicist Paul Davies had put it into words of startling poignancy:

> There is a deep compulsion to believe in the idea that the entire universe, including all the apparently concrete matter that assails our senses, is . . . convoluted nothingness, that in the end the world will turn out to be a sculpture of pure emptiness, a self-organized void.

The theory lost its vagueness, took on shape in Jacob's mind: if energy and matter are a consequence of spacial activity, is not space-time, then, the ultimate level of existence, the primeval Originator? Is it here, in space-time, that our search for the Creator ends?

Perhaps. There are those among the scientists who think that space-time has always existed or that it was self-created. In the words of Paul Davies: "entirely from within its own physical nature, the universe infuses itself with all the energy necessary to create and animate matter, driving its own explosive origin." Most cosmologists believe that the universe emerged spontaneously out of an *absolute* vacuum, an unimaginable nothingness where even space and time had no being.

But if space-time could emerge from this nothingness, did this not mean, necessarily, that somehow the "absolute" nothingness had, after all, a potential? The thought was inescapable. It had to be so. For without a potential, there could not have been an event.

Jacob smiled to himself. Do those modern mathematicians and physicists and astronomers and cosmologists know that medieval mystics and early Chassids referred to God as "No Thing"? They believed that Nothingness became active and brought forth creation. Was this intuition? Could it be that what we experience as space-time is part of the "absolute vacuum," which has become active in a special way? If the "absolute nothing" contained a quality, a potential from which space-time and in consequence everything else issued, was this nothingness then the ultimate level of existence? Was *this* the Deity? Or was there a creative level even more remote?

*   *   *

The word "supernatural" did not have much currency in Jacob Harald's vocabulary. Whatever existed was nature. But, of course, there could be levels of nature inaccessible to us. Space-time, a great "nothingness," or an indefinable existence beyond the "nothingness"—where was the Ultimate to be found, that fundamental Ultimate whence everything else originated?

Suddenly, a liberating thought occurred to Jacob Harald, a thought that for the moment ended his tortuous speculations. He said to himself, it does not matter that science cannot tell me which is the original level of existence. I do not have to know *exactly where* the chain of events that led to the formation of my world originates. It is enough that I know there is—there truly is —a primary level, an Existence that brought my world into being. Maybe scientists will change their minds about the exactitudes of the how and where and from what and into what. Errors will be found and corrected and found and corrected. . . . But this does not change the knowledge that there *is* the Primary. Spinoza called it "Substance"; the renowned physicist David Bohm calls it "the ground, which is the beginning and ending of everything."

From this Originating Existence flows all the measureless beauty, the love, the ecstasy, the setting sun, the grain of barley and the firefly. This is the living God. To this creative and sustaining strength, Jacob Harald knew, all his adoration, the gratitude of his entire self, was directed. Don't be afraid, it called out in him to a vast throng of despondent believers. The God of the stars, the God of your heart is more real than your mythologies ever told you. Science has not taken away the essential centre of your fantastic myths. On the contrary! Their central mystery has turned out to be reality; not less mysterious for that, far from less mysterious. But real.

Jacob understood that henceforth he would speak the words of the liturgy with a new conviction:

> *Shema* Israel—Hear, Oh Israel: The Lord is our God, The Lord is One! . . . Blessed is the Lord, the Source of Life. . . . This is our truth: the One God calls forth being from nothingness and makes all things one.

* * *

Looking up, Eve saw Jacob standing before her. There was pure exaltation in his eyes. "I have it now," he said excitedly. "I know how I should have spoken to Pierre. If I could have explained to him my concept in a coherent manner, I am sure he would have been able to draw his own conclusion. He would have understood how absurd it is in our day, with our knowledge, to imagine that God is someone who 'forsakes' people."

Eve closed her book and turned to Jacob, giving him her full attention."Why don't you phone Pierre now? Ask him to come over next weekend," she suggested.

"Maybe *you'd* better invite him. Phone him tomorrow when we're back in town." In the years to come, in the vortex of his unhappiness, Jacob could never explain to himself why he had said this nor why Eve had agreed to it.

She hesitated. Then she said, "OK. I'll give him a ring tomorrow. I'll phone him at the store." And she got up and went to the kitchen to fix supper.

* * *

Later that evening, Jacob had an immense desire to explain his thoughts and to hear Eve's reactions; but he could tell she wanted to finish her book, so he did not say anything. He didn't have to. Eve was aware he needed to talk, and it was she who insisted on discussing how he proposed to speak to Pierre. She had not half his education; she was a dietitian with modest formal academic training. But she read with a proud appetite, she was interested in everything that interested him and several things besides, and she was never afraid to criticize with utter honesty what he said. The vitality of her intelligence usually gave him a cleaner impetus than the judgment of learned colleagues, which he suspected was at times blinkered with an inveterate fear of competition and made stale with the conventions of their profession.

It was late, and they were still sitting at the kitchen table under the light of their Scandinavian lamp. It spread a comfortable, diffused brightness. Eve and Jacob had chosen it for the simplicity of its design that seemed to exude a cheerful confidence and easily blended into the uncluttered, rustic surroundings. Jacob had expounded at length. Now he looked at Eve expectantly. He leaned into the curving back of his captain's chair, his elbows firmly planted on the arm rests and his hands gripping their front ends.

"I think . . . this is what I have felt—very vaguely—for a long time," she said. "Only I wasn't able to say it to myself so clearly. Thank you for doing this. . . ." Her eyes caressed him. A pause. Then she said tentatively, "Would you mind very much if I played the devil's advocate—for a moment?"

"Of course not. On the contrary, I'd rather hear the objections from you. I want to have arguments ready in case he wants to quarrel with me."

Eve took the lid off the little brown glass pot on the table and refilled both mugs with hot, sweet, soothing liquid of milk and cocoa and sugar.

He liked the way she was tilting the pot. There was something protective in her movement. "Tell me."

She struggled to find a right way to say it. She thought about such things sometimes; but now it was difficult. "You say the Originating Existence is parent to everything; and because of this, in your view, this Existence is God. It's just that. . . . I mean when people speak about God, they don't just mean the Creator. Usually, they think about His love. It's to an all-knowing, loving Father people pray. Or Mother. Nowadays. Can the Originating Existence love us; do you think? Or respond to a prayer?"

An uncomfortable feeling that started in the mind and echoed somewhere among sore muscles in his lower back made Jacob get up and walk about the room. He was preparing a counteroffensive, not, in the first place, against Eve's questionings, which were, of course, legitimate, natural, and quite to be expected, but against something inside of himself, something he badly wanted to ignore. "But that's just it! That's what I'm trying to say!" He sounded impatient. He knew the weight of what she had said, felt how much there was unready, unformulated in his mind, and he fought the inadequacy. He was thinking aloud: "People have always been told that God is the loving, omniscient Creator, and so now they believe that such attributes are necessary for God to be God. And when they can't find evidence for all of them, they promptly conclude that the Divine does not exist.

"You see, mine is the opposite approach. I do not say, to be God, the Originating Existence must have such-and-such attributes. I say, here I stand—I am aware of an immeasurably wonderful Creator. I therefore cannot have any doubt concerning the reality of God. I stand before Him in awe—and I shall try to comprehend what His attributes are."

Jacob knew he had not answered her questions.

For a while Eve thought about what he had said. She saw his helplessness and herself became helpless in an effort to tide him over. But the weakness passed. The body has powerful remedies when the mind reaches into mist. "Come," she said quietly, and she took Jacob by the hand. They walked into the bedroom. They were tired. They did not make love tonight, but they lay in each other's arms so that each could feel the entire length of the other's body—the warm flesh moulding itself to the form of the other. When things can be so beautifully simple, do we have to question at all? Do we have to search? Speculate? Everything was light and peaceful in their minds. They felt at one in their thoughts, in their understanding of life, in their little island place as it sailed about the universe; and they felt as if they were swimming away together into a gentle infinity.

In The City

III

Early next morning, the Haralds drove back to town. They were in excellent spirit. Jacob hurried right away to a meeting of the advisory committee at City Hall, where proposals for subsidized housing were to be discussed with some of the aldermen. As Professor Harald, he had had his fill of meetings. During his teaching years, he had served on many of the faculty committees, and it was fair to say that he had developed a chronic aversion to that outpouring of personality that invariably characterized them. It was no different this morning. One of the participants was again holding forth endlessly, "using fifty words where one sufficed," and Jacob reflected on how often in the privacy of his office he had reprimanded students for this heinous transgression. Here, his inborn politeness prevented him from intervening. Usually, this made him very fidgety. But such was his good humour this morning that he relaxed even during this protracted annoyance.

He was hungry as he hurried home and looking forward to Eve's welcome, to her embrace, to their passionate caresses and kisses that were scattered throughout the day like bursts of sunlight.

*   *   *

She met him in the hallway. Her worried eyes and strained greeting signalled at once that something unpleasant had happened, and his thoughts, in panic, leapt to the children and the new grandchild.

"I phoned Pierre at the store. He wasn't there."

"Is he ill? Did you phone him at home?"

"I did. He isn't there either."

Jacob's impatience rose sharply. The news affected him. "Maybe he went to see the dentist or something. Didn't you ask at the store whether he'll be back in the afternoon?"

"I asked.—He won't be back. It's two months since they let him go."

"Let him go?! Two months?" They looked at each other. Eve silently began to serve lunch.

"We must phone him in the evening," said Jacob.

"It may be better if we drive over there. He didn't tell us he lost his job. He won't talk on the telephone about a thing like that."

"We'll go there late-ish—when he's likely to be home."

*   *   *

They drove to Pierre's place about half past nine in the evening. He had a small furnished apartment in a somewhat run-down fourplex. Jacob and Eve climbed the stairs and knocked repeatedly on his door. No reply. They returned to the street and walked around the house. His windows were dark. For a long while they waited in the car, looking at the painted brick facade, pale yellow and mottled here and there like the flesh of an overripe banana. Maybe Pierre had gone to the movies. Maybe he was visiting somewhere. Eventually, they drove home.

At six forty-five in the morning, Eve was on the telephone. It wasn't likely that Pierre, who always lacked energy and had difficulties getting himself out of bed, would leave the house before seven. But there was no answer. "Perhaps he's found another job and has to leave early," Jacob suggested.

*   *   *

At nightfall they tried again. They let the telephone ring twelve times. After that, they decided to drive back to Pierre's and to inquire at his neighbour's apartment. A young woman came to the door followed by a half-clad toddler with a fever blister on the upper lip. She had no contact with Pierre Rezekier, she said in mangled English. "Me and him—we never talk." Maybe the landlady downstairs would be able to help.

But nothing useful was gleaned there either. "Are you friends of his?" asked the elderly woman.

"Yes. We are anxious to get in touch with him. It's important."

"Mr. Rezekier doesn't live here any more. Matter of fact, his lease was up. He owed me for a couple of months. But then he paid up; so I let him stay for a few more days. He left yesterday. Early in the morning." They had missed Pierre by a few hours.

"Didn't he give you a forwarding address?"

"No, he didn't. He asked me to look after his violin and some books. So I guess he intends to come back. If you ask *me*, I don't think he knew where he was going."

The Haralds left—disturbed to the very core. They didn't put it into words right away, but as the night wore on, they confessed their fears. That Pierre had left the violin and the books did not seem in the least reassuring. For a long time, they couldn't say it. Finally, Eve clutched Jacob's arm and blurted it out: "I am afraid! It looks to me—as if he wanted to go away—I mean altogether."

Jacob dismissed it half-heartedly: "What would he want to do that for? I can't imagine. . . ." But he knew and Eve knew that they could imagine it only too well. Pierre had lost a job that had fed him, modestly, for the past fifteen years. They gathered he had not been a very successful salesman, and he had no other marketable skills. A mind like Pierre's could play all sorts of dangerous tricks.

A relief organization had brought him to Canada after the

war; one of a group of orphaned youngsters, all of them with corrosive memories, and some of them with terrible emotional problems. In most cases, time, like scar tissue, had slowly encapsuled the devastation in their minds. They had learned how to cope one way or an other. But Pierre was one of those people who had never really healed. His mind was not without talent, but it was traumatized, incapable of the focus, the discipline necessary to succeed. For many years he had worked in a warehouse. Then he had strained his back.

How many winters ago had they met Pierre? Five or six? He had attended Professor Harald's evening classes on Milton and metaphysical poetry. This was Jacob's most successful course. His evening lectures in the large amphitheatre had drawn well over a hundred and fifty students year after year. Many were not even registered in an arts program. They came for the joy of listening to Professor Harald's famous eloquence and to take part in the marvelous discussions that followed each lecture. Debates in his class always left people with the feeling that they had come into contact with vitally significant problems; and no one else gave such encouragement as he did whenever a student came up with an idea of some originality and sense.

And so, in spite of the avalanche of writing that had to be dealt with, Jacob had fished out something from Pierre's essays. They were not particularly well written, but something out of the ordinary had impressed him, a passionate concern with issues, an attempt to apply philosophical ideas to everyday life; and sometimes Jacob had detected in them also a humour of peculiar effervescence. At the end of each lecture, there was always the usual mob of people clustering around Jacob's desk, and Pierre had always been among them, and most often he was the last to leave. One night, Jacob had asked him to come to dinner the following Sunday, and it was embarrassing how absurdly grateful he had been for the invitation, how pathetically enthusiastic in his praise of Eve's cooking. Nevertheless, a friendship of sorts had slowly developed. The Haralds had never known anyone like Pierre Rezekier. Such a very odd name. "Unusual," they had tactfully called it; and Pierre had told them how his father actually started out as František Rezek from Pravonín in Bohemia. That was a pretty ordinary name where he came from, Pierre had laughed. An uncle in the family was named Pospíšil, which in Czech means 'he hurried', and even this wouldn't startle anyone in that part of the world. Many people were called Vyskočil, which meant 'he jumped out'; or Dokoupil 'he bought more', Chytil 'he caught', Navrátil 'he restored'. And—watch this one—Přecechtěl, 'nevertheless he wanted.' Intriguing thought, don't you think? I wonder what the ancestor of Mr. Přecechtěl wanted, nevertheless, in spite of everything?" Pierre always had some interesting bits of information ready. And he told them how his father had married into a Hungarian family, Jewish emigrés, who lived in Tours, and had entered there his father-in-law's small jewelry business. Shortly after that he added the "ier" to his name because, Pierre explained with a smile, he thought this would make him more French. "It was more like Prunier, the name of our doctor."

* * *

Pierre himself was born in France, and from the way he described his early years, they gathered he had loved France impetuously, fervently, with the patriotism of a young boy. "Till June 8, 1940. That was the day I lost it," he announced, "at four o'clock in the afternoon."

They were scandalized. "It couldn't have been very deep if you lost it like that."

"It was extremely deep," Pierre insisted. "Only, you see, it was based on a misunderstanding. On that day I suddenly began to understand everything much better. You see, there were rumours that the German troops had broken through on the roads to Rouen. People said the government was leaving Paris, and we were terribly afraid we might soon be occupied by the bosch altogether. But then again, we heard the government was going to open up shop in Tours. So we thought that perhaps it was all an exaggeration. Maybe our troops would regroup, make a stand. My father, who was not a little deaf, talked of running to join them even though he had been rejected by the military. Mother thought things probably weren't half as bad as people made them out to be.

"My parents didn't want to leave town. Here was our little family store, my parents' livelihood. And here was the apartment. They had saved up for so many years to furnish it nicely. They really didn't know what to do for the best.

"We were all packing rucksacks, just in case one did have to flee the city. We were putting in warm clothes and raisins and nuts, and lemon-flavoured hard candies against thirst, and some favourite items, small photographs and such. My parents stuffed in jewelry from the store, and my sister put in her diary. I still remember that. It was bound in red morocco and she always kept it locked. The key she wore on a ribbon around her neck, although mother said it spoiled the look of the little necklace she had received for her twelfth birthday. And I put in the medal I had won the summer before in a children's race at Trouville and a magnifying glass Grandpapa had given me. . . . Funny how little details like this stick with you.

"And then my parents became more and more worried because there was no word from my grandparents. Grandmaman Kemeny had gone to bring her sister Ilona from an old ladies' home near Blois. Aunt Ilona had bad gallstone trouble, and that morning, Dr. Prunier—he was a very kind old man, and he had a car—that morning he took Grandmaman to Blois to persuade her to come and have the operation. They were expected back hours ago, and still, there was no word. We had the radio on all the time, and we knew things didn't go well. My mother tried to phone Grandpapa, but she couldn't get a connection. So, at last, my father sent me to Grandpapa's apartment to see whether they had come back.

"I ran the few blocks and found Grandpapa in a daze. Instead of packing a rucksack, he was walking around, just looking at a picture here and a little knickknack there. When I told him he should start packing, he sat down at the piano, hiding his face in his hands: "Where can we go? How shall we live?" And no, there was no sign of Grandmaman and Aunt Ilona. He was an old man and quite distraught.

"I ran back home. When I came to our house . . . (well, it didn't belong to us; but my parents had lived there since the day they were married, and both my sister and I were born on the dining room table in our apartment) so, when I came to our house, the concierge was standing on the sidewalk chatting with some neighbours. He barred my way, and he said I couldn't go in. I dodged around him and got hold of the door handle, but the door was locked.

"I shouted, 'I have to go up!' I didn't understand at all what this was about. He just shook his head with what looked like moral indignation, as if I had asked for something to which I wasn't entitled. He said, 'Now you can't go in and out like this.' And suddenly, suddenly I understood. This concierge whom I had known all my life as a friendly man with an unkempt moustache, this man with whom my parents had always been on good terms, this concierge *knew* that the bosch was about to overrun the city, and he was already adapting himself to the new regime, welcoming the chicanery they would introduce for the Jewish population. I screamed 'I must go home! I've got to go up to my parents!' Well, after a few minutes of remonstration, the stupidity of the situation began to dawn in his little fascist mind, and he unlocked the door. You see, on this day, for the first time, I experienced the lack of it—I mean *of égalité*. Here, this man, he wanted to take from me the *liberté* to go home. I won't even talk of *fraternité*. I asked myself, 'Is this what people carry around underneath their politeness?' This was the hour when I realized I didn't really belong."

* * *

The Haralds had questioned Pierre. Why couldn't they all escape to Portugal? So many had managed to get across the border. But Pierre didn't really want to talk about it. The bosch swept down too fast, overtaking many who were fleeing south. Yes, his family knew there were many heroic Frenchmen who were hiding Jews and risking their own lives to do it. Some acquaintances disappeared overnight. But, of course, one had to know how to contact the right people. And how were his parents to know with whom to get in touch? They didn't speak French all that well. They hadn't made many friends in this provincial city. They didn't know any politicians. They didn't know any farmers. The doctor lived in a small apartment and, at any rate, he said his housekeeper couldn't be trusted. He didn't know anyone with a safe place, anyone brave enough to take them in. And the two people his parents could think of who might have helped—the owner of a little restaurant, who had pronounced left-wing sympathies, and a local newspaperman, who was a great liberal—those two had already gone underground. They had disappeared without a trace.

It was too late. The family was trapped. Grandpapa Kemeny consoled them. People wouldn't have taken them in anyway. Seven people, not to mention the foreign accents. They would be much too difficult to hide, even in a cellar or attic. Poor Aunt Ilona, who might get another gallbladder attack any minute—what were they to do with her if she took ill and began to moan and cry aloud during an attack? And as for the children—Vera and Pierre—well, they weren't in any danger. Who would want to harm a child. Nevertheless, at night, Pierre heard his parents discuss the possibility of asking an old teacher at the Lycée to look after him and his sister till the war was over. They would offer him gold jewelry from the store. So, if the worse came to worst and the family was to be deported, the children would be in good hands. But when the worst came, it was indescribably worse than any one could have imagined. Eventually, the Germans deported them all. Pierre refused to speak about that. He was the only one to survive.

* * *

After the war he had tried to find other members of his family, the Kemenys who had lived in Nagykanizsa and Debrezin; and the many relatives in Czechoslovakia, especially an uncle and aunt from Teplice Šanov, where he had spent two glorious vacations. He scanned the lists of survivors of the concentration camps. There were agencies that published those lists and tried to match people who were searching for one another. For weeks, months, years, he had been poring over those lists, and he had kept on hoping, always hoping to find a familiar name. At last, he wrote to the authorities in the towns where his relatives had lived. Was there no record? Had they no information on what had become of them?

Yes, in most cases, a few scant data were available. So-and-so had been deported and had not returned. Presumed dead. Letters from Czechoslovakia with official stamps and reference numbers enclosed official lists. Here the Germans had kept exact records of their crimes. Each person's name and birth date was given and the last address where he or she had lived before deportation. Then came the date on which this person had been taken from his home to the interim concentration camp of Terezín and the number of the transport that had brought him there. And then followed the date and another ominous transport number showing further transportation from Terezín to the death camps of the East. Sometimes a terse note said the number indicated this transport was destined for extermination. But not even those of Pierre's family whose transports were not so clearly slated for immediate annihilation had ever returned from the camps; uncles, aunts, cousins, Grandmother Rezek, who was nearly eighty when she was taken away, and two children aged only three and four were among them.

And in spite of the official letters, Pierre kept on scanning the lists in refugee and ethnic periodicals. Survivors were looking for relatives and friends. For years he was hoping, always hoping. Slowly the advertisements grew sparse. But decades later, here and there, he would still come across the notice of a persistent searcher. It was like a cry in the void.

*   *   *

Here in Canada, Pierre had not made many friends either with fellow immigrants or with people at work. He did not frequent functions at the Jewish Community Centre, where he might have found congenial company. As far as the Haralds knew, he belonged to no clubs, nor was he active in any organizations. Right now, they were probably the only ones to whom he could turn if he needed support.

"We must do something," said Eve.

"What can we do?"

"The police."

Jacob didn't expect that the police could be of much help, but Eve insisted anyway.

It was almost midnight when they arrived at the station. The nearest constable sat at a desk and was occupied with some manual. His mouth shut abruptly on a yawn when they approached. "What can I do for you?" He was friendly, glad to set his official capabilities in motion.

"We want to report a missing person," said Eve. Her voice, stupidly, cracked a little. "He hasn't been heard from for almost two days." The constable gave her a searching, paternal glance.

"The name?"

"Pierre Rezekier," Jacob spelled it out.

"Age?" They hesitated. They didn't know. He must be at least fifty; but he looked so much younger. "Is he a relative of yours?"

"No. A friend."

"Well—how is he missing?" Eve suddenly realized the absurdity of their expectations here. "He lost his job," she ventured. "He didn't tell us. . . . He left no address. . . . We *must* find him."

The constable's eyes were steady, "Did he take anything with him? Something that belonged to you?"

"No! No, no. . . ." They both shook their heads, almost their entire bodies. Jacob felt embarrassed. He was ready to leave.

"Is it possible that Mr. Rezekier might be suffering from amnesia, or—do you have any reason to believe there could have been some foul play?" Again, Eve shook her head. "No, it hardly could be that." He had given up his lodgings and had paid up his rent before he left.

"This is a free country," said the constable. "If an adult decides he wants to move on without telling his friends and we don't have anything on him, we have no right to go after him. Besides, he could be anywhere, couldn't he. He could have left the country, for all we know."

Eve pleaded: "What we are afraid of . . . perhaps. . . ."

Jacob came to her aid. "Officer, Mr. Rezekier was rather. . . . He was very depressed. We're afraid he may have done something to himself."

Now the man looked at them sympathetically. "Did he threaten suicide?" he asked.

"No. Never."

"There's not much we can do. We can't put guards on every bridge. It wouldn't do much good even if we could. There are too many ways for a man to take his life if he chooses to do so.

Maybe your best bet would be the YMCA or the Salvation Army. Look in at some of the other shelters, too. You might place an advertisement in the newspapers, perhaps. But that's expensive. Of course, if it's worth it to you, you can always hire a private detective; but that would cost you a bundle, and unless you can give the man something to go on, you'd probably be wasting your money. . . . Anyway, best of luck. Sorry we can't be of more help. . . . Yes, if you'll give us your telephone number we'll let you know if we should hear. . . ."

* * *

The following day, when Jacob went to the soup kitchen, Eve came with him to help with the potatoes so that they could get out early. They drove first to the Y and then to the Salvation Army, but no one had heard of Pierre. They looked in at another shelter and were shown into a small busy-looking office. A grey-haired gentleman in a dark suit listened to their story. He consulted a card index and made a telephone call. "Mr. Rezekier has not been with us. Not unless he used a pseudonym," he said. "Have you tried any other shelter? Maybe he has taken a cheap furnished room somewhere."

"Our fear is . . . what we are really afraid of is that—" Eve was pleading for reassurance.

The transparent eyes of the gentleman measured her. "That he killed himself?"

"Yes," said Eve. It was as if she hoped some help, some magical solution could come from the man.

"It's a pity that he didn't come to you when he was in trouble. When he had friends like you." The gentleman looked at their casual, prosperous-looking clothes, and in his hard, transparent blue eyes they read the question, "Whatever drives you here? Whatever did you do to him that made him go away?"

They left more worried than they had come.

* * *

In the course of the next few days, they phoned all the shelters. They went to the library and looked up recent newspapers. They phoned everyone who had advertised a furnished room and asked whether Pierre Rezekier was living there. The replies came angry, hurried, sweet, lilting, curt, regretful, wondering, business-like, shrill, broken-voiced, old. It took hours. Eve objected. This was crazy. But she helped with the phoning.

They looked timidly through the dailies, hoping not to find a notice of someone drowned or discovered with his wrists slashed in some alleyway. And as they did not read anything suspicious, they consoled each other. If he had drowned, his body, surely, would have been found by now. If he had done harm to himself, the newspapers would have reported it. Of course, he might have attempted something and not succeeded. They phoned the hospitals.

There remained one other frightening possibility. If he committed suicide somewhere else, the local papers would not carry it. He could have walked into the bush somewhere. A man could disappear that way. It was a cruel thought that tortured them and became particularly virulent at night. If something of that kind had happened, they would never find out.

And all the time they hoped for a letter, a postcard, a telephone call. They became angry with Pierre. How dare he treat them like this. "Of course, he doesn't owe us any explanations. We haven't been that close," mused Jacob.

"No, we weren't. Maybe that's it. He had enough of us and of this city, and he's gone to try his luck somewhere else. Let's forget about him until he sees fit to contact us in a civilized manner.

* * *

Jacob knew Eve was right, and as if by agreement, they stopped talking about Pierre. But one evening, when they happened to drive past Micki Boudreau's apartment block, Eve made Jacob park the car and ran to see if Micki still lived there. She returned in triumph, "Yes, her name is still on the mailbox. Maybe she knows something." They rang the apartment bell.

"Who is it?"

"Professor Harald."

"Who?"

Eve asserted herself quickly, "It's Eve Harald . . . Don't you remember us? We are friends of Pierre Rezekier. You've been to our place. . . ."

"Please come up." The buzzer went immediately, and they were admitted to the foyer.

Potted plants, much too perfect to be real. A lot of gilt and mirrors under subdued light. The carpeting in the elevator and in the corridor was mauve and soft. When they reached the apartment, they found Micki ready to go out. In her late thirties, she still looked as attractive as ever. Her full, wide lips were smiling. Her bleached hair that stood away from her head in straight little spikes was cropped so short, it made her head look too small above the enormous padded shoulders of a fashionably long and bulky coat. But she still had a certain flair that made extreme clothes look handsome on her.

"What can I do for you? . . . . Forgive me, I was almost out the door. . . ."

They told her. But no, she hadn't heard from Pierre, not since they had broken off about two years ago. "We aren't in touch at all," she smiled, and then added with genuine sympathy, "Geez—I'm sorry he lost his job."

The three of them left together. "Can we drive you somewhere?" asked Eve as the elevator was descending.

Miss Boudreau's face turned an annoyed red. "No thank you, I have my car," she said with testy emphasis. "Funny, people always ask single women whether they need a lift. It sounds as if a single woman couldn't afford a car or wasn't able to drive or something. . . . Geez. . . . "

Eve's face turned even redder than Miss Boudreau's. "I assure you I didn't mean it like this at all." To her relief they had reached street level, and Miss Boudreau stayed in the elevator to go to the garage below. Their parting was swift. What explanation could I possibly have offered her? thought Eve. How *did* I mean it? She felt reprimanded and, in consequence, thoroughly wretched.

As far as Pierre was concerned, the Haralds knew that every promising avenue had been explored.

"I shouldn't have said this to her. I offended her," Eve remarked tentatively, looking for reassurance.

Jacob's preoccupation with the road was intense, although there was no traffic on this dusky back street. "You meant well." He didn't want to make room for more uncomfortable hindsights.

"I feel bad about it. I really shouldn't have said that."

"Nonsense," said Jacob accelerating as if to escape her recriminations. Something in the old Dodge vibrated, asking for attention. It made him nervous.

"I should have thought more clearly. . . ."

"Stop it. . . . It doesn't matter." Recognizing his own tendency only too clearly, he became irritable when it surfaced in her, which luckily happened very seldom. Altogether, there is too much self-reproach, Jacob thought. It was no good coming here with our worries. We shouldn't have bothered Miss Boudreau. . . .

IV

Of course, they did not give up hope altogether. Not by any means. Any day now, they might get mail from Pierre or a telephone call. Proud son-of-a-gun, he was waiting until he had re-established himself. Once a new job was propping him up, he was surely going to contact them. The mail slot at their front door spewed heaps of bills and fourth-class junk and relentless, desperately urgent requests for donations, numbing in their quantity, their regularity, their pounding frequency. Occasionally, a calligraphic letter from an ancient relative appeared with information on recent sightings of orioles, flickers, cardinals, and other spectacular fowl; or palm-beachy postcards, innocent as Disney cartoons, blew in from Florida, where friends, munching pompano and grouper, were soaking up vitamin D. From the children came hungrily expected notes, whose infrequency, lack of regularity, and sparseness were grinding on their nerves, causing pointed inquiries. Berni wasn't too bad about writing, but Susan preferred the telephone, and there was always a certain artificiality and sameness about these timed conversations (even though the tone of voice compensated to some degree), and they were left hungry afterwards. Nothing from Pierre.

*   *   *

On Sunday, Jacob went downtown for a walk. The sky was overcast and hardly anyone was about. The streets were clean, grey, and dull. A city crew in a fit of tidiness had removed all the fliers and posters; poorly printed leaflets; rain-bleached and wrinkled, scribbled, typed, xeroxed invitations; mod and startling graphics, which local art groups had stuck on trees and

42

utility poles wherever a surface hospitable to thumb-tack or staple could be found; and the naked wooden poles and bare trees vanished into the general tedium of the street. All the summer vendors with their carts full of flowers and fruit and even the chip wagons with their comforting buckets of hot fried potatoes had gone to hibernate. In a doorway, a glum-looking pigeon was pecking at nothing. Only a few cars were taking people to the movies or to some well-heated restaurant for a late Sunday brunch. A feeling of boredom swept over Jacob, such as he had not known since the days of his youth before he and Eve had met.

Ahead of him, a man with long, dirty hair straggling from the rim of his bald crown was accosting a young couple in jeans and black leather jackets. They were tightly clinging to each other, their bodies rubbing as they walked, his arm around her shoulders and hers around his waist. "Could you spare a dollar?" They ignored the man. Standing at the curb, he pretended he was interested in watching them go, her buttocks shifting under her tight jeans and her blond locks, untidy and frizzy, falling prettily down her back. He pretended not to see Jacob.

Maybe this is the moment to cross to the other side of the street. I don't want this greasy individual to talk to me.

"D'you think you could spare a dollar?" The man's eyes, pinkish inflamed, were possibly hostile, quite possibly malicious. It used to be a dime, Jacob thought. And then maybe a quarter. Now it's a dollar. What's he going to spend it on if he gets it—a drink or cigarettes? More likely on drugs. Most probably he is half stoned already. Am I going to support this? Jacob passed him, revulsion and anger forcing a reflux from his hiatal hernia, a sour burning right into his throat. He walked to the next street corner. There he stopped. Let us suppose. . . . Theoretically. . . . Suppose, only for a moment of course and only for the sake of argument, I mean. . . . Supposing this dollar is actually needed. If that creature without a proper overcoat is actually hungry. . . . Jacob turned angrily, explaining to himself his reluctance as a natural reaction of one who knows he is victim of a fraud. Why do I have to punish myself? I am a chicken that offers itself to be plucked. He sauntered back, his hand groping through various pockets. The fellow watched him, expectancy rising all over his face. He almost smiled when he saw a two-dollar bill emerge from Jacob's wallet. "Thank you very much!—Could you possibly make it five?" Jacob walked away. He could feel the pink stare, envious, disappointed. The truth was, he had given away the only money he had on him. He was enjoying the warmth of a good lunch, and it infuriated him to know that he would have been unable to refuse if there had been more.

* * *

He had never subscribed to the theory that the poor were bound always to be with us, and he despised the whole, vast, inefficient machinery that rattled along without making noticeable inroads. Evidence of its inefficiency always depressed him. It was a reproach. Maybe it would have been better to make one's mark in the fields of economics or political science. One had imagined when quite young that literature, properly approached, could improve people, so that the improvement of economics and politics and scores of other matters would automatically follow. But during years of teaching, had there been any impact at all? In the bleakness of this moment, Professor Harald doubted it. Maybe the only result of his approach to literature had been the backstabbing by some academic would-be assassins who thought he should give more emphasis to analyses of literary techniques and thus, unavoidably, spend less time on the psychology, the social and philosophical content of the books. But perhaps it was not absurd and not too late, even now. Maybe he could still begin a systematic study of economics and go into politics instead of enjoying himself with books on archaeology. It was a trend of thought that was particularly unwelcome at this time because it led Jacob toward a subject he had promised himself to avoid. It had to do with the value of the dollar and the predicaments caused by the scarcity thereof.

It didn't take much to make him brood over the generous quantities of macadamia nuts Pierre had always insisted on bringing as hostess gifts. Obviously, he had chosen them because they were expensive, precious, worthy of their hospitality. A dollar is a dollar, Jacob thought, feeling very uncomfortable. Maybe we should have told him that we didn't really like them. For this truth, by how many dollars would he be better off now? The dike, so carefully tended in Jacob's mind, was giving way: If I had been less brusque when he came to me with this terrible question, he would have had the courage to confide in us when he was in trouble.

* * *

The November air was chilly and damp. Jacob forced his mind away, focused on something else, but the low, utilitarian facades, grimy grey or grimy brick or grimy whatever, above lettered boards advertising business of sundry kinds and display cases overstuffed with merchandise, could not hold it. His mind slid off them as if it were independent of his will.

An old lady in her best coat, cotton gloves, and a felt hat over neat white curls was passing a row of closed stores: a beauty parlour, a pizza place, a second-hand bookstore, ladies' fashions, a trust company, sporting goods. . . . Jacob noticed her earrings. They were conspicuous: a large glittering circle of rhinestones around a sky-blue centre. Slowly, stiffly she walked, as if she had nowhere in particular to go, nothing in particular to do, no one to meet. Why was she dressed up like this? Was she hoping, perhaps, that somehow, something of interest might come her way, that some unexpected encounter might break the monotony? Were these earrings a cry for love, for companionship? She walked by, looking straight ahead.

Suddenly, for a moment, there was Pierre accosting people on a half-deserted city street. Pierre—unshaven, his coat threadbare and dirty. In Toronto. In Montreal. In Winnipeg. They would never know.

*   *   *

Jacob felt lonely, which didn't happen very often. Normally, he and Eve shared their evenings and Sunday afternoons. He had never joined a men's club, and it pleased him that Eve had never craved the togetherness of the henhouse. They both felt that segregation was to be avoided wherever possible. But today Eve had trotted off to a party strictly for ladies. She had gone to a kitchen shower given by a friend for a newly engaged niece. Tucked under her arm was a gift-wrapped cookbook with vegetarian menus, a beautiful creation of her own. I should have invited someone for a game of chess, Jacob thought.

In front of St. John's church, a sign in big, black letters said: "Deep in their roots all flowers keep the light."

The damp cold began to penetrate Jacob's coat. He walked faster and turned down a path that led to the canal, wading through crisply rustling leaves, drinking in a pungency that tasted of childhood walks in the park. A few youngsters on bikes were overtaking him and disappeared around the bend, where a copse of nude honeysuckle bushes and spruce blocked the view. All the flowerbeds were empty and carefully raked, ready for the winter. The water was low and muddy and the quay deserted. He was conscious of a vague, empty miserableness.

*   *   *

If only Pierre would come back . . . if he came back today, I think I could make him understand the absurdity of his question. I truly could.

But then again, could I? Could I really? At the cottage, at that ecstatic moment when his gratitude, his adoration had risen toward the Ultimate, toward this Originating Existence, everything had seemed so clear, so simple. He had longed for a chance to explain to Pierre his concept of God. Surely, Pierre would see. Now, suddenly, he was not so sure. He could imagine Pierre's pained, skeptical smile. He could hear him say, "You are not speaking about God at all. God is the name we give to the Creator who is also the omniscient loving Father to whom we can pray, the just and merciful Judge. The originating existence—whether it is energy, or space-time, or a nothingness that gave birth to space-time—this originating existence is nature. Can we pray to the originating existence? If we are created by a force of nature that does not know us and does not care and cannot help us—how can we call this creator 'God'? Is this not the creed of the atheist?" For Pierre, there would be only the two alternatives: God was an omniscient Father in whose power it was to rescue the innocent from peril and whose mysterious refusal to help filled one with anguish, confusion, despair. If the cosmos was born from a natural force that had no power to quench the flames of Nazi hell, then man was alone.

Pierre would not see. He would not see at all. Again, the feeling of helplessness came over Jacob Harald. He remembered some of his PhD candidates whose doctoral dissertations it had been his task to supervise. They had come to his office glowing, filled with ideas and satisfaction, their eyes tired from working through the nights, and it had been his lot to have to point out their shortcomings, the lack of logic, the factual error, the hidden flaws. He remembered the despair in their eyes and the cry of sudden, horrified recognition: "I have no thesis!" The assembled construct had disappeared. Today he felt like his students. He could see it now. Pierre would reject his arguments.

*   *   *

Feeling unsure, losing direction, suspecting that getting entangled in Pierre's imagined objections was leading him into a quagmire of unpromising speculation, he was yet compelled to zero in. Something in him was insistent, tried to organize itself, speaking in its silent way and breaking, breaking through that strongest of all barriers that separates not being from being, the unconscious from the conscious—only to find denial. Of that he was sure. Yes, there would be denial. He felt an unaccustomed frailty in him, like a fever. He wanted to go home but was not going. Perversely he remained in thrall to the winding path along the dismal, empty canal.

He saw hordes of people swarming like ants over the mountainside, down valleys, over hills—looking for truth, thirsting for truth. They scattered and became dry leaves to be walked over, rolled over by the tires of bicycles—whispering in a low wind that lifted them briefly. They will kill for their truth, and it will turn out to be a lie, and they will kill for another lie, and another. . . . And they will have the truth—the real truth—only when they are no longer willing to kill for it. But then they will go flabby, and a truth nobody is willing to fight for is trampled under foot. That is the tragedy. . . .

Jacob was forcing himself into some coherence. After all, there had to be a way if one made oneself think—think with a clear head. One could ignore the fever. Clarity was there, veiled under layers and layers of mist in which floated like seaweed the disappointments of millennia—but it was there. . . . He was focusing now as sharply as he could.

*   *   *

How to tell Pierre, how to explain! Eve was right. An answer for Pierre had to bring the concept of God closer to the primeval yearning that makes infants grasp the hem of a parent's coat: "You know all my troubles. Love me! Feel with me! Protect me!" This, most probably, is what Pierre needs, I am sure, Jacob thought. Nothing else will be enough. But can one, so late in the twentieth century, satisfy such cravings, he wondered, satisfy them and ignore everything science has taught us? Even if one had the stomach to embark on such a rocky voyage, could this give an intelligent man like Pierre what he needs?

Can there be any rational way that would allow us to think of the Originating Existence as omniscient? Something in Jacob was urging him on. To be all-knowing—what precisely does this mean? What is knowledge? Is it consciousness? Awareness? Yes, but quite broadly. In the human being, surely, it involves all the sensitivities of the body, all emotions and instincts, and the entire spectrum of the mind that absorbs meteoric showers of information, thinking, reasoning—and so is led to judge, to bring forth a will that produces action. A symphony of experience played by the most scintillating of virtuosos, electric activity inside our brain cells.

Jacob was walking along the canal bed at an even pace now. He did not notice the resolute, stout woman in the red ski jacket who was briskly walking her cocker spaniel. The lone joggers who occasionally passed him were invisible. The landscape had become transparent. He was looking deep into a thought.

"It's this way," Jacob murmured to himself. "When we speak of knowing, we refer to information absorbed." And it's got a strongly directive potential, he added silently. Clever little brats that we are, we use it mainly to direct our action for survival or to make life more pleasant—our own and that of favoured others, for the most part. So, knowing seems to be an important factor in the constructive process of nature.

Let's see, thought Jacob, let's have a look at what happens

when we go back a little along the evolutionary path. What does electric activity do in the brains of animals? Abstract notions, reasoning power, analytical thinking appear to be absent: but animals know. And how often does their instinct turn out to be more reliable than our intellectuality? Wild animals don't get poisoned nibbling toadstools. They don't have to take a clumsy, roundabout way—think, worry, test, analyse, draw conclusions—to find out what's edible. Can I build a shelter for my family? It would probably be a fearful mess, Jacob thought wryly. But the little Amazonian caciques make a nest that is woven from blades of grass and suspended from the branch of a tree, yet strong enough to support the weight of the parent birds and their young. And caciques do not have to take courses in strength of materials, and they don't study structural analysis before they perform these feats of stupendous engineering sophistication. It's pretty clear. Instinct must contain a built-in directive that calls to action. Yes, animals do know.

In human beings, knowing *precedes* most of conscious action. I pick a berry because I *know* it's a raspberry, and I *know* it's good. The further back we go, the tighter the union of the directive knowledge and the action.

And why not go back further and further—back to the more primitive. In an amoeba, ingesting food seems almost as automatic as digesting it. Even here, we may still suspect traces of preceding knowledge as the amoeba extends itself over a food organism, choosing some algae rather than grains of sand; though its knowledge can hardly be differentiated from that of a sperm when it seeks out and burrows into an egg. And there we don't assume previous knowledge at all. We consider the directive information—that is, the factor determining the direction of the sperm's activity—to be simultaneous or almost simultaneous with the action, both of them the result of physical and chemical process.

Yet, what is human knowing (this important preliminary to action) but the result of physical and chemical doings, the interplay of electric charges in the brain? Seen from this perspective, human knowing, our possession of information, appears to be merely a particular mode of something infinitely wider.

* * *

"This is it, this is it . . ," Jacob murmured to himself. Maybe here is what I should hold on to. He did not feel the cold now. He wanted to penetrate deeply, probe like a frenzied prospector for the hidden wealth. Back! Still further back! Into the labyrinth of inorganic matter, into the world of atoms, into the realm of the quanta. He began to formulate it. Electric impulse enables me to know that I want to live. Electric impulse enables a sperm to "know" where the egg is located. And it is clear that electric impulse is involved also in the geometric dance, all this capturing and changing and holding, enmeshing, and arranging that goes on among atomic particles when they combine and form patterns and objects and ourselves. And can we say that their automatic mode of "knowing" is less effective than our intellect in bringing about meaningful action? But in the subatomic particle, action and the directive "information" seem completely fused. More than that: all differentiation between the particle itself, its electric charge, and the action with its directive information becomes blurred.

Jacob felt a bold idea tunnelling out from his subconscious. When it came out into the open, it looked altogether flamboyant: I, when I am hungry and rush out to buy a loaf of bread, and the atom in a growing quartz crystal, when it links up appropriately, becoming part of the crystal's wonderful symmetry, are kindred spirits, sparks flying from the great invisible fire—glowing each of us in our own mode of knowledge. It is all one—all part of one great constructive thrust. . . Jacob closed his eyes.

* * *

A cannonade of bellowing laughter assaulted his mind. It shook the city and reverberated all around him in a thunder of merriment. He recognized the voice; obviously it was Robert Potter's, welling up maliciously from the caverns of the Physics Department. "There is no constructive thrust!" the voice shouted. "Only chance, crude, common-or-garden-chance that brings particles together. When their electric charges happen to fit, they hang together—crudely speaking."

Jacob scowled. "Do you know Paul Davies?" He's one of your own, a physicist; and very highly thought of, too. I read in one of his books that the statistical chance of the sun being formed rather than a black hole in space is One followed by a hundred billion billion zeros. If the formation of the cosmos depended on chance, then the likelihood of the cosmos being formed is One in roughly One followed by a thousand billion billion billion zeros, at least."

"So what!" Potter said. "Given a tremendous time span, everything could come together by chance. I see no proof of a thrust! And what are you babbling about directive knowledge?"

"You should watch your language, my boy," came Peter Besterman's voice snarling out of the Department of Philosophy. "Tch, tch, tch . . . 'directive'! That smacks positively of teleology. Nature doesn't aim. Basically things happen by chance."

"Chance! Chance!" Mel Henry from Biology was chiming in.

"You misunderstand me—all of you!" Jacob cried. "The lot of you! Listen to me! Please listen!"

"We are listening, and we don't like what we hear," said Potter in a voice that was straight and firm like a slide-rule made of brass.

I shouldn't have made a good lawyer, Jacob thought. I am not arguing at my best when set upon. But he succeeded in sounding superior with a tinge of nonchalance. "Then listen again," he said. "Whether electric charge in a woman's brain prompts her to buy clothes alluring to a man, or whether electric charge directs a particle to link up with another particle, such happenings can and do have significant constructive consequences. So this is what I mean by 'constructive thrust'."

They didn't reply. It felt almost like praise. Jacob grew bolder: "And since you speak of chance—how is it that a cow, instead of giving ordinary milk, secretes colostrum—just when the newly born calf needs it for protection while it's own immune system isn't fully developed. That's rather mysterious, don't you think? That doesn't look like coincidence to me."

"My dear good fellow," chimed Mel Henry (in his agreeable English public school accent, which Emma Coghill, Chairperson of Mathematics, had once referred to as "cute" and "sexy"), "my dear good fellow, there is a perfectly good, comparatively simple explanation for this. Some of the cow's ancestors, presumably, produced something like colostrum by lucky chance. The young of these primordial creatures profited from this. They were healthier than all the others, and therefore they had a much better chance to produce offspring. In time, through a proliferation of their genes, the production of colostrum became a characteristic of all the members of the species."

"Very plausible," said Jacob. "But this doesn't take into account why, after a few days, just when the newborn calf's own immune system has matured and is ready to take over, the colostrum disappears. When the need is gone, the cow stops manufacturing. Pure, pure chance?"

"I don't know the answer to that one," conceded Mel as cheerfully as ever. "Maybe some day we'll find out." He was a handsome young fellow with bushy hair, and he looked very pleased with himself.

"I don't deny evolutionary process—I wouldn't think of denying the importance of chance the way you describe it," said Jacob. "You know me better than that, Mel." He was trying to sound conciliatory now yet unable to prevent himself from getting wrought up and raising his voice.

*   *   *

"But explain to me this," he cried. "Isn't there something about our own immune system that's rather hard to fit into the usual pattern—evolution functioning through chance and natural selection? Didn't you yourself tell us in that public lecture of yours how astounding it is—this cooperation in a sequence complex beyond our ken—how T cells, B cells, effector cells, killer cells, helper cells, suppressor cells, and memory cells work together, signal to each other, travel about in our bodies and congregate at the site of trouble when foreign particles or bacteria or viruses invade our bodies, how they agglutinate intruders until they stick together as ineffectual bundles, and how they coat them and make it possible for the powerful macrophage cells to get hold of them and gobble them up. Didn't you tell us all that?"

"With much greater precision, I trust," interjected Mel Henry with a benevolent smile and nodding indulgently.

"And so, now you are going to tell me how it's all chance and mechanics, though how this is possible you don't know. Aren't you going to tell me this?" Jacob waited for a moment. Irritated. "Why don't you answer? . . . I can guess why you don't. You are quiet because there is something else about the immune system, something *extremely peculiar*." He paused, conscious of treading on thin ice below which extended the vast territory of a science whose intricacies and barely explored subtleties were only peripherally familiar to him. But he felt he was holding a trump card, and he was reckless now.

"You can't get out of this one, Mel!" he cried. "I remember you said the B cells in our immune system are produced in an almost infinite variety of shapes, each equipped to produce a highly individualized antibody, a substance that can fight intruders, provided they are of a corresponding type. So when an intruder, such as a virus, shows up, there will be one cell (or maybe a few) that will be able to 'recognize' it, match it; one might say, 'fit it like a lock over a key': apprehend it! But, of course, these culprits don't normally arrive singly. They come in packs, and the body needs more than just one or maybe a few of the matching cells that can fight them.

"How well I remember your words, Mel!" cried Jacob with glee. "You said as soon as one of those culprits has been seized, something spectacular begins to happen. The entire immune system is alarmed, and the particular cell that was able to 'recognize' the intruder begins to divide, proliferate, producing in massive quantities copies of itself, all able to make antibodies which can attack invaders of the same type as the apprehended culprit. Next time, when a different type of menace appears inside our body, a cell of a different shape will 'recognize' it, and it will be this particular cell that will replicate itself a myriad times over. And together with its copies, it will produce new antibodies, all specifically suited to cope with the new invaders. Can *this* have come about by chance?"

No one answered Jacob's question.

"It's almost as if a commander had only one gun to blast away a hostile bomber, and when a squadron of them arrives, presto, the gun turns into an entire arsenal. Next time there is only one torpedo wherewith to destroy a hostile battleship, but as soon as a whole fleet of them arrives, presto: The torpedo begins to multiply."

"The immune system recognizes never-before-encountered invaders, bolsters its fighting power, and attacks them. Does this not indicate that matter recognizes need and responds to need? Physical and chemical activities in the brain tell us when and how we should defend ourselves. Physical and chemical reactions trigger the immune system to wage its fabulous battles.

Does this so called 'automatic' activity not suggest a mode of knowledge? And doesn't it show that matter not only builds but when possible also tries to protect what is built?"

There was silence. Jacob didn't know whether he had impressed them enormously, or whether they had grown tired of him and had gone away.

He was inching towards a logical conclusion. He whispered: "In God, knowing and action are one." And silently he added, "It is an all-encompassing knowledge, utterly pervasive: the material universe is founded on the continuous, inherently informed activity of subatomic particles. So the knowing of the Originating Existence, who forms the particles, in a very real sense, reaches into all being."

* * *

He was sitting on a bench by the canal jotting down ideas on the unused summer pages of his pocket calendar. Now the lines began to curl and intertwine, luxuriating over page after page. A cold and dreary curtain of dusk was on the canal. Jacob shivered but remained where he was, riveted by a strange uneasiness, which he could not explain to himself. The impact of a clarity freshly gained, so elating normally when it was achieved after much concentration, was muted by the conviction that there was, after all, a gap somewhere, an important incompleteness. He tried to fasten his mind on something obvious. Something concrete. The houses on the hill stood closed and so remote—as if they weren't just on the other side of the canal. Bare, spindly twigs on trees marked his mind with acid discomfort. He felt a need for something soft and warm. Healing roundings. He was turning there for protection, knowing that this was not how the gap would be closed. It was a refuge sought spontaneously. And Jacob felt the fever in him now unmistakably.

The seeker of clarities knew love. He knew it even though the fever was trembling inside of him. All his love was for life itself; and the people he loved—and had loved, and still loved, and would love always in every breath—were the lustre in that vortex and its infinity, and he wanted them with unending hunger as much as he wanted to breathe and think. And while he was thinking it, the cold did not bother him. Why have these lines come into my head just now? If consciousness were nothing but a moment of sun, a stirring in the penis or the brain. . . . He shook his head. No, this was not what he had written then—though it might have been. If consciousness were nothing. . . . How did it go? How did it go? He remembered the day—a cool, cloudy November day in Vancouver. They had friends over for some food and good talk the night before. There had been a lot of laughter, too. And in the morning they finished those delicious left-over open-faced sandwiches (salami and pickled cucumber and hard-boiled eggs and mayonnaise and even a bit of smoked salmon on rye—all those wonderful things Eve didn't want him to touch anymore because of the saturated fat and the cholesterol and the curing and the smoking and the salt). They had them for brunch. And it felt so good that morning thinking and talking about the night before, after the lovemaking, after the long Saturday morning sleep. It was a light, bright, good feeling.

In the afternoon he and Eve went down to the beach. Eve said she wanted to get a lamp stand, and he said they didn't just float in on every tide. But sure enough, an enticing piece of driftwood was being gently cradled in the waves toward the shore, and Eve waded into the water and captured it, but it was too heavy, soaked full of water, and he helped her get it home, each of them holding on at one end. And people on the way were looking at them and smiling and making remarks because they knew what was going to happen to that piece of driftwood. For several months it was left in the basement locker room of their apartment building until it was dry and had lost its heaviness, and for weeks afterwards Eve rubbed it patiently with sandpaper and then with linseed oil. It became an impressive lampstand. They still kept it in their living room. Such a happy day. . . . He wondered what made him think of it just now. Oh yes. That day before brunch they had played Mendelssohn's Violin Concerto on the radio, and while he was listening, he was writing those lines. Surely, he could recall them. . . .

> To know the liquid fire in the air!
> To feel and know—
> If consciousness were holding no joy
> But the colour of green, or raindrops
> On a sunlit pine
> Or berries on a shrub in autumn winds
> Blowing their tidal laughter;
> If awareness gave no more
> Than one note vibrant burning on a string
> Or an equation understood and solved
> Yes, even half solved;
> If it were no more than a caress
> Of young fluttering wings
> Or one poor question
> Asked from surging desire;
> If it were nothing
> But a moment of sky
> Pale and fading beyond the islands—
> Even then it would be
> Triumph irrevocable
> Worth all the myriad ages
> In fossil existence—the eons in vapour
> Burning in hydrogen, freezing in iron—
> Tossing in chaos
> Of primeval torrents
> And distant motions of fiery nebulae.
> Even then it would be worth
> The fear at the heart
> Of aging accelerating time
> The deeper chord

—If this will enter—
Like memory of wheels in the night
Always resounding
In the most distant cavern refuge
Of our senses.
Even then

It would still be worth
The endless journey.

Such a happy day. I must remind Eve when I get home, he thought. And he felt very fortunate. Love has built a shell around me, a kind of invisible armour, he was thinking. All my life I have been so loved that, even if I found myself utterly alone in the world, ignored, shunned, disliked, I should still feel beloved and lovable. Mom and Dad were so delighted to have me, Eve lets me know every hour of the day how much happiness she derives from my presence—even if I were utterly disfigured now, I should still feel handsome. And such trust in me have they always shown that, no matter how wildly people may scoff at my words, I shall still retain confidence in this, my own measure of wisdom.

This last was thought with defiance. He had not bothered sending out those lines. Obscurity was in fashion then far more than now—the artfully distorted sentence, the fragmented, mangled grammar pretending spontaneity. An aura of being cerebral was not out of favour, but idea, if present, had to be veiled, clothed, shrouded, swathed. In the reputable publications it was drowned, suffocated, inaccessible. *A poem should not mean but be.* Most of his colleagues quoted this—as if it were established fact proved by scientific method. Editors and reviewers in respectable publications despised naked ideas. To say it clearly was like sending out your wife naked onto the piazza. Some of his students would come to him and show him their rejection slips—furious or crushed, and usually both. Well, he didn't need this. He was, for himself, quietly but firmly convinced that there existed ideas that were in themselves poetic and needed no artistic apology. Jacob felt tired, almost sleepy. He saw his father on the bed that was to be his deathbed. He was half smiling, saying to Jacob, "One day there will be radios with pictures in every house. It won't be so long now. Somebody will sing a song in New York and people thousands of miles away will be able to see him actually standing there." He looked at Jacob with a wistful smile, so full of longing. "It will be in your lifetime," he said. And Jacob, overcome with the pain of it, took his father's hands between his own. They were the most wonderful hands, beautifully formed and proportioned, manly and sensitive. And Jacob, trying to be reassuring said, "You'll see it, too, Dad." His father nodded and smiled, and Jacob didn't know whether he believed him, or whether he just wanted to make his son believe that he believed, to help him, to make it easier. . . . And Jacob, even now, was overcome with the pain of it. . . . And even now, he felt the surging of passionate love for this gentle human being.

And his mother? A vivacious lady, slim and wearing trim clothes, lively about her housework, and arriving like a breeze of summer in the workroom, where her husband was cutting fine cloth, sewing it into handsome garments, fitting them on wealthy customers. When there was a rush job, her energy peaked. She would help her husband and his three employees with the basting and finishing. And often it was she who did the accounts. In the evening, when his father put Mozart or Beethoven on the turntable, she would curl up with worn books of poetry and novels from the old country. Uneducated as they were in any formal sense, his parents had given him his respect for learning, his love for the arts. In her widowhood, his mother took charge of the tailoring business her husband had built and eventually turned it into a retail store that was easier for her to manage.

Jacob saw her clearly as she stood in the kitchen the night he came home ashamed, remorseful, quite crushed after a hockey game. The team was blaming him. The coach was reproachful. Barry Kozak had been so close to the puck, but he, Jacob, was closer, and instead of passing it to Barry, who was much better at it, by far the best player on the team; instead of letting Barry have the chance—Barry, who would surely have scored—he had to show off, take it away from Barry, and himself try for the goal, knowing his own mediocrity, how unlikely it was that he would succeed; and, of course, the opportunity was lost. It might have been a tie. As it was, because of him, they had lost the game. And against their archrivals, too, that snooty team from Borden High.

Jacob was prepared. He expected his mother to carry on where the coach had left off, only with a little more tact. "You have to learn how to work with other people. . . that's what it's all about. . . . As long as you recognize that you've made a mistake, it'll be all right. . . ."

She didn't give him any of this. She said, "You wanted to do something splendid, and you didn't want someone else to do it for you. Maybe you aren't the right boy to be on a team." She stroked his hair. "Would you like a pair of skis for your next birthday?" He nodded, furiously fighting the tears. She looked into his eyes. "We'll see what we can do. But no racing or jumping! Do you hear me? No competition! I don't want you to break your neck for a bit of nothing. Just get out there into the snow . . . ," she knew him through and through, entirely. And suddenly, in spite of all his shame and misery, a great joy broke free and completely fused with her person. Even now, he could feel for her what he had felt then at barely fifteen.

*   *   *

How many kinds of love are there?

His children and the first grandchild. He sighed. Yes, he loved them too. With passion. Only it seemed to him that his feelings for them were of the nature of a permanent anxiety, a nervous desire to be reassured about their welfare. With Eve, it was the exact opposite. What he felt for her was brushing away all the grit and clutter. It was always in his consciousness that he loved her. Madly. She was perpetual spring in his blood. There was a stirring of the penis even at the thought of how she was rubbing herself against him like a kitten, that habit of clawing and making little responsive movements and purring noises when he stroked her. Sometimes he told her he didn't know who was more of a cat, she or Sir Cougar Coeur-de-chat, their tortoise-shell feline who did his utmost to be human. How often they laughed when they were together! Such a completely private hoard of comedy. And Eve was light and graceful as a dancer even now, and sometimes, when he was too tired to get up, she would dance alone, dance for him, like a ballerina—free, with this immense joy, all music and motion, gliding, bending, displaying her own fantastic choreography, her arms and hands in some strange way enveloping and caressing him in spite of the distance. He loved her charm, her face, her body, every nuance he knew so well. But then again, she was unexplored— with the depth of the ocean, its mysterious ecstasies, intellectually and bodily calling him into a corolla of infinite being. Yes, he loved her with passion. But he had never tried to define for himself what love was.

My love has many strands, Jacob thought. Can there possibly be a common denominator in what I feel as a parent, as a child, as a lover? And what about my love for a place, for music, for ideas? Love can be living in thoughts, emotions, sensations, instincts—and before that: back, further back, is there, can there be in the primeval cosmic beginnings—a glimmer of it?

I want all that I love to exist and to prosper and to be close to me, said Jacob in his mind; to exist, exist, exist always—to

BE! And if this is what love is, can there be a more clear expression of it than the act of creation itself, the bringing into being? Is the love I feel a mode of that which constitutes the constructive thrust of matter, the workings of energy? If creativity can be equated with an act of love, can there be love more all-encompassing than that of Originating Existence?

And perhaps that which by the name of love is welling up in our human consciousness, when fully understood, is a mode in the constructive reachings of nature, an iridescence in God's affirming strength.

*   *   *

Pierre wouldn't understand this, said Jacob to himself and immediately countered, I am only pretending because I haven't got a chance to tell him.

Pierre would probably shake his head and then make an impossible comparison, like saying, "A loving Father I can speak to and get a reply. No? Jews have always spoken to God. They always imagined they could petition Him: A loving Father answers a prayer. That's the whole point."

Oh Pierre, Jacob thought, *Mon pauvre enfant*, you want Him to take you by the hand. But a hand can have many forms. In the fog-bound Vancouver nights, when he was lying in bed (quite possibly a century ago), Jacob could hear the dark, regular chords of the foghorn sounding from the North shore across Burrard Inlet, guiding whatever homing ship was plying its way. Like a father's hand, safe and strong, Jacob had often thought while he was lying in his warm bed, half asleep. It always felt good, knowing that the oum-haa . . . oum-haa . . . oum-haa . . . would keep on coming faithfully to anyone who might be out there in danger and blind among the dark waters. And sometimes, hearing the full proud voice of ships when they proclaimed the passing of the narrows, he thought gratefully: they're home now. Now they're gliding into the harbour. . . .

Hands can have many forms. . . .

His hands? You must look for them in your brain cells, in your muscles. . . . Energy is pulling you, pushing you. Originating Existence equips you, gives you abilities; that is the answer to your prayer. From here on, it's a do-it-yourself job. Sure, you can present your petition, as long as you know that action is likely to be the most effective prayer. As long as you don't expect to be hired just because, on the way to the interview, you helped an old lady across the street. The Originating Existence works only within the logic of its own laws. And the answer to that particular prayer is in the fact that you are leaving the old lady standing safely on the sidewalk on the other side of the street. Do you see what I mean?

*   *   *

Pierre would draw himself up and say haughtily (as he had done on a previous occasion), "I would appreciate it if you'd give me some credit. You don't have to point out to me that water is wet." And then he would come back and say irritably, "And what if the abilities I am given are weak? Isn't this just what we pray for? Increased strength?"

Ah yes, the silent prayer, the secret prayers of the heart. Yes, Pierre, I do think the Originating Existence can answer them if you reach out with all your might, if you put yourself in accord with Its natural laws.

"Reach out? I wouldn't know how to begin." Jacob could hear Pierre's voice and see the impatient, sudden toss of his head. "How does one do this reaching out?"

Well, Pierre, maybe the talent for it is not yet fully developed in us. That's where communal worship comes in, I suppose. It carries you. It helps when you want to reach out and you don't know how.

"But how does one do this?!"

Jacob felt awkward. There was no way he could formulate it

adequately; but he kept on trying. It was like trying to drive a car up an icy hill.

Maybe you've heard a physician say that the will to live is a most important factor in a patient's recovery. That's been known for a long time. Now they maintain that supportive thoughts, trusting thoughts, when they concentrate on our immune system, can actually strengthen that system. When we strain with all our might toward the life engendering, the life sustaining, our strength is increased, renewed. . . .

That he couldn't say any of this to Pierre and perhaps would never have the opportunity to do so left Jacob drained. An emotional exhaustion came over him. He was walking very erect through centre town. The contours of the office towers rose sharp and black against a harsh brightness in the western sky. Overhead, in a dense sheet of dark, the strato-cumuli were spreading night. Unexpectedly, quite unbidden, Pierre's face was before Jacob. Not so much his face, it was a disconcerting expression in Pierre's eyes—the way he had observed it one evening about two years ago.

*   *   *

Ron, their son-in-law, had brought Susan for a six-week's stay with them. She was pregnant, and his firm was sending him to the Middle East and Asia to help their customers install and operate new equipment. Berni was home, too, for a brief spell, looking for job opportunities in the anthropology departments of various universities. On Saturday night they had Pierre over with Miss Boudreau. At that time they were hoping he might marry her, considering the way he had talked to them about her. Eve had already started worrying about what would make a suitable wedding present for them.

Across the street, they saw them park in Micki's neat little red Chevy. Pierre's nineteen-year-old Ford was about to expire and looked it. Evidently they had decided to arrive in style. For a moment the Haralds thought Pierre had bought a new car and had let Miss Boudreau drive it; but it was she who locked the doors, and she put the keys in her purse.

They did their best to welcome her with friendly interest and warmth, but they soon had to accept the fact that she was not going to be at ease in their company. She never shed her polite, quiet formality. With her boxy fashionable clothes, long, glossy red fingernails, and flawlessly applied eye makeup, she had the appearance of a woman who was used to presenting herself to public scrutiny with confidence. It occurred to Eve that Pierre was showing her off like a trophy.

They never allowed the conversation to flag, and Pierre was helpful in this, showing much interest in Ron's impending trip and perhaps more than a little envy, too. "Don't you wish you could accompany your husband?" he asked Susan, who countered with a vehement, "I wouldn't set foot in countries who oppress women and keep them in harems, and don't even let them drive a car.—Would you?" she said turning to Miss Boudreau.

"I shouldn't like to live in a harem," replied Micki, avoiding a direct answer.

"If you went to such countries, you would have an opportunity to talk to the women there, and you could speak about the subject with a bit more knowledge," said Berni, goading Susan. It was a habit of his that Jacob and Eve had hoped he would have outgrown by now.

"Don't give Susan ideas," said Ron, only half joking. "If she starts discussing her views with ladies who inhabit harems, she'll get herself into trouble. She'll start a revolution. I don't want to have to run to the Canadian government, begging them to get my pregnant wife out of some exotic jail."

"I don't have to travel to find a need for revolution. There is enough for us to do right here," declared Susan, and turning again to Miss Boudreau, she said, "You are in business. Don't you think it's time for more women to be in top management?

People have no idea how scandalously few women make top decisions. We need legislation. If necessary, we'll have to force employers!"

Micki's smile was faint. "It would be very good if there were more women in high jobs," she said. "Myself—I guess I am lucky. The head of Ladies' Wear has been appointed one of our vice presidents. So there is quite a bit of moving up in our firm. My boss is going to be the new buyer, and she has promised me—in the new year I'll be her assistant. So I guess I have some hope." She gave a pleased, modest little laugh.

"But there should be more women who break out of the traditional women's fields. Why aren't there more women in oil or transport or—" Susan suddenly seemed to realize that she was putting Micki's achievement down, and she quickly said, "There should be many more women like you—women who are going to make their mark in the business world."

To which Miss Boudreau quite simply replied, "I have no choice. I have to work."

* * *

Later, after Micki and Pierre had left and the family was helping Eve clear away the dishes, Susan gave vent to what evidently was agitating her sisterly sensitivities.

"It's disgusting," she said, "how many women there are like Micki: good looking, capable, intelligent, really nice persons, and the men won't marry them!"

"Maybe *she* doesn't want to marry *him;* has this occurred to you?" asked Berni with his vexatious logic.

"She does," Susan insisted. "Did you notice the way she said, 'I have to work. I have no choice'? Maybe she wants a child. She isn't that young. Did you notice how she mothers Pierre? How she chose that piece of chocolate square for him: 'Look, here is a corner—you like the corner, don't you—*gla-*

çage on three sides! So much icing!' And when she got up to leave: 'I'm afraid we have to go now. Pierre has to help with the inventory. They're starting early.'"

It was true. They had noticed something of the kind.

"He's exploiting her," Susan insisted, talking herself into a flurry of disapproval. "He's using her as his chauffeur!"

"His Ford is all but a wreck," Jacob quickly interjected. "She probably wouldn't want to be seen in it."

"And they don't even live together," Susan went on. "He won't even make that much of a commitment. He probably leaves his own place in a mess. If he lived with her, she'd want him to share the housework. He's got all the advantages . . . ." The predictability of Susan's habitual speeches irritated them even though they often agreed with her. Ron looked a trifle subdued. Maybe he didn't do much sharing of housework either.

*   *   *

A few weeks later, they extended another invitation to Pierre and Micki. They had bought their new refrigerator from Pierre (actually spending more money on it than they had originally intended to let him have more profit), and they wanted him to see it in all its beauty proudly installed in their kitchen. Then they were all going to have dinner together to celebrate. Ron, of course, had left for the Middle East, and Berni was in Halifax, where he had landed another temporary job. This time he was substituting for a lady professor who was having a baby. Pierre turned up alone, driving the ramshackle Ford. Micki, he said was sorry: a last-minute thing at work. She couldn't come. After dinner, when they were sitting in the living room and Pierre was sipping his Cointreau, Susan quite suddenly, to her parents' unspeakable mortification shedding all restraint, in a abrupt attack bluntly said to Pierre, "Why don't you marry Micki Boudreau?"—leaving them aghast and wondering how they could ever make amends for her impudence.

She had driven it home incisively. For a second he looked at her with narrowed eyes as if he couldn't quite believe that such audacity was possible in this house. Then he looked away, and for a moment they thought he would let it pass, but he turned on her. "Maybe I should ask *you* to marry me!" He said it with savage hostility. And they were afraid she would counter this confused, senseless, totally inappropriate remark with some wounding irony, of which she was quite capable. But she sat there looking at Pierre with a half smile, as if she were slightly amused.

There followed a pause. A seemingly endless pause. And somehow, slowly, the usual flickering discontent of Pierre's personality that seemed concentrated in his outburst dissolved. He looked into Susan's face with a great, still seriousness, a strange, intent expression in his eyes. Jacob remembered wondering whether Eve, too, was noticing the transformation. Afterwards he didn't ask her, and she never mentioned anything about it. But it was Eve who broke the silence.

Looking at Susan she said, "I just remembered: I promised Vicki Cohen to return the book that's on my bedside table. She may need it later tonight for her discussion group. Would you mind very much if I asked you to take it over to her?"

"No problem," Susan said, and in a very quiet, dignified way left the room.

"Are you watching anything interesting on TV these days?" Pierre asked almost lightheartedly. And the evening flowed on normally, uneventfully.

Miss Boudreau's name was not mentioned again, and it soon became clear that she and Pierre were no longer seeing each other.

* * *

Jacob was walking through the dusky streets more slowly now. That disconcerting expression on Pierre's face was before him. He didn't want to think about it because to speculate about the expression on someone's face or in his eyes was surely futile. The margin of error is bound to be enormous, he thought. Too many possibilities. Was that embarrassment he had seen? It would make sense. How awkward for Pierre to be asked why he didn't marry Miss Boudreau, when maybe the rupture between them had occurred that very day. Or was it regret because he had lashed out at Susan? Reproach because her impertinence had made him utter an absurdity? It could have been any of these emotions. Yet none of them really seemed to fit what Jacob had seen. Something had briefly come into his mind that evening. It was hard to admit it, but Pierre had looked at Susan with the earnestness of a man who wanted to take the woman he loved into his arms. It wasn't a lustful gaze, Jacob had to acknowledge. That element was missing. It was a deep, serious stillness. Jacob had known it then. His entire interpretation of something so tenuous was an extravagance of his own imagination; and he knew it now. It was not only unlikely. It could make one laugh. Before that evening when Pierre had brought Micki to visit, he and Susan had hardly seen each other; and Susan's conduct when she assaulted him like a forward child hadn't been exactly endearing. At the moment when he gazed at her so intently, she didn't even look pretty. Jacob had seen some of his acquaintances become more beautiful during pregnancy. But this had not been the case with Susan or her mother. Pregnancy exhausted them. Susan was sitting there looking a bit unkempt, and in that unattractive pose (comfortable no doubt and justified by her condition, but hardly likely to stir romantic feelings), leaning back, her head thrust forward, her rounded belly almost parallel with the ceiling, and her legs slightly apart. Jacob could not imagine that any man could have fallen in love with her at that moment. But what, then, *did* that strange expression signify? Jacob at last dismissed it. It doesn't matter, he thought. It never did matter. What can it matter today?!

* * *

The streetlamps flared into brightness. He realized it was late. And still he could not banish Pierre. With no prospects in any direction, Pierre had needed something, had perhaps been groping toward a centrality. He came to *us,* Jacob thought. He came to us, and we were helpless.

Hurrying now, he was aware that he was alone in the street and quite a distance from where he had left his car, and he hurried toward home, to Eve, eager to discuss with her every flicker of thought, hoping that whatever oppressed him would dissolve in her reassuring words. The western sky had grown dark. The windows on some of the empty floors in the office towers were lit now, switched on by some lonely commissionaire on duty or turned on automatically. Jacob shuddered. There was in him a deep uneasiness which perhaps had nothing to do with Pierre, a vague disturbance reminiscent of the undefined primeval gloom that sometimes in his childhood had invaded him on Sunday nights. It loosened its grip when he thought of Eve but did not disappear. It remained like a barely acknowledged, veiled fear.

He tried to shore up thoughts concerning the moments of clarity. There would be gifts for Pierre if he came back. But could such fragments be enough? Can this be enough? Can this be enough? Can this be enough? Can this be enough. . . ?

On The Road to Yad Vashem

V

This time, however, Jacob did not talk to Eve about his explorations. She had waited for him angry and reproachful, had fretted and worried, and at last was hugely relieved when he finally showed up. After supper, he went to bed because he noticed the strange little throbbings that always told him that he was in a fever. It turned into a bad cold, an influenza probably, to judge by the lingering aches and a feeling of chronic fatigue that caused, and in a vicious circle, was caused by, a dullness, a dissatisfaction, a downcast and burdened mind. Late in February, he developed pneumonia, and it was June before he had regained enough strength to live up to his various obligations.

* * *

But all this lay behind him now. During the past three and a half years, he had recovered sufficiently to do all the things he had planned for his retirement; most of them, at any rate. The archaeological expedition to the Mediterranean had to be postponed, not because of his health, but because the roof of the cottage needed mending, and they had to purchase a new car, and after thirty years of impeccable service, the washing machine had to be replaced; and Berni, whose degree in anthropology did not seem to have any market value at all, needed money to go back to school and retrain.

Jacob rarely brooded about Pierre. At least, he did not often permit himself to speculate. But at the back of his mind, the suspicion, the fear, the doubts existed still. Sometimes he looked at Eve and wondered whether she too still worried, and he wanted to ask her but dared not. Perhaps she had forgotten, and his question would bring it all back and cause her pain. Then one day, he did ask, and when she made no reply, he broke without restraint: "What if he is dead?! What if I let him go like that when he needed our friendship?"

To Jacob's surprise, she said very calmly, "I'm convinced he will show up one of these days."

Did she really believe this? Or did she say it because his voice had given him away and she knew how he suffered? He did not raise the topic again, but the memory of Pierre blighted the congenital exuberance of his "Hi there, little rabbit (Why are you so small?)! . . . Why, hello Revenue Canada Income Tax Return form! . . . Welcome little leaf! . . . Hello my life!" He could go on for days performing his tasks, even enjoying himself reading, writing letters, going to the theatre, to concerts, watching television, inviting friends, and attending social gatherings. He could give himself to the flow of agreeable events, and the memory would keep itself discretely subdued. But then suddenly, when there was poignancy, a passage of music, or a conversation that was especially animated, some beautiful formation of sunlit cloud, even a gust of his favourite perfume from the back of Eve's little earlobe—when his breast expanded in well-being, the feeling of joy subsided in mid-flight, blasted by the conviction that he had failed Pierre when his help was urgently needed. "Hi, little rabbit, why are you. . . ."

*　*　*

Sometimes Jacob was certain that he was battling the onset of mental illness, and he was ready to confide in a psychiatrist. But then again, talking about it would be painful, and a doctor would tell him that his remorse was unreasonable, that he expected too much of himself. And he knew this without medical advice. Of course his regret was unreasonable. Quite absurd as a matter of fact. The man had hurled at him a totally unreasonable question. How, in the name of common sense, could he have expected a reasonable reply! And on the spot, yet! Without giving anyone a chance to think about it. Totally unreasonable. —When his thoughts proceeded on these lines, Jacob felt a good deal better. He knew he was right. Nevertheless, he was glad when those thoughts at the back of his mind kept quiet for a while.

If I had clarified my ideas before that weekend at the cottage, I could have countered his question. I could have given him an answer that might have consoled him. It would have lifted our friendship to a different level. I might have had an opportunity to do some real good. Is this the price we pay when we don't put our house in order, when we drift, when we don't know what we believe in? If my children had asked me that terrible question, I should have clarified my faith years before I met Pierre. Why did they never ask? Were they afraid? Did I fail them, too? What purpose was there in all my teaching? How much did my students need it—ultimately? Here, with Pierre, there was a real opportunity. If only. . . .

In time, Jacob made a determined effort to give up those tortured speculations altogether. He no longer formed distinct arguments in his mind. What was left was only the vague feeling of blight, of regret, of no longer being able to experience to the fullest those moments of carefree joy that nourish the roots of a happy life. "Hi, little rabbit, why . . . why are you. . . ."

*   *   *

Their financial situation meanwhile had improved. A savings plan had matured and the new investment supplemented their income so that, at last, they could make arrangements for a Mediterranean sojourn. It had to be modified, shortened somewhat, but they were to see all the most important archaeological sites, even, at the end, the coast of Anatolia with a few days in the Troad.

* * *

They spent two weeks in Egypt and two in Greece, and they were so hungry for all there was to do, experience, learn, explore, that Jacob began to have doubts about the efficacy of the schedules he had so laboriously prepared. "It's probably all wrong," he said more than once. "We should have concentrated on just one country at a time. We should have spent a month in each, maybe two or three." But of course this was patently ludicrous. Eve joked it away. "And what do you suggest we should have used for money?" They could never have afforded it.

Their Egyptian days were a bonfire that consumed rapidly a profusion of exciting, astonishing moments and left them dazed in the continual change of sounds and smells and sights. Emotions suddenly welled up in pleasure when architecture, ancient and modern, rose from the desert in grandeur or left them cringing at the decay that flitted past their eyes when their bus gathered speed, and again expanded the breast at the elegant sweep of Alexandria's Marine Drive, where they walked along the ocean against a bracing wind, away from the unabating, charming, annoying, interesting, exasperating chatter of a band of tourists whom they had joined in Cairo.

The pace was so hectic, so crowded and varied that, for the first time, even that faint, persistent ache was forced from Jacob's mind. But in the silent streets of Delos it returned. The small, still island with its lifeless walls and empty foundations now open to the sun offered no defence, and the vague regret at the back of his mind would no longer disappear. Jacob mutely called it his "neurosis," and he knew that he had to live with it the way a man with a physical handicap has to live with his affliction.

There were truly stupendous moments, of course. Eve threw her arms around Jacob with unexplainable tears, and they saw the declining sunlight mellow over the Aegean beyond the columns of Cape Sunion, their integrity, their serene beauty that seemed to say, "Only he could conceive us who had transcended all human grief." Jacob and Eve knew that what moved them so had been the destination of millions of travellers, and that their response was only a repetition of un-counted experience. Jacob had no doubt most of his former colleagues at the university would turn up their noses at the naivety of Eve's enthusiasm. But such snobbery was merely a quirk of civilization. And Eve, as if she knew what he was thinking, said, "Good fresh bread and spring water taste superb, no matter what multitude shares in the experience. It becomes part of the self. Everything here will always remain our own, our very personal own."

A pair of dolphins played near their ship off Santorini on their way to Crete. Jacob and Eve stood on deck and watched them rise from the water side by side, their motion through the air tightly synchronized, their bodies like a single organism, a black athlete controlled but easy in graceful flight at a curve smooth as from the brush of a genius, and their return with a splash and spray as if the blue water, the incredibly blue water, were happy to have them back. . . . Again and again they rose. Eve called them "the perfect lovers from the sea." Tourists were swarming all over the deck. Everybody was watching the dol-phins. So Jacob and Eve couldn't let each other know ade-quately how the oneness of these beautiful creatures echoed in their own bodies. But they moved closer, close enough for Eve to press her arm against her husband's side.

* * *

In Jerusalem they rented a minuscule apartment that belonged to a youngish bachelor, an assistant professor who had gone to the United States as an exchange lecturer at one of the universities there. The place was not comfortable, rather skimpily furnished, and not particularly well cared for. There was a bed with a sagging mattress and a misanthropic, hard cot, neither of them quite fit for Jacob's long legs. All supply of heated water (one couldn't really call it *hot* water) remained sporadic, and the plumbing was altogether capricious. No, they didn't like it at all, but the place was comparatively inexpensive.

Luckily, they had worked out a pleasant routine which kept them away from home for most of the day. In the morning they visited the sites they wanted to explore, and every afternoon they went to the library of the Hebrew University to study and gain as much background information as possible for next morning's adventure. Later in the afternoon, they strolled along Yehuda Street or through the Old City, window shopping, admiring, relaxing, letting its fairy-tale dinginess, its protean humanity and craftsmanship, which crowded the labyrinth of narrow streets, tantalize the imagination; or they treated themselves to some unmitigated pampering and went for a swim in the magnificently landscaped garden pool at the King David Hotel. All of this was most enjoyable.

But back in their claustrophobic lodgings, they often wondered what made them stay here so far away from their comfortable home, where there were books and a radio and a TV that always spoke to them in a language they could understand; and where hot water came out of the tap without fail; where there was a toilet that always flushed with vigour; and where everything gleamed from years of loving attention. Sometimes they thought it had all been a terrible mistake—coming here for such an extended period. Two weeks, surely, might have sufficed. Poor Sir Cou, accustomed as he was to a lot of petting and the occasional unscheduled tidbit, was probably pining miserably in the care of the young home-minder. There was no air-conditioning in this apartment, and when the nights became unbearably stuffy, they fled to Caesarea, to Haifa, and from there to Lake Kinereth and the Galil.

*   *   *

And then Tsefat. They came to the holy city of Tsefat. In the holy city, almost three thousand feet above the sea, old houses crumbling in the sun cluster atop a mountain and scatter upward to where crusaders built their stronghold, Foulques d'Anjou, more than half a millennium ago. From the terraced park that cordons excavations, the camera takes in the lake in the distance below, the Golan Heights even, and far away, land that is Jordan. Eve said, "It won't be any good. It will just be a few insignificant streaks in the distance."

"You'll be glad to have it, to remember," said Jacob and kept on pressing the button on his camera. Clicking.

They were walking endlessly. Later in the afternoon, their sightseeing expedition led them to visit the synagogues of Rabbi Luria. Ishak Luria. The man they called Ha'Ari, The Lion. He had prayed here, surrounded by his followers, igniting their spirit with his mystic fire. Eve was walking slowly ahead on the hot, dusty path to the edifice, which stretched along a shelf on the hillside. Jacob stopped. Heavy perspiration was on his face and his back. The heat was not only physically debilitating, it did something to his will. No energy, he thought. Not enough protein, maybe. Must be careful. Must talk to Eve about that. Maybe more strenuous exercise necessary. Regularly. Maybe not enough control altogether. That scorching light. Why am I standing here instead of trying to get out of it quickly? Same reason why I let thoughts bother me; sometimes. Not enough control.

He looked at the long, low wall stretching away in the

glaring sun. He was too tired to climb the few steps. The Lion had willpower, Jacob thought. Admirable will power. To leave one's cushioned place in a wealthy home and the jollity of friends and to live alone in a shack like a pauper, this needs, at the very least, some power to manage oneself. Ishak Luria had stayed like this for a year on the banks of the Nile, thinking, speculating, wrestling until it was time; and then he emerged in strength. It was then that he became The Lion.

We haven't had such heat since we came here, Jacob thought. It's too much heat. Even sunglasses don't help enough against this glare. There was in him a giving way to an old secret exhaustion which he badly wanted to conquer and a vague desire that in this land of the cabalists, he might be touched by the strength and fire of the sages who had lived here four hundred years ago. For an instant he was unsure whether it was just a thought that had come into his head, or whether he had actually murmured the words: If your spirit was freed of torments at last, even if that freedom was bought with desperate, lonely struggles, be my guide!

Just for a moment, what he had felt rather than thought precipitated into words, into a totally irrational hope that something here might help him clean the senseless remorse from the deep layers of his mind, help him rid himself also of that barely admitted oppressiveness which occasionally troubled him. The experience was fleeting, banished as soon as he was fully conscious of it. A preposterous extravagance. He had caught the little boy in a daydream, and he dismissed it as thoroughly alien to his view of how things came about in this world.

*   *   *

Inside the synagogue, a young man with a yarmulke was recounting history for a group of tourists. The women had covered up in deference to the prescribed standards of modesty which orthodoxy here strictly enforced. Eve had tied two corners of a multicoloured piece of chiffon under her chin. It covered her chignon and fell over her bare arms down below the knees. To Jacob, she looked as if she had stepped from an oriental painting, from among the curlicues and gold leaf. Now she was turning slightly, a habit of hers always to make sure she wasn't standing in anyone's way, blocking anyone's view. A short, stocky woman with heavy, dark eyebrows was right behind her, and Eve made way to let her come closer to the speaker.

*   *   *

The woman had draped a heavy cardigan over her head and sleeveless arms. She must be melting, poor thing, thought Jacob, still wiping the sweat off his face. Why on earth would she bring this woolly object on a day like this, he wondered. Then he noticed that her clothes looked skimpy and cheap. She probably had nothing more suitable to bring along.

Eve was the first to interrupt with a question, and the young man replied earnestly, eagerly, and at length, and obviously pleased with himself. Other people joined in. Some were clearly much more knowledgeable than the Haralds. How I remember this! Jacob thought, grimly recalling certain conferences he had attended. Questions that reveal one's urge to prove one's erudition rather than a thirst for information. He tried but could not fight his ill-humour. The group moved about the sanctuary. Admiration was lavished on the ornate covers of old Torah scrolls. Jacob did not follow. He became absent-minded and restless.

All those tourists coming here by the hundreds, by the thousands. Knowing so much and knowing so little. So spellbound because here is some of their history, their heritage. But the soul of this place, the Lurianic cabala—what is it to them?

Ishak Luria's vision of how the universe began and of its glorious ending when all the splinters of light that have scattered from the Godhood will be gathered in and return—how much of this do they know or even want to learn? The world has no time for Luria's poetry. The world has other worries. And maybe he struggled for nothing—in the long run.

But I, I want to learn from you, Jacob thought. Vaguely. With an emotion more than with his mind. Teach *me!* I need energy. I need a healing will to be free of absurd regrets. Help me! Even if I have to go through fire. Teach me how to do this. In spite of himself, Jacob was looking about him with a sense of expectation. Was there, could there be among these walls in some way. . . . something. . . . an impression perhaps, an idea, an experience, something to guide one. . . . ? But there was nothing. It had just been a feeling, of course.

Altogether laughable. He had not really expected anything. The place was tranquil. Everything looked clean. Eminently concrete. Well-dusted, lovingly cared for by loyal, respectful hands. Nothing more. The spirit of the cabalists eluded him. He could find no trace of the strength and fervour that had flourished here.

*   *   *

When they stepped outside, the sun was still high and unutterably bright on the pale, terraced blocks of stone. They were fumbling for their sunglasses. Buildings with arched apertures on steep, dry, overgrown slopes. Houses with vegetation sprouting from walls. A few cypress trees. A lonely donkey with nothing to do. Down below, on the side of the hill, a large tract of scorched brush. High up in the distance, a pole with electric wires, proof that the twentieth century was laying claim to the hills of Tsefat.

The Haralds were making their way down the stony lane,

when Eve surreptitiously tugged at Jacob's shirtsleeve. She was excited. "Please take this—you must take this!"

He saw a strange girl, maybe fourteen or sixteen, pleasantly plump, with loose black hair and a lovely full mouth. She was sitting on one of the steps where another lane-way branched off to lead up the parched slope. A tree gave her a little shade. And she smiled at them. Her flowery skirt was gathered at the waist of an open, white blouse, and a fringed dark shawl was thrown over her shoulders. She was barefoot, but from her ears dangled heavy, splendidly ornate silver earrings; and she had with her a young goat, a cream-coloured animal with a black face.

"Maybe she doesn't like to be photographed." Jacob once had a disconcerting experience. He was cautious. But Eve was determined. She approached the girl and asked permission. Then she gesticulated. But she only got a non-committal smile.

Two middle-aged ladies who had just left the synagogue and were walking behind them stopped. The Haralds had noticed them before. The shorter, darker one with the heavy eyebrows and the woolly cardigan in her hand wore a plain, dark blue skirt and a striped T-shirt; the other, the slim one, was in a khaki safari suit, and her face was shielded by a wide-brimmed hat. Now the shorter one, the olive-skinned, vivacious woman, addressed the girl, who immediately began to arrange and spread the hem of her skirt.

"She says she doesn't mind being photographed." They were surprised to hear an unmistakable New York accent, Brooklyn probably, and they thanked the lady profusely for her help. Eve seized the opportunity:

"Is she an Arab girl?"

"No," said the lady, and after a brief conversation in Hebrew, she added, "She says she came here from Morocco six years ago."

Jacob went to work with his Nikon, a present for his sixtieth birthday. Eve was perceiving his difficulties and, as always, she was ready to help.

"Please—we want the goat, too!"

The Brooklyn lady obligingly translated, and the girl pulled the goat close, putting an arm around the flanks of the animal. But now her shoulder rose at an unbecoming angle.

Again, Eve remonstrated, and again the Brooklyn lady translated. The girl obediently released the goat, which promptly turned around to pull some vegetation from between the crevices of the stone steps.

"No, please, no!"

Eve was flustered. The lady translated. Jacob was waiting patiently, adjusting his Nikon. With some difficulty, the goat was turned around to face the camera. The girl was no longer smiling.

"Oh, please, could you please ask her to smile? Just the way she did before?"

With an inscrutable glance at Eve, the lady translated. A smile returned. It was no longer the same sunny smile they had seen when they first discovered her. Eve was exasperated, but she lost courage and kept quiet.

The camera clicked once, twice. Jacob took some money from his wallet, but the girl hid her hands and said something to the olive-skinned lady.

"She says you should send her a photograph."

"OK—If they turn out, I will."

The lady took down the girl's name and address and handed it to Jacob.

"I do admire your Ivrit. You seem to be completely fluent," said Eve.

"I live in Tsefat. I paint. I have been here for the past fifteen years. Yes. But my friend is only a visitor. She comes from Toronto, Canada."

* * *

There followed the usual fuss most people think as necessary as paying the tax-man when they meet compatriots in some out-of-the-way place far from home. It took a while to establish that they had not a single mutual acquaintance or friend or relative in Toronto, nor indeed, anywhere else in the world.

When the Haralds had renewed their thanks and wished the Torontonian a safe and enjoyable vacation, the two women walked ahead towards the town.

After a hurried conference, Eve caught up with them. "We wondered—would you ladies care to have tea with us? We are staying at the Rimon Inn."

The face of the Brooklynite lit up. "My favourite place. I go there on special occasions—like my birthday. When I can afford it." And turning to her friend she laughed, "I'm so glad you'll see it. It's beautiful. I always think it's a hide-away for honeymooners or runaway lovers."

She kept on exclaiming, and the Haralds were pleased with themselves when they saw her pleasure. They were walking through the courtyards of the inn. Arching doorways, trees, balconies with richly trailing vines, and potted flowers on stairways and in low niches; everywhere tubs with vegetation, brilliant splashes of sun-drenched colour against the massive cut-stone walls.

"Every time we turn a corner, there is a surprise!" cried the painter, whose name was Mitzi. "This is what I call superb architecture. It's always like an unexpected treat, and in spite of this, nothing is forced, nothing is incongruent." She was having a marvellous time. "Look at this composition. Just Look! The space, and the contrast in these lines and colours—it's inevitable. It emerges naturally—like a crystal or a plant."

When they passed through the lobby, she became subdued, almost reverent. "Such noble austerity . . ." she whispered, her elbow lightly nudging her friend and with one sweeping motion of her head taking in the enormously high ceiling, the bold stairs, and the walls of simple stone and glass. Later, at the table in the pleasantly intimate vaulted dining room, she continued with her rhapsody. "I believe architecture like this imposes its own standard on those who enter."

"Not necessarily," said Eve. "I don't believe that living in a well-designed house makes people necessarily better human beings."

"Of course not; not when you are thinking of people's morals. I'm not talking about ethics. Morals don't come into this at all." The Haralds didn't mind being contradicted. Mitzi had the kind of spunk they enjoyed. She said, "what I mean is that living in a well-designed house or even just being for a while in a beautiful building influences one's style, the way one pictures oneself, or at least the way one would like to be. It's an inspiration for living—aesthetically."

"Architecture certainly influences one's mood," said Jacob.

"It's not only that. It's much more than that," Mitzi insisted. "People who grow up where there is attractive space around them—interesting organization of shape—they are much more likely to do quality work. They have an understanding of quality. I think that's why, for instance, Italian artisans are usually tops. I once travelled through the countryside near Naples. There were some stone hovels, really a rural slum, and you know, even they were aesthetic. In their basic design, they were beautiful. It's like this all around the Mediterranean, at least in the older parts; haven't you noticed? Also, I think good architecture has something to do with a basic *joie de vivre*. . . ." The arrival of a platter with delicious fish from Lake Kinereth interrupted her.

"Have you read Pirsig on quality?" she asked before delicately attacking her salad. "You really should read Pirsig."

* * *

After the meal they stepped out onto the deck. Beyond the gardens and terraced houses with Mediterranean roofs, flat roofs and roofs frilly with convex tile, there stretched the mountains of Galilee, forested, green, an open range of gently curved elevations. Earth-coloured patches dotted with young trees were marking the lower reaches. Lovingly tended soil.

They let the painter select a spot she particularly liked, and she wanted to be near some rimonim, the pomegranate shrubs from which the inn took its name. They sat in this quiet corner, and she was telling them about her life in New York before her divorce, and how she had gone to art school in San Francisco and finally had settled here in Tsefat. Marketa, the woman from Toronto, was quiet most of the time. She told them that originally she had come from Prague, and that she got her Canadian citizenship twenty-eight years ago; but that was all.

Mitzi compensated for her reticence. More than compensated for it. She adored talking about her work, and thriving on the Haralds' interest, positively blooming, she was going on about it with a lust that was disarming. "Lately I have concentrated on painting portraits. Very exciting ones. This has become the real, the serious ambition of my life. Believe me when I say they are fantastic. Of course, I could never be interested in anything conventional. Anyone who knows me will tell you that. I couldn't have people sit for me, give them something they can show their friends twenty years from now: Look how pretty I was! That's for the make-up department." Her efforts to impress were too honest to grate on one's nerves: "I am an artist. I have a responsibility. These portraits I am doing now are very different. I do hope you'll have time to come and see them. I feel it's a real breakthrough. Imagine very smooth and sweeping lines—almost like brushwork in ink, although I am using acrylics and oil (she made a dramatic gesture with her hand)—and against a stark, white background. You have to imagine faces that are noble, serene, classical almost—you know what

I mean. But over the face, I mount an actual, three-dimensional wire cage, coloured wire—black or red or green, all sorts, depending on the portrait. And the wire is twisted so that it clearly forms a face that is the same as the portrait on the canvas underneath; only it's grotesque, it's distorted with misery: with anger or jealousy, or sadness, or hatred. . . . You understand. Very few people do, of course. They won't take the trouble. Most people don't want true originality. They never did. Look at Van Gogh. When they come here, people want souvenirs of Tsefat. So I paint the city. That's how I make a living. . . ."

"Her landscapes are extraordinary. I'm taking three of them home with me," said Marketa. They wondered whether it was true or just a friendly sales pitch. "There's something of the mystery of Tsefat in them," she said. "Even the houses seem alive. They're dancing almost. I think Mitzi is influenced by some of the work of Shoshana Vilensky. . . . Don't you think you are?" She was turning to the painter.

"Maybe," Mitzi said, and in an unmistakable moodswing began to tear at the rimon leaf she had been rubbing between her fingers. The Haralds noted that her friend had made no remark about the portraits, and the omission was not lost on Mitzi, either. She challenged Marketa with a straight stare: "My portraits are still at an experimental stage. As I told you. Come back in two years, and you'll see." The irritated voice seemed to make Marketa shrink back into herself. Her pale, somewhat tired features were fading into the pale khaki of her safari outfit.

* * *

Eve determined that it had been rude of them to leave her out of the conversation, and that something had to be done for her, quickly. "And you, Marketa, is this your first visit to Israel?" she asked, her kind eyes full of amiable expectation.

"No. I was here before. Two years ago I was here."

"And you loved it so much, you had to come back." Eve said it with an encouraging smile in her voice.

"I loved it, yes. I was here for a whole month.—But you see, I did not go to Yad Vashem. When I was here before."

They said nothing.

Marketa apparently interpreted their silence as a reproach. She seemed to have a need to apologize. "I could not face it, then. I absolutely was unable to face it."

"And now?" asked Jacob.

"Yes. This time I am going to see it. I came back especially. I am on my way to Yad Vashem. I am leaving Tsefat early tomorrow morning."

There was a hesitation.

"What made you change your mind?" Jacob knew the question was too probing, too intrusive, but he could not help himself.

"You see, I was so afraid I might see someone—my mother or my father or my little brother or some relative or a friend. I know they have pictures there—I have seen pictures like that— with dead bodies, murdered; or people with a chain around the neck, waiting to be hanged, or waiting behind barbed wire. Sometimes on those pictures one can make out the faces very clearly. I was so afraid that. . . ."

"And now you have overcome your fear." Jacob could feel Eve's astonished, embarrassed eyes on him. He knew this was tactless, but there was a strange compulsion in him. It was obvious that the woman was under some strain. He knew he should leave her alone.

"Yes. I have."

A pause.

"What made you change your mind?" In heaven's name! Why did he ask this? Why couldn't he leave it! Eve became fidgety. He could see she was frantic to find something to say, something innocent that would sound natural and steer him away from this impertinent interrogation. Her mouth was twitching. He felt sorry for her and prepared to be reproached afterwards, but he needed an explanation.

"Last year I had an experience that made me change my mind." The woman called Marketa spoke very slowly. "Not an experience really, just a conversation. But it changed what I was able to do. You see—two years ago I *couldn't* have gone to Yad Vashem. Now I can."

"It must be very difficult," said Jacob. Their eyes met for an instant, and something in her seemed to respond. It made her go on.

"You see, I was in England when the war broke out. I had won a British Council scholarship to take English courses—at the Polytechnic in London; so I wasn't in Prague when the Germans marched in. This saved me. I stayed in England. I was the only one of my family who got out.

"Of course, I knew quite a lot of what was going on in Czechoslovakia during the war, and afterwards, when we found out that it was worse, so much worse than our worst fears—I didn't spare myself. I did read the reports in the newspapers and I saw the photographs. Eisenhower. Standing there looking down at the open pit with those enormous . . . those enormous multitudes of starved bodies at his feet all lying there the way they had been thrown in, and pictures of men and women on the road dead, some people half naked in a heap on the ground with their private parts showing; and those living skeletons unable to digest food." She seemed to be short of breath as if she were fighting an attack of asthma. "The photographs of the crematoria. For a long time I used to lie awake before dawn every morning trying to feel what it must have been like.

"I wondered where my family. . . . I wondered how. . . . I actually tried to feel the full force of it—can you understand this? I was with them—how it was in those cattle cars where people were forced in, so many that some died standing. . . . and behind those barbed wires waiting to die, despairing of any help ever reaching there. For years I tried actually to feel it. It was awful. Awful. I thought I had to do this. I thought it would be disloyal not to feel what they must have felt. But you see, I wasn't there when it happened, and I knew that I didn't ultimately grasp it all—the horror. I gave up trying. I told myself they wouldn't have *wanted* me to know this ultimate fear and despair. . . . Somehow—I felt released.

"Then, when I came to Israel two years ago—visiting Yad Vashem was like going back to the brink of hell—when I had persuaded myself already that it wasn't my duty to enter there. I thought, if I go, it will start again, this compulsion to try and feel what they must have felt—I was too afraid." Marketa played with her broadcloth hat, her fingers nervously rolling and twisting the soft, stitched brim.

"And then, about a year ago, I went to do some research in a library. In the school where I teach, we decided the kids didn't know enough about the holocaust and that we should tell them more about it, and they chose me. I just couldn't refuse. So I went to get some specific data . . . figures and dates, you know, and names of official government publications.

"I had to get some help from the librarian, and when she heard why I was there, she began to talk about herself and about the people she had known in the camps. You see, she is a survivor of Auschwitz.

"There were two girls she particularly remembered, girls who were her friends. . . ."

Marketa trailed off. She might have left it at that; but Jacob could not leave it: "Yes?" He knew he was not being tactless at all. He knew he was helping her. An acute kinship told him that she, too, was compelled, and that something pressed her to tell them, just as he was unable to stop goading her.

* * *

"You see. . . . This librarian . . . her name is Mrs. L. They were teenagers, she and her friends; and one day Bronia had a bellyache, and it kept her at the latrine too long and she was late at roll-call, and the little girl-warder with fashion-model makeup who was in charge of them told her she'd be punished. And then the girl-warder left the yard, ostentatiously, as if to consult with someone in authority, and when she came back, she said to Bronia, 'Tomorrow you'll be shot.' She said it just like that. . . . Everybody tried to calm Bronia. A woman was weeping, and many were angry because Bronia let herself go so much. They told her if she didn't get on with her work, she'd only make things worse for herself. And the girl-warder walked away as if to make more exact inquiries, and when she came back, she said: 'At half past two. That's definite. Tomorrow afternoon.'

"Most of the inmates didn't believe her. They were convinced that girl had no influence in the camp. She was only threatening people to make their nerves tingle. She liked to torment them. But the thirty or more hours till half past two next day, and even later, till three, till four, till Bronia could believe that it wouldn't happen. . . . They had no watches, of course, and there were no clocks. When the factory whistle blew it must have been one. She couldn't know whether it was two o'clock now or half-past two or three. They could come even if it was only two. And they could come after three. And how could one be sure even after four o'clock, even after six when the trucks arrived—a truck!!— that turned out to be just an ordinary truck that had come for the wood. . . . At sundown her hands were aching from chopping and stacking wood, and in the dark one still didn't know . . . (How can one ever unmake this?!) And when they didn't come—did this mean a reprieve? Or were they merely late? There were executions constantly. In front of a camp workshop there was sawdust on the floor, still damp and sticky and brown where police dogs had been set upon a man until he was dead. Perhaps it was only a delay, and they were still coming to take her away. And what was the time? It was driving one mad not to know exactly what the time was. But it didn't matter. They could come any time. Towards morning she began to hope. But then perhaps they had only changed the day. . . ."

*   *   *

Marketa cradled her brow in her fingers. She seemed out of breath. "Bronia survived. This was her experience. The other one . . . the other one was—Mrs. L. said Sala became her best friend. But that was at another time, I think. A different camp. Sala still had her mother with her."

In a moment of silence, Jacob thought that Marketa was going to scream and scream without end.

But she forced it into speech: "There was that great mass of people there lined up waiting. And one by one, they had to come forward and parade before some puny scum. . . .

"A Nazi was strutting around there, wielding a baton as if he were the leader of a band pointing to and fro, and he decided who was to go to one side, the right side, and who was to go to the other side. And those who were young and strong (And Mrs. L. was among them) were all sent to the right, to be taken to a labour camp later on. But the old and the weak and sickly ones he sent to the other side, and they were to be taken somewhere else. Not all of them knew that for those on the left the gas chamber was already prepared, and the crematoria of Auschwitz were gaping to swallow them up. But some guessed. And some found out and knew what was happening. Mrs. L. said they were standing there in absolute panic and agony.

"Sala was only seventeen. When she had to come forward, she was waved to the right where the lucky ones were waiting to be taken to the factories. So she was safe—at least for the moment. In another age, in another place, I suppose such a girl would have worried about what dress she would wear for the next dance at the local high school. Instead, this girl stood there sick with fear watching her mother, who now had to parade before that Nazi who did the selecting. Her mother was still young, only about forty. But Mrs. L. said she looked much younger, like thirty-five maybe or less. She was full of strength and good health, a beautiful human being who might have survived. She would have been able to get through the next stage of that grisly selection procedure, where the women had to parade naked before a group of male Nazis—They looked each of them over, and anyone who had a blemish on her body, perhaps a scar or even just a pimple, they condemned to the gas chamber.

Sala watched her mother and she had to wait and she watched the baton (where was it going to point?!) And then the baton pointed—to the right! And then she saw her mother walking towards her. In the middle of this ghastliness, this. . . . Suddenly—there was that moment of relief. A streak of joy. . . . You can imagine. . . . She was only a child—And when her mother reached her, they embraced. For this one moment they hugged each other.

"But the Nazi had seen. He had seen! And he came over angry. What was going on, he wanted to know. What was it they were so happy about? And Sala, by way of apology, said it was because they would be together now, and because this was her mother. And the man looked at her mother, who was still young and strong and beautiful, and he said: 'If she has a daughter as big as you, then she is too old for us here.'"

Marketa stared at them. It was as if something had been torn open.

She paused. "I can't bear to think this to the end. The mother forced to the other side. . . . The daughter near madness. . . .

"When I heard this, I thought I would drown in hate. My mind wouldn't let it be true and I was in this raving choking despair because it *was* true. It was. . . ! For the first time, I think for the first time I could feel the full weight—as if I myself had been there. Only for an instant. Only for a moment. The mind can't sustain this. But for this one instant—I think I knew."

*   *   *

"And then it came to me. What right did I have to stay away from Yad Vashem? No matter how it was going to affect me! My mother, my father, my young brother. . . . and all those others. They had to live with this not just for an instant but for days, weeks, months, even years—who knows?!—the constant threat to be murdered today, tomorrow, to see the people you love 'selected,' torn away to be murdered, and the only choice to die with them, to commit suicide perhaps by provoking the sadists in charge with some trifling disobedience; or to steel oneself with the hope, the desperate will to survive so that one could tell it all, so that perhaps one day one might be able to let the world know. And millions had this will and did not succeed and realized they would never have a chance to tell the world, never be able to accuse, never be able to scream it into the living day, not knowing whether anyone will be left to tell how dastardly, how agonizingly they were done to death. . . .

"I knew then that I had to go to Yad Vashem and look at their faces—at least to see their names in the pages there—to look at them and say, 'I do know. I have come. I am here. And though I have not suffered with you the way you have suffered, I am here to share with you in the only way I can share. And I shall remember and I shall never let the world forget it, not as long as I have breath. . . .'" She was crying. She cried convulsed in her appalling, irremediable injury.

After a while, the ladies left, and the Haralds promised the painter to visit her studio in the morning.

They stood at the window of their room. The land of the cabalists lay before them in dusk. Ragged veils of mist, faintly billowing, were drifting among the hills.

VI

It was impossible to shake this off. It was as if the agony of that girl and her mother had etched itself into Jacob's mind. He had not been ignorant of the historical facts—of course not. There was the gigantic volume of information that had bellowed and oozed out of Europe at the end of the war, when troops of the United Nations were advancing across the continent uncovering the reign of death behind electrified wire fences, discovering the pits filled with the naked corpses of murdered civilians. He remembered the newsreels laying it bare, the deliberate starvation, the whole rabid brutality. He had indelible memories of pictures sent home by horrified press photographers. Countless books. Testimonies of survivors. The trial papers, revealing how the infamous decisions were made. No, he had not been ignorant all these years. But it is one thing to receive information, and quite another thing really to understand it.

During the war, they had never gotten around to sending him beyond England. He was put behind a desk because of his fluent command of German, learned in childhood from his father, a native of Vienna; his perfectly good Russian, learned from his mother; and his remarkably elegant French, acquired when his parents, who were decades ahead of their time, had insisted that a Canadian boy should be proficient in this tongue. So he had no personal experience of what had gone on over there on the continent. Other soldiers told him, buddies who returned from the continent, shaken. They had seen with their own eyes. One of the Jewish soldiers, an Austrian whose family had disappeared into the extermination camps, returned with a nervous breakdown. Jacob could hear the prolonged, piercing screams rising in fury, could see the thrashing fist, down and down battering the night. And Jacob had thought he understood. Now he knew he had never been even remotely near. For the first time, somehow, it got inside of him: a glimpse of how it must have been, a glimpse—not just of stated, stark facts but of the terror, the aghast helplessness of those who had to suffer there; and the experience was searing him to the last, the utmost corner of the self. He felt nausea. His very skin revolted. Waves of nervous itching swept over him.

It was the moment of Jacob's most profound understanding of evil. Of course, he had been angry before, incensed the way any inherently decent person was bound to be incensed. But it had been a detached kind of anger, born from an astonishment that such viciousness was possible. He had never before felt this wrenching paroxysm of real gut hate.

This time it was reaching into his consciousness differently, and he was beside himself. What was this *thing* that was capable of this? If there were a hell, it would close its gates against it because eternal hell was too good a place, eternal damnation inadequate punishment for this. No Dante, no Shakespeare could have invented this cruelty; no novelist, not the most frenzied maker of horror movies could have dreamed this up. No mind in which the last vestiges of humanity were alive could conceive it. This Nazi's action could stem only from a mind at the nadir of depravity, evil through and through. It was inconceivable that such a thing could happen, and yet—it had happened.

*   *   *

Jacob remembered an American sociologist who had come to give a lecture at the university. The man had argued that, of course, he was not trying to whitewash the Nazis; he was merely trying to explain them. They had been totally wrong of course, misguided by their leadership, misled because of erroneous premises and false conclusions. But wrong as they were, so the lecturer had insisted, one should consider that in their own erring minds, they had imagined they were doing the right thing. They had been persuaded that the Jews were a dreadful danger to the Reich, and thus their actions were prompted by a feeling of duty toward the fatherland.

A professor from the history department got up and reminded the lecturer that Hitler insisted on transporting thousands upon thousands of Hungarian Jews to the gas chambers in Poland, although he knew that the trains so employed were urgently needed to take reinforcements to the collapsing eastern front. The decision to murder those helpless, innocent people was given preference over what clearly was in the best interest of the Reich.

The lecturer remained unperturbed: yes, this was the insane Nazi leadership, but the ordinary guy didn't know how bad the military situation in the East was for them, so they just kept on doing what they imagined was right.

Jacob groaned. He wished he could have this miserable sociologist right here in front of him. He wanted to scream into the man's miserable little ears that were deaf to the cries of outrage: See here! Here you have an example of a guy who was by no means top scum. Just an underling. Medium grade. That one was not insane in the ordinary sense of the word. No, his brain functioned. He could differentiate between those who were young and healthy and could work, and those who were elderly and weak. The choice had already been made when it was decided that the girl's mother was strong enough to go to a factory. With their own eyes they had chosen her as one who was young and healthy enough to do the work. When he forced her away and condemned her to die, he knew he was not doing it to benefit his fatherland, which badly needed her labour. That Nazi did not act out of misguided patriotism. Jacob would have liked to scream it into the throat of this numb-witted lecturer. What we were confronted with was evil, abject, inexcusable evil.

*   *   *

Suddenly Jacob, too, was compelled to try and imagine what it must have been like in those camps. He tried to put himself there with his boundless hunger for life and with years of life ahead of him, and suddenly, without any reason, without any necessity, he was to die—now—immediately—he was to be taken to a place where he would be choked by lethal gas. Jacob felt his scalp crawl. Or Eve and the children were being driven away to be choked by gas. Why?

Simply because some puny Nazi twerp decided he wasn't going to allow them to live, wasn't going to allow them to have any more air to breathe.... And there was nothing one could do about it, no redress at all.... And again, Jacob imagined himself ailing, in pain, or Eve and the children in need of medical attention, and instead of help, instead of kindness (such immense efforts were made by civilized humanity to mitigate pain, to heal the sick—and here—) instead of doctors and nurses and hospitals and medication and support—the gas chambers! An implosion of horror, a revulsion at this reign of filth, a fear, a despair suddenly understood, although it remained ultimately unimaginable, made him feel physically sick.

It began to haunt him in terrible dreams in which there was no hope of dawn. Sometimes Eve heard him gasp, and she rescued him from his sleep.

*   *   *

Has this woman from Toronto infected me with her need to imagine? Why am I constantly compelled to get near this, trying to understand the ultimate terror of it even while I try so hard to escape it? Am I trying to relive the sickness of it so that I can discover some solution, some ending that's different from what happened in truth? What for? It was a futile instinct, of course. In the past, when he had read some disturbing novel, seen some horror film or a tragic play, he could never rest his mind until he had invented a different ending, had convinced himself that it was all unnecessary, that he himself, in such circumstances, would have acted otherwise, that the disaster could have been averted. He could never accept the inevitability of disaster, always felt that the hero of the piece might have escaped it. And perhaps he was groping for a way out even now.

He knew it was without purpose; and yet he had to ask himself whether some action, some mode of speech perhaps could have saved Sala's mother. And he knew there was nothing. Unarmed men and women, surrounded by barbed electrified wire against men safe on high scaffoldings, their machine guns trained on the crowd; men and women tricked with promises of showers to undress; naked against specially trained, savage dogs. . . . But a word? Was there, after all, not some word that could have made a difference? The language was barren of such a word; nothing could have penetrated that unspeakable denseness. He could as little have prevented Sala's mother from being forced away as he could have stopped with his body the locked cattle cars crammed with human beings starving, suffocating. . . . There was nothing he could have done if he had been there. But he could not accept the inevitability of this, just as he could not accept the rest of it as an unavoidable calamity. Somebody could have prevented it. At some point it had been preventable. This he knew. He thought of the politicians of the nations and those who had made them what they were. And he knew that they, too, emotionally obese and slippery in their smooth, ever-so-realistic arguments of what was politic and economic, in their giant capacity to organize death and their refusal to organize life, had murdered Sala's mother, for at the passport offices that were beleaguered by frantic, frightened people begging for safety in happier lands, behind the polished desks of their foreign missions, they had refused to be their sisters' keeper.

As the old reports became vivid again in his mind with their endless, rending sequence of ungraspable facts, a dark, almost unbearable question began to invade him. How was such evil possible? How—how could it seep into a universe of such wonder, such magnificence, such infinite potential for happiness? . . . But is the Originating Existence not the source of *everything?* Jacob hesitated. He suddenly recognized that he was, in essence, asking the very question Pierre had asked him. Had he become a victim of the same plague? Was this contagious? Caught from the traumatized minds of these survivors? Had he caught their disease? Was the poison lingering still and inflicting wounds decades after the Nazis had been defeated?

*   *   *

His feeling of guilt was wiped away. How could he have ever thought he was capable of giving Pierre a meaningful answer? Yes, he could have shown Pierre, on the basis of science, that the Creator existed. Yes, he could probably have won Pierre to the understanding that the Creator was omnipresent and in a certain sense all-knowing, loving, and answering prayers. Pierre might have accepted this. But did this ultimately answer his question?

*   *   *

Suddenly Jacob was aware of it: all the time he had repressed something. Often there had been doubts, even at moments of exaltation; there had been issues he could not come to grips with. Something important had been left out. Something very central. Vaguely unacknowledged, it had been there all along. Now it came pouring out like foul pus from a festering gash that at last was lacerated, and he was stunned to see the putrefaction. The great WHY brought forth. The Tree of Knowledge was yielding its fruit. He could no longer shrug it all off with a facile, "See it whole! To you the horse's dung may be dirt, but to a sparrow it's a feast!" Not at the touch of real evil. If the Originating Existence was from Itself producing the entirety of the universe, everything there was—how then—how then—? Jacob was piercing into what felt like a sealed, bound opaqueness, something that could never be lifted, resolved, healed. He did not even want to complete the thought. It negated the very structure within which he could function safely, joy-fully, and in peace. But what—what was this evil—in the midst of creation? The question had to be asked, and it left him in panic.

Was not here the reason why Spinoza had been excommuni-cated by the orthodox, the reason why religious naturalists were treated with derision and shunned by traditional believers? Was it not because, inevitably, when you equated the Creator with creation, or when you argued that creation was part of Him, you implied that the evil, as well as the good, was an actual part of Divinity? The thought was intolerable. A cul-de-sac! The way that led into the cave with no exit. A hell where the adventurous mind went mad.

"It is written!" the orthodox have cried through the ages. Jews, Christians, and so many others. "It is written!" And their patient acceptance of evil as an ordained portion of mankind had always repelled Jacob. They call God all-powerful and then proceed to ascribe to Him all the ills that torture the world, completely oblivious to the blasphemy that hides in such piety. He had always felt that his own thinking was greatly superior. Now it seemed to him that his own sophisticated approach implied an equal affront, or worse. And he didn't know how this was to be borne.

Like Mordecai Kaplan, the Reconstructionist, Jacob had always believed that God was that particular—Principle? Pro-cess? Force? that created goodness in the world. Though it had been a faith he could only vaguely sense, this had remained his creed for most of his life. When at last he had found his way to a science-inspired concept of the Originating Existence whence flowed all being, at that moment of clarity, he had felt only awe, only the joy, only the wonder.

Now he could no longer avert his consciousness from the logically ensuing question. Is evil a natural, normal part of being? Does evil, ultimately, not matter in nature? Is the Originating Existence neutral, unconcerned with the suffering of individuals? Jacob refused this notion as if he had been stung. There was a sinking pain in him as if he would die.

*　　*　　*

Were good and evil, after all, only an invention of the human intellect, as Shakespeare wrote? In Hamlet's words, *there is nothing either good or bad, but thinking makes it so.* Jacob rejected this. He rejected it with his brain, his stomach, his nerves, every fibre, every atom.

Might as well play footsie with the sociologists who maintain that good and evil are only acquired notions, Jacob thought. It was a sneer that burned in his hiatal hernia. He had known quite a few such sociologists. Concepts of what's good and what's evil, they said, depend on one's upbringing, and therefore they vary from society to society, from culture to culture. So don't you go looking for absolute touchstones against which to measure good and evil, because there ain't any. Ever so objective. Ever so smug. . . . The burning rising from his stomach increased. Might as well tango with existentialists, he thought, the great minds of our time who have said to mankind, Blow society! It's the individual who is the arbiter between right and wrong. If you've got to do a deed so you can fulfil yourself, become "authentically" you, then for you, that deed is right. It's good. Touchstone? Why, it's the self! Each on its own—a conflagration of selves battling each other in their terrible, sad freedom. How he had argued about it with his undergraduates. . . . !

The issue, after all, was not new. It was as ancient as could be. He had discussed it in his youth. He had discussed it in class. Good and evil! The eternal conundrum. But the questioning had never before affected his fundamental thoughts.

*   *   *

He had never before been dragged into such bottomless darkness. Grief had always been shared: in a deep friendship with his mother after his father's death; with Eve after his mother was gone. This time, for the first time, there was no confiding in anyone. Eve's constant efforts to get to the bottom of it became a burden. "Don't you enjoy the view? You are so quiet—what are you thinking? Is there a problem? You never go to bed at ten; did we overdo the walking maybe? Are you tired?" She knew him too well. She knew an evasive answer when she heard one, and she felt shut out and became restive, constantly alert, watching him with that worried expression that said, "What have I done? Tell me!" But he couldn't give in. He was determined not to infect her with his unhappy thoughts.

She, too, had been appalled that afternoon at the Rimon Inn. There was an angry outburst to the point of tears a few days later. But something had toughened her mind. She came from a broken home; she was the product of stormy years when a man and a woman, both impatient, full of strong opposing convictions and passionate, had quarrelled without restraint about everything from art to politics. She had learned early not to keep on brooding over insoluble problems and grief that can't be mended. Jacob was not going to undermine her strength now with ideas that challenged the very centrality of their existence. His own confidence was in shreds. He needed to know that he lived in a universe that, in its ground and essence, was benevolent and beautiful; needed, needed, needed it. He couldn't explain to himself why it was, but he felt he could not be without this knowledge, and he would not take it away from Eve.

He searched his memory for clues, anything that might help, and he learned to dissimulate, faking attentiveness and interest when, in truth, he wanted to be alone, thinking.

He provided himself with tools designed to confound Eve's vigilance. He started buying more newspapers and magazines, and in a secondhand bookstore, he acquired a copy of Wright's *The Pottery of Palestine*. But though Eve did not say anything, he knew that she noticed when he failed to turn the pages as often as could be expected. Or maybe he only imagined she knew, casting about as he was for something he could use as a lifeline, or at least as a prop to hold on to.

*   *   *

Many of his friends had embraced a benevolent humanism. A few years ago, Joe Baxter, who was secretary of their local humanist organization, had tried to recruit Jacob at somebody's midsummer night barbecue. They were sitting with their glasses of Chablis and plates of broiled food that vaguely tasted of charcoal in a more remote corner of the garden. "Mankind," Joe said, while thoughtfully gnawing his corn-on-the-cob, "mankind finds itself in a formidable cosmos. The only thing for us to do is manage as best we can. For consolation, we have to look to each other, that is, to people in whom there is some kindness, a little bit of gentleness. That's where we can hope to get help."

Jacob remembered his own reply. "Sure," he said. "I can buy that."

"In that case," Joe went on purposefully, "you are likely to make a very good humanist."

"Except that I believe there has to be a touchstone outside

the human by which to measure good and evil," Jacob retorted.

Joe carefully put away the empty cob. "Why must there be?" he asked. "Why insist on something so—ehm—esoteric, so un-provable? You have a good, reliable touchstone—the standard of your peers, intelligent people of good will. For an adult, mature mind, this has to be enough."

"Let me never be so adult!" Jacob cried under his breath; but he knew Joe needed more substantial debate. "What defence can you put up if a kid comes to you and spouts a few gems like, 'Thank you very much, I don't want to be your peer. *You* be as gentle and kind as you like, you bleeding-heart liberal, you milk-sop, you meek do-gooder. I, for my part, shall be as ruthless as I can because I have found out that being a swine pays very good dividends. And you show me why my point of view is not every bit as good as yours. As a matter of fact, I, for one, believe it is much superior.' Now, what can you say to this kid if there is no criterion for good and evil but human opinion? After all, he or she is human, too."

The lamplight was on Joe Baxter's silvery hair, and his red-cheeked face brimmed with amusement as he passed Jacob a plate of date squares and Chinese chews. "I would naturally be very upset with this kid," he said, "very upset, indeed, if he or she were mine. I suppose I would do my best to educate the little monster; I'd try to point out that being reasonable and caring is likely to be more advantageous in the long run."

Jacob remembered sneering at Baxter. "Socrates tried it. So have quite a few others, if memory serves me. How far did it get them?"

Poor Joe Baxter was very disappointed. "True, my friend," he said, "education hasn't done its job, so far, We can only try. Humanism isn't perfect. But at least it doesn't expect people to believe in moral laws other than those made by human beings when there is nothing to prove that such other laws exist. Besides, does it help when people are religious and believe in higher laws?

I wish I had a cent for every beastly, damn-awful thing perpetrated by a believer."

Jacob's parry came swift: "But when a man thinks there is no law higher than the human, and he imagines his opinion is as good a the next fellow's, he feels he has the *right* to do whatever he likes. At least, when a believer commits evil (Thou shalt not . . .—a true believer, I mean), then he knows he is doing wrong; in which case we are already a step ahead."

*   *   *

Remembering the conversation now, Jacob saw something very attractive in humanist doctrine. Perhaps a kind of salvation could be found in a creed so firmly placed in human experience. But he knew almost at once it was fruitless. This was a restricted world of lost ambition. They seemed to him lost wanderers on an arid field, doling out the meagre produce, not daring to hope they might ever find a land more fertile than this.

For Jacob this wasn't enough. It never would be. If there was no touchstone other than human opinion, then in cosmic terms, the decent were no better than the cruel. Everybody acted simply in accordance with his own preference. And in such a world, there was no triumph even if one defeated evil. He could never make peace with this. It was not enough that evil lay defeated. One had to know that one was right to defeat it, justified beyond considerations of one's own advantage.

And because he did not know how he could ever crawl out of the darkness into which he had fallen, his spirit was in perpetual pain. He thought of others who had suffered in such torments. He thought of Bunyan and Kierkegaard, of their leap into faith that had saved them. And he knew that no leap of faith was possible for him. He did not seek belief. He wanted knowledge. He did not seek myth. He needed science-based fact. And science had unequivocally made him conclude that everything,

EVERYTHING there was, resulted from the activity of Originating Existence.

*   *   *

Why not take the straight road? Escape. The sermon of a rabbi. Well remembered. A splendid sermon. The congregation was advised to make peace with the fact that we may never understand the meaning of the Holocaust. Yes, why not take the straight road? Did this not promise freedom? But everything in Jacob revolted at this challenge. He wanted to shout, contradict, write to the rabbi even now, so many years later, tell him he could never accept such a solution. But it was unlikely that he could count on the rabbi's sympathy. He would point out that Jacob's distress was the logical consequence of his heresy. If one believed that the entire universe and *everything in it* were part of the Creator, then, of course, one could not find peace in an unquestioning, trusting faith, in axioms that drew on tradition, on established beliefs.

*   *   *

Eve was concerned. "Do you not feel well? Does anything depress you? Shouldn't you see a doctor? Are you angry with me for some reason?"

"But darling! Why should I be angry with you?" He fended her off, poor little Eve, by pleading tiredness and succeeded only in making her more worried.

As long as the issue was before him, he would have to probe, seek, burrow, search, tear his world asunder. But perhaps his misery could be stilled if the entire issue were banished from his mind altogether. Yes, why think about it? The world will swirl on in its gravitational valley whether I think about it or not. People will go and murder even if I could prove to them beyond the slightest doubt that the cosmos itself condemns their barbarities, and some people will sacrifice themselves to save a life even if no one tells them about altruism or gives a damn, for that matter. They'll do it out of sheer instinct. So what is so important about my wanting to live in a cosmos that isn't to blame for the murder and somehow reaches toward goodness? Maybe such longings are of no consequence. Supposing I make up my mind not to think about theology and ethics. Supposing I were like other people: live without thinking about such problems, without caring about what the larger world is like . . . mind my own business. Why shouldn't I? Jacob tried for a while.

* * *

It was as if the sun had set, and what was left was a substitute that merely enabled him to function 'daytime style', as he called it (remembering how the neighbourhood diner at home served a "Russian style" borscht, a tedious imitation of the Russian borscht on his mother's table). There was no glow in his day, no ecstasy, no brilliance.

He reflected on the purpose of his professional life. Had he not spent years, decades, to probe the wisdom of vast civilizations? And there was nothing in all the literature that could help him now. Anacreon, from the far away shores of Ionia, and Omar Khayyam, out of the sleepy perfume of his beautiful quatrains—nothing but the old song of forgetfulness. Enjoy. Accept what is beautiful on earth. Man cannot hope for more. Voltaire: cultivate your garden. Give your life to the necessities at hand. Live it usefully. All very attractive, most reasonable, even desirable. Jacob thought he ought to profit from these uncounted writings he had studied, mulled over, analysed with such fervour and persistence. What good were they now? Maybe I should have pelted the poor kids with exercises in the use of oxymorons and metonymy and synecdoche and gone on at length about foreshadowing and denouement and connotation and denotation as some of those boys and girls I know are doing in their classrooms. Maybe it all comes to the same thing in the end. He was clawing at it masochistically without really believing what he made himself think.

The lustre was gone. There was no glow in his day, no ecstasy, no brilliance.

A glimmer perhaps, yes, something that shone enticingly in one of Yeats' little dramas, his *Player Queen*, and there was a similar one by Ugo Betti, *The Queen and the Rebels*. In both, a low-born woman puts on a mask and pretends to be the queen. The pretense forces her to assume royal manners and royal responsibility, and in doing so, she actually becomes, in the truest sense, a queen. The mask is able to transform. You choose a mask, and the masquerade turns into reality.

If I pretend to be a happy man, try to think only the thoughts of a happy man, concentrate on all the enjoyments that come my way and act like a happy man—shall I in the end not emerge happy?

*   *   *

They returned to Jerusalem because of a lecture series on the latest archaeological finds, about which there was as yet very little information in the current literature. It was offered by a scholar of international renown, who had personal knowledge of the digs, and they had been looking forward to this for weeks.

A sinewy Arab in white trousers and a black, open shirt stood at the curb selling hummus and falafel. To Eve's surprise, Jacob stopped and purchased two helpings of each. He shunned street vendors as a rule, mistrusting the hygienic precautions of their enterprises—if there were precautions at all. They had seen lusty flies dancing about trays of buns displayed in one of the Old City streets. But this man had spread out sheets of polyethylene to protect his tubs. So Jacob was throwing to the winds his normal rule of never eating between meals. Eve was on the verge of reminding him that falafel were deep-fried, and that people who had any consideration for their health did not eat anything fried. But Jacob had been so down; she was glad to see his initiative and swallowed her words.

Enjoy! Enjoy! He said to himself as he carefully savoured the creamy, tangy, lemony yellow of the hummus and the darker, peppery garlic and cumin taste of the crispy-coated falafel. "This is good food!" he called back to the vendor as they continued their walk.

The man smiled and nodded. Then the smile was disconcertingly turned off, and he looked away.

Eve made a barely perceptible sound, like a cat that is pushed against slightly by careless people. She was annoyed. Not with the man; not with herself. She was annoyed with the world that created issues instead of preventing them. There had been too much lately. I don't want to be disliked, she thought. I haven't done anything wrong. It came to her how pampered she was, for she felt acutely the injustice of being deprived of a smile. And she reflected on how it must feel to be unjustly insulted, or starved, or maimed. And she thought of all the people in the world who have unjustly been deprived of their lives. And she wanted to cry; and she felt a need to talk to Jacob about this; but she saw him eat his food with obvious pleasure, and she was glad to see him recover from his gloom, and she kept it to herself. "They sure know how to cook," she said instead. "We really shouldn't be eating this, but it's so good!"

Jacob didn't reply. She didn't know whether he had heard her. There was a look of concentration on his face as he continued carefully and single-mindedly to savour the content of the pita bread in his hand.

*   *   *

"Let's go and spend a day or two in Tel Aviv before the lectures start," she said, and she was grateful and relieved when Jacob responded at once and made reservations in the attractively situated Plaza Hotel. She had not expected such enthusiasm nor such readiness to splurge some more and so soon after their northern excursion. It was an immense pleasure to stroll together, to sit in a café where natives and tourists came to drink espresso and refreshing concoctions of milk and fruit, to observe the passersby and to look at the sea. "Maybe we should go to Jaffa and see one of the nightclubs," he suggested. Clearly he was working himself out of his glumness. "I'd love that," she said. She was radiant.

Remember the mask. It is not too difficult to keep the mask in place when the guitars are calling to your heart in their Mediterranean tongue, a language so erotic and so full of pity. The air is filled with anticipation. It is youth, excitement. The mask fits well. It may never have to come off at all. The voices are young and so are the melodies.

"Summer love. . . . Suddenly now, suddenly today. . . ." A woman across the table translates for them the Hebrew words. She speaks to them in a curious mélange of English, German, and Yiddish. She laughs and gesticulates in frustration because she can't find the right expression. The band begins a familiar melody. She gestures to the Haralds: "This is for you also— many tourist like. . . ." They are swept into the circle of a hora. Everybody is clasping hands. Eve on his left. In his right hand he holds the hand of a slim young girl with long black hair. She looks up to him with large, dark, glistening, adoring eyes. He can feel she wants to be near him. Not like a daughter. Like a young woman who is attracted to a handsome older man.

Hava nagila hava nagila
Hava nagila venees' mecha

The rhythmic steps come easily.

Hava ne ranena hava ne ranena

Those who do not dance clap their hands and sing. More and more people are joining the circle.

Let us rejoice
Let us be happy
Let us sing

The man on Eve's left makes some jocular remark. They laugh. But now there is no more time, the music accelerates, no more words, no more—they dance in synchronized rhythm—together—breath and pulse—with every step—at one—faster, together—the circle is one living being, each link adding energy and receiving the energy of the whole

Hava ne ranena hava ne ranena

I am one with my people, I am happy. . . . The faces are moist and red and laughter is in their eyes, in their dishevelled hair, in the tight grip of their hands, in the carefree open-necked shirts and bouncing skirts, laughter is in me, I am happy. . . .

Uru achim
Belev sameach
Wake up, brother
With a happy heart

He had learned this song as a child. . . .

U-ru a-chim b'lev
Sa-me-ach

The circle dissolves. It forms a long chain winding itself

along tables and out into the open, into the summer night and back again. The music stops. I am happy, yes happy, happy, happy.

* * *

It might have worked. If he had been in Canada with all his tasks and responsibilities, perhaps he would have been able to keep himself suspended in this elation. It might have worked for a long time. But here in Jerusalem, the hours of enforced leisure that might have been priceless to an unburdened mind renewed his pain. The pain followed him into the lecture room; it was with him when he swam in the pool: all around him flowers and lawn and palm trees and people enjoying the sunshine. Eve in a new bathing suit, slender and attractively curved. But the pain in his spirit would not be stilled. It sounded inside him, a persistent, piercing tone.

About this time, something happened that Jacob considered a particularly lucky coincidence. Here perhaps was help for him. As they entered the King David Hotel for their afternoon swim, they almost literally ran into Ryan and Caroline Elbtree. It was more than twenty years since they had seen each other. Jacob and Ryan had both been associate professors then, involved in the same faculty squabbles and concerns over salaries, admission standards, and student ineptitudes. In the perennial ado, they had become more than acquaintances. They had served together on the executive of the faculty staff association. They had seen each other often on social occasions. Their wives were in the same car pool taking each other's kids to school. One could say they had been friends. Ryan, in the end, gave up his teaching career. He was a psychologist, and after he had published a respectable number of learned articles, he moved to Cleveland, where his wife's family was socially prominent, and founded a clinic for people with behavioural problems. Apparently he was doing exceedingly well. The Elbtrees had come to Jerusalem because Ryan was to present a paper at an international convention, and they were staying at the King David.

*   *   *

During the following week, the two couples met often. They dined together and went for walks. Once, when the ladies were engrossed with some store windows, admiring brass and silver work, Jacob steered the conversation toward religion. It was not difficult to do, considering the place. And then, almost spontaneously, Jacob spoke to Ryan about his problem. He did not tell him about the pain. Of course not. He just remarked, in a general way, on how modern science had opened the way to acceptance of a natural religion, to a cognition that the Creator was a natural force. He tried to convey to Ryan the joy inherent in this idea. Belief in the Deity was no longer a matter of hopeful faith. It was recognition of science-based fact. There could no longer be any doubt that the living Creator existed. But in this natural religion, when one considered the findings of scientific research, EVERYTHING was one; the creation had come into being from the Creator Himself. And in this case, what about evil? Was it not an intolerably perplexing issue?

*   *   *

Ryan did not look at Jacob. He was lighting a cigar, a thing Jacob despised. (In London, during the war—was it a Major Novotny or Novotek? Impossible to remember. He had told Jacob it was high time he started smoking. It was more "manly" he said. And Jacob had shot back: "Really? Is that why every prostitute smokes?" And where there had been only dislike for Jacob before, there was then savage contempt. Ah, well. . . . Jacob chuckled. He could take that. In retrospect now, it even seemed quite humorous.) "Does this—problem—interfere with your activities?" Ryan asked with a knowing expression on his face.

"Of course not."

Ryan was looking straight ahead. "I think this isn't something you or I will ever resolve. So why burden yourself with it." Jacob very nearly replied with a quote from Bernard Shaw. Lady Britomart reprimanding her daughter: *"Really, Barbara, you go on as if religion were a pleasant subject."* And Undershaft coming to his daughter's aid: *"It is the only one that capable people really care for."* But Jacob checked himself. Instead, he said: "I can't not burden myself. After all, it is a root question. It determines our attitude to the fundamentals of life." There was some urgency in his tone.

Ryan looked at him sideways. Fleetingly. "If you should find that this keeps you from functioning, get professional help."

"Why should it?" Jacob was furious. Chiefly with himself. He had opened himself to real friendship, and it was cast in his face. His tone must have given him away.

Again he longed to speak to Eve, but his pity prevented him. She was not to be plagued as he was. He must not plant disturbing thoughts in her mind. He wanted to protect her no matter how alone he was in this.

Unpleasant memories came crowding in. A film they had seen on television a few months ago. Who had made that film? Was it the *National Geographic?* A lioness standing over a warthog, tearing pieces of flesh from him, feeding while the hog was wreathing in agony; and insects—unbearable photographs where all the horror was magnified so that it couldn't be overlooked, couldn't be concealed any more by that merciful dimension that normally shields us from it—the minuteness, its invisibility all gone. It was there! Creatures torturing each other

—the living hell of their daily repast.

Jacob felt sick. This was evil, too. And quite recently—large, suffering, reproachful eyes deeply sunk in skeletal features. Bellies distending horribly below protruding ribs—like a macabre mocking of the emptiness inside. A silent crying on parched African plains, TV flitting past the dying sigh, the noisy stomach; the cameras a safe barrier between the viewer and smell and disease. You could switch off the TV, and the pining away in the barren African countryside disappeared. For all the pity and ministering organizations and millions of collected dollars which these pictures on the TV screen had brought into action, the very idea of people after dinner sinking into their soft upholstery to watch the drought-stricken, dying peasants was obscene.

*   *   *

One image in particular had stayed with Jacob. A dying girl, maybe twelve, maybe older. The reporter commented that doctors in the refugee camp were asking her family whether they would permit them to try and save her. Yes, they accepted the offer. The camera showed the girl sitting upright and doctors trying to make her swallow some liquid. She stared helplessly. The doctors gave up. The reporter, a good-looking guy with curly black hair, explained in his competent, calm voice that had just the right hint of pity: "Artificial feeding is out of the question in this place. We are in wild hill country. Hundreds of people die here every day of starvation. There is no transport connecting them with the outside world. There's a lack of roads, and the ferocious warfare is preventing adequate supplies from getting through. . . ."

"Why doesn't he scream?" asked Eve. "Is this to console us, this conviction that there's nothing anyone can do, that she is beyond help?"

But was she? Jacob was still wrestling with this now. He remembered Eve muttering as they sat there watching the unwatchable: "I bet you anything there'd be a way if the doctors or the reporter needed help. There'd be a helicopter conjured into the sky at night, or something. It's so easy to insert tubes with liquid food. Such a simple apparatus. In every mediocre hospital, they take intravenous feeding for granted nowadays. . . ."

A few moments later, the viewers were told that the girl was dead. An elder of the family had covered her with a sheet and had placed his hand over her mouth and nose. Almost insane, Jacob tried to enter the mind of that child as she felt the trusted hand beginning to cut off her air.

Only the flies in the camp were thriving and frisky, living it up, feeding on sticky excretions from people's eyes, people too weak to lift their bony hands to chase them away.

At night, Eve was calling Jacob her Venetian lion, who enfolded her with his wings. She did not realize that he was clinging to her with despair in his breast.

Evil was endless and pervasive. All suffering had become cliché: hundreds of millions of people without clean water, without access to vaccines, often without the most primitive medicine. What else is new? The statistics have long ago ceased to be fit copy for the front page or the prime-time interview. That reporter on TV ought to have screamed, thought Jacob. Yes, he ought to have screamed. Until there was no sound left on this earth but his scream. Uproariously bizarre: people worrying about atom bombs over Ottawa or Manhattan. When you endure those unmentionable little tricks governments are capable of in some out-of-sight police cubicle—or a kidnapper decides you are a dandy commodity to prove he means business and makes his blackmailees dance for him in panic—or when your butt is blown down from the sky or blown sky high with a little explosive toy from what the media so romantically call 'terrorists'—or when you squeal in the hands of some murderous little punk—then for you, the catastrophe today does not differ from any future Armageddon. For you, the worst is happening now, and it happens every day. It reared up as from a den of pythons.

And that chorus of poor crackpots and hysterical do-gooders lamenting, protesting, allowed to let off steam—is it nothing but a requiem for our lakes and streams? For the great rain forest? The shy animals that have scattered into the night forever, the lost magic in the leaves and roots of little plants? The delicate, ailing air? Jacob heard a cold greed whistling in the wind. It whistled an old tune, a tune wrinkled with history, blistered like industrial slime on a dying pond: *après nous le déluge.*

* * *

In the name of heaven! One could not even give an apple to a child without offering poison. Jacob pushed away the cafeteria apple crisp though he didn't know where the apples came from and whether the growers here used the techniques that had recently been introduced in North America. "Be sure to eat the skin," his mother had always admonished him. "It's in the skin that all the best nutrients hide." When their own children were small, they began to wash the skin very carefully to get rid of the residues of pesticides. And later, washing would no longer do because farmers and dealers were spraying the apples with a preservative wax that didn't come off. You couldn't be sure. There was less spoilage and fewer financial losses, but the people could no longer eat what was best. Never mind. They peeled the apples and ate what was left. But then, science found a way to treat the apple trees with systemic chemicals which made the apples grow bigger and prettier with red cheeks, and it made them firmer, and it made them stay longer on the tree and last longer on the shelf. So the growers had fewer losses, and the dealers had prettier merchandise and fewer losses, and both were very happy. But then, scientists found out that the daminozide, which now permeated the flesh of the apples, was carcinogenic, and that when the apples were heated (say, a housewife baked the apples for dinner or made apple stew for a sick child), the daminozide broke down into dimethylhydrazine and other stuff and became more carcinogenic still.

At that, the manufacturers of daminozide engaged researchers and told them to look and see whether those alarmists and scaredy-cats who didn't want daminozide and dimethylhydrazine in their food had a case; and the scientists started a long, elaborate testing program, and while everybody was waiting for the result, the bureaucrats very politely suggested to the apple industry that they use as little of the stuff as possible. Of course, they could have ripped those chemicals right off the market. Jacob could only surmise why they wouldn't; but he had it clear enough: Once a farmer or a canning plant operator or a dealer had profit from a handy little gimmick like this, you can't take it away without making him very angry. And angry farmers and processors and dealers are prone to making the government unhappy. And unhappy politicians are afraid of what may happen come election time, particularly when the big chemical industry is involved with all that money and all those jobs. . . . And because the apple growers were so pleased with the fruit they were raising on daminozide, the peach growers hurried to use it too, and so did the cherry growers and the vintners. Of course, everybody was quite convinced that the amount of carcinogen in the fruit was too small to harm anyone. But then, they couldn't be one hundred percent sure. As they said to the upset consumers who badgered them over the phone: "Nothing in life is a hundred percent. And you can't hold back progress." Sometimes, the poor consumers won a battle and a detested chemical disappeared. But no sooner was it gone, five others replaced it.

Mulling over such matters, Jacob felt clammy with perspiration. The shirt stuck to his back, and the sweat was not the sweat of the heat at noon, and it was not the sweat of happy exertion. The sweat was cold as from a fever. It was a sick feeling. There were uncounted problems. He thought he should choose one and devote all his energy, all his waking hours to fight in its cause. Perhaps he could make some small difference yet. But there were too many iniquities. A conflagration of crimes. He was unable to decide where to turn. Each year the nations were spending eight hundred billion dollars on armaments, while one in four human beings went hungry. Millions of castrated women, mutilated in their childhood, were suffering the consequences to the end of their days. Pecuniary Westerners, lured by sleazy travel agents to buy tours of the child-brothels in Southeast Asia (the latest piquancy of package-deals!) were spreading their diseases. Jacob wanted to cry with disgust and anger and pity.

There was too much. The mind found no refuge, and it could neither grasp nor catalogue all the ills forced upon its consciousness. For years his mind had registered shock after shock, and it had been able to confine the disturbances to the periphery. Now it all became central and vivid. Two years ago, in the States, at the James Joyce Symposium, he had lost his way to a restaurant and found you could stumble into an international trade fair and be met by hotshot sales personnel who looked and talked as if they were in electronics or agricultural machinery, though what they offered was hard-core pornography, a plethora of sadistic perversions. Then again, you couldn't as a stranger walk into a schoolyard nowadays without being right away suspected by the teachers of peddling pot or crack, or worse. Jacob almost laughed when he remembered the commotion. He had gone in to see the back of the building because the architecture was interesting. Two women teachers had pounced on him. Luckily, he remembered that Nancy Cops, a former student of his, was teaching here. The women were apologetic. They were doing their duty. There had been cases where eight- and ten-year-olds had been involved, and at a high school across town, a sixteen-year-old student had died sniffing glue. "But don't you worry," said one of the teachers in a feeble attempt to be humorous. "The kids didn't suspect you. *They* know who the pushers are!" Entire generations were growing up in this millstream (and how efficient they had become, today's *dark Satanic mills!*). Generations were being raised in the shadow play of media glamour and media violence, where appetites were teased and understanding blunted, perpetually, grindingly, a fit *hors d'oeuvre* to a more sinister diet. He saw them fan out in countless directions, concretizing their fantasies with dirty needles shooting death into their veins, lording it in laboratories elegantly inventing death, or quite unspectacularly voting into office many a blundering set of zeros, preferring lower taxes to public housing and courting the rat and cockroach at the rim of the crib, courting the hydra-headed forms of death that feed on poverty. . . . And the past blurred into the present and contaminated the future.

* * *

Jacob saw himself rush from the room, a small throbbing frog in his cupped hands and heard the voice of the master of the realm shout after him, "Jacob! Where the devil are you taking that frog?" as the door slammed on the last biology class. He remembered rushing into the greenery of the park, into the dark, moist paradise of the pond. . . . In the classrooms, did it still go on today? This was bearing down on him now—youngsters who never in their lives would be called upon to use what they had learned in biology class, inexpertly killing small creatures— learning to dissect ("invaluable first-hand information" said the course description), though the system that so adamantly insisted on imparting this "practical" knowledge never made them acquire the skill to produce a wearable coat or to repair properly the torn binding of a book! All these years, Jacob had been glad he had rescued that little amphibian—lucky, lucky chap who had been handed to Jacob Harald. Now, suddenly, the triumph was blighted. A sickening picture. Had he delivered the creature to being slowly digested alive inside the body of a snake? His tortured mind returned fleetingly to the humanists. Yes, Joe Baxter, we live in a formidable cosmos. . . . .

And he began to blame Pierre, whose insane question had started him on a path that led into ever deepening, darkening, suffocating despair: but for you, I could now enjoy every minute of the grandest vacation I am ever likely to have instead of wrestling with an impossible problem that no one can solve. I am like a man who jumps in to rescue someone from a whirlpool and himself is sucked under and pulled into the depth.

Even as he was thinking these thoughts, he rejected them as trite and unworthy; and he fought them, wanting to shake it all off and still found himself crying, silently, inwardly, without tears. It was as if he had been skinned, and the exposed flesh was hurting and sensitized to the slightest touch.

Wherever he cast his attention, evil flared up. A dish of grilled sole on a restaurant menu brought back a weekend long buried in the fragmented, chaotic years before the advent of Eve. He had gone on the first and only fishing trip of his life.

A fellow whose father owned a lodge near Kenora had invited three of them to stay for a week. Mercifully, the weather was bad the first couple of days, and they sat around and had good talks with a lawyer from Winnipeg and the two girls who waited at the tables. On Sunday, the rain and the wind stopped, and it was warm and still, and the clouds hung misty and low, "just right," Jacob was told, and they took out the skiff to get some doré. But all Jacob could remember now was Howard Sands having robust fun when he pulled the struggling, fighting fish out of the water, enjoying its desperate splashing as it resisted what lodged so viciously in its mouth tried to loosen its flesh from the piercing hook, dangling from the line quite hysterical gasping and choking wildly flayed the air—until wounded, it was flung back into the water, too small to be taken. . . . Jacob was able to hitch a ride back to Kenora and took the train home. Howard Sands had never forgiven him for that. Even years later, when they saw each other occasionally at meetings of the Learned Societies, Howard cut him, and his wife cut Eve as if she, too, were to blame.

*   *   *

Jacob felt awkward now as he scanned the menu. He loved to eat fish. It was more-or-less the only kind of meat he allowed himself on a regular basis, and it was important to him because he worried about not getting enough protein, about becoming seriously ill if he didn't get enough of the right kind of protein. Eve, who was a determined vegetarian (though she prepared meat for him without protest whenever he brought it home), hadn't been able to dispell his fears. Now he was agonizing over the Kenora episode, and he despised himself. Whom was he reproaching? Sports fishermen with their repugnant buckets of live bait? Was he himself any better? Did he give any thought to the fishing trawlers with their choking load that supplied his dinner table? The hypocrisy of it! Did he or did he not permit himself to buy neat packets wrapped in transparent plastic, displaying dainty frozen fish fillets that never gave a hint they had once been part of an animal?! At least the fishermen were honest enough about getting their meal. And the fish, at least, had been swimming around for a while as happy as a fish could be. What about those neat little trays with chicken breasts he sometimes got at the supermarket? He thought of the hidden-away, crammed cages so favoured by the proponents of the factory farm, where creatures live in squalid confinement from the day they are born to the day they are killed, without one comforting ray of the sun, without a breath of the sky. It was lack of imagination. A refusal to know the pain of dumb living things. And Jacob squirmed, feeling tainted and hurt, and not knowing where to turn.

Back at the apartment, he snapped at Eve angrily because she was taking down her braid for the second time, and he feared they would be late for their lecture.

"I can't go like this! I've got to pin it up properly!" she insisted, impatiently fumbling with the hardware, and in this hurry doing it badly and once more undoing the whole thing. He saw her worried, hunted, hurt expression and wanted to apologize, but he left the room.

* * *

Why did he suddenly have to think of every ill the media had thrown his way in the course of the years? All this information was on him, stinging like pesky insects. A swarm. Troubling him. From the horror of Spanish bull rings, with their public ostentation, to so-called "festivals" (mostly illegal now) where mindless crowds were cheering still the ancient sadistic rituals and having their bellylaughs watching harmless creatures (a donkey, or some rabbits, or a bear, or geese—depending on where in the world the gruesome ceremony was taking place) being tortured until they were dead; from the illegal but persistent hanging of dogs and burning of cats destined for the gourmet tables of Asia to the legal horror of stockyards all over the globe and the very legal hair-raising experiments conducted on animals by streamlined producers of cosmetics in search of yet another new lotion to improve their customers' complexion—mankind blotted from its awareness any pain other than its own. And humanity was too stupid even to prevent its own disasters. They came like clouds of poison gas that forced one to stay ever alert, never allowed one to sink into quiet resignation, for one didn't know what would be overtaking one next; and by paradox, they came like a tidal wave that obliterated one's outrage.

He dreamed the earth was covered with a labyrinth of narrow passages whose walls were red-hot iron, and he was pushing Eve ahead of him, his arms down her sides to shield her, and his arms became scorched and shrivelled as he kept on touching the walls.

His awareness of evil had become so acute that he could not free himself, no matter where he went or what he did.

A young man he overheard at the university during a break between lectures told his friends he was training as swimmer and hoped one day to make the Olympic team of his country. The word at once conjured bitter recollections of how the world had congregated at the Olympics in Nazi Germany—regardless (!), and how the games had proceeded in Munich after nine Jewish athletes had been murdered in their dorms. . . . And he broke into the conversation, blurting out loud that the games, which in ancient Greece had celebrated the magnificence of the human body, had now become a debased sham, a lure for youngsters willing to risk fatal disease and the loss of their manhood in order to win a medal! The bodies of athletes a mockery: their muscles artificially puffed with chemicals! "Anything for a few moments of ballyhoo and buckets full of loot," he shouted at the swimmer, who replied with an intimidated stare. "Let's go," said one of the young men, and they all walked out into the sunlight of the campus. They treat me like a crazy old man, thought Jacob. He could see Eve was upset. "You were right of course," she said. "But did this improve anything?"

A beautiful diamond pendant in a store window flared into his consciousness with the brutality of the sun that strikes down on the black townships of South Africa. What sordid iniquities had played midwife when the diamond was ripped from the womb?

On Hamelech George Avenue, a brightly coloured sari glistening in turquoise and gold reminded him of a brief article he had read this morning in a British newspaper. It hadn't made the front page. An epidemic of burnings in India: women burned alive by in-laws who wanted new brides with richer dowries for their sons.

And over and over again he asked, where is nature in this? And he cried out from the depth of his blood: Is this how it is bound to be?

*　　*　　*

And what were those growls coming out of the radio staining the smooth voice of the announcer like vomit? Or did they come from his own throat? Something about international governmental investigation. Reports on children, many children, sold by starving families; and criminal networks using such children to take from them organs for eagerly awaited transplants, removing the eyes of retarded children and selling them to recipients tired of waiting for a legal donation. How to tear this knowledge from one's brain?! How to clean it from the face of the planet?! How to help these poorest of the most poor. They were entitled to the next pair of eyes available through a Last Will bequest. Humanity owed them at least this much if it was technically possible to give it.

He wrote letters, offered money for an operation. And he hated himself for his ineffectualness and his weakness in confrontations with ever new enormities, which surfaced like corpses from the depth of a sewer. And his stomach began to hurt. From the billions and billions' worth of weaponry stockpiled by madmen who already had enough armaments to murder every living thing many times over to so humble an action as the cooking of an apple, humanity was mired in evil. He was floundering in a stinking, rotting morass. Jacob felt defeated. His humanist friends were right. Voltaire was right. Even the rabbi who said we should give up trying to understand evil was right. Perhaps, after all, the only way to escape the despair was resolutely to put all thought of religion from his mind. For good.

* * *

The telephone rang. Eve said the Elbtrees had returned from their prolonged sightseeing tour of the country. They had rented a car, and they wanted them to come for a little drive and have tea.

There was a pleasant, cool breeze where they sat amidst the unobtrusive elegance, the subdued chatter of people on vacation, the friendly service. The Elbtrees were on their second bit of pâtisserie, delectable morsels of hazelnut and chocolate and whipped cream spiked with coffee. The dainty paraphernalia of afternoon tea and glasses of iced water stood before them on the table.

The Elbtrees looked very right in these surroundings. Probably they had bought their clothes in California or Florida. Ryan quite imposing in his quiet, silky blazer; Caroline, her grey hair smartly coiffed, was in a pale pink dress, very simple, with matching pearls. A shimmering cardigan of pink and white yarn was thrown over her shoulders. It occurred to Eve that this was the kind of mother Susan wanted to have. With her discreet, expertly applied makeup, she was wearing her age as proudly and gracefully as the impressive, sparkling rings on her beautiful and flawlessly manicured hands. A warm, rose polish on her nails blended perfectly with her clothes and her lips.

Jacob suspected that Eve felt poorly dressed next to her. He could always tell by the way she tried to make up for the difference in appearance. She was going out of her way to be witty, entertaining, interested in what Ryan had to say.

Poor little Eve. She could have saved herself the trouble. Ryan obviously needed no encouragement, and he wasn't willing to share the star performance with a woman. He all but ignored her efforts. He talked about conditions in Italy during the war when he had served there as a rear gunner. It was good to see how the country had changed. They had spent their vacations in Italy two years ago. And what a difference! He talked about their travels and where they had eaten the most remarkable meals, where the shopping had been the most worthwhile, the shows they had seen. The Haralds had always known Ryan was an excellent raconteur, and today, as their host, he seemed to feel specially obliged to entertain them. Probably king of the country club, Jacob thought. Caroline sat with a pleased smile on her face. Sometimes she reminded Ryan of an extra detail or turned to Eve with an explanatory remark. Her civility was above reproach. She was friendly, her tone was gentle. Nevertheless, Jacob thought (as he had occasionally in the past) he could detect something like an ever-so-slight condescension. He didn't quite know whether it was in her eyes or in her voice.

Eve had extremely sensitive antennae ready to monitor even the faintest messages of that ilk, and she must have picked up something, for she seemed determined to have her say, to let her personality glow more than anyone's emerald possibly could. The Elbtrees watched her with some indulgence.

"And talking of buses, there was this marvellous anecdote the driver of the Egged bus line told us on the way to Tiberias." The Elbtrees looked apprehensive. Surely, she wasn't actually going to tell them a joke. But indeed, she was.

"It's about the Egged bus driver who came to the pearly gate. There was Saint Peter, of course, and when he saw the bus driver he immediately said, 'Come right in, we are very happy to have you. Make yourself comfortable!' Well, at the same time, there was a rabbi who also arrived at the pearly gate, and he also wanted to be let in. But Saint Peter said, 'I am very sorry, you will have to go—to the other place.'" Eve's index finger pointed repeatedly and meaningfully downward. "The rabbi was absolutely flabbergasted. He said, 'I have been such a pious man all my life, I taught the children how to pray, I kept the Shabbat, I gave to the poor, I did everything I was supposed to do; why on earth should I go down there?!'—'Well,' said Saint Peter, 'I'll tell you how it is. It's true you led a good life. You followed all the rules. But did you really influence anyone? Be honest, eh? Did they listen to you? Did you make them pray? Did they keep the Shabbat?' The rabbi shook his head. 'There you are,' Saint Peter said. 'So this is why you can't come in here.' Now, the rabbi was a reasonable man. He said, 'All right, I can understand this. I accept it. But what about the bus driver? He was let in!' 'Ah,' said Saint Peter, 'Did you ever see that bus driver—how he filled up his bus and then went down those hairpin curves a *hundred* miles an hour?—*He* made people pray!'"

There was an explosion of loud laughter. Eve was triumphant. But Jacob knew and she knew that they did not admire her. In their world, a woman who wanted to be considered a lady did not tell jokes. They thought her quaint. At home in Cleveland, she would hardly have been a member of their more intimate circle.

* * *

They were still chuckling when a youngish man in a short-sleeved jersey stopped at their table. "I see you're having fun," he said to Ryan. His wife, a very tall woman with a black, vividly embroidered stole greeted Caroline. They were quickly introduced as Professor and Mrs. Jamieson from London, England, who were here for the convention. Ryan asked them whether they would like to join the company, and chairs were politely moved to make room while Ryan helped Paul Jamieson bring two chairs from a neighbouring table. They sat down between the Elbtrees and ordered tea and croissants. A pleasant couple. They seemed very sure of themselves. Jamieson had a broad, high forehead and piercing dark brown eyes. He leaned forward and asked Jacob whether he, too, had come to Jerusalem to present a paper. But when he found that Jacob wasn't participating in the convention and, indeed, wasn't even a psychologist, and moreover wasn't very talkative (and altogether seemed a bit of a bore and maybe also a bit stuck-up), he lost interest and henceforth addressed himself only to Ryan. Jacob was aware of the impression he had made but did not bother to improve it. He noticed that Eve didn't fare much better. Caroline and Mrs Jamieson had much more to say to each other than to Eve and included her only now and then, and probably more from politeness than inclination. They were discussing the beauty of the Arabic embroideries one could purchase in the Old City and compared them with embroideries in other parts of the world where they had been, notably Greece and Hungary. The two men were exchanging convention gossip: the incoming president of their association, the likely choice of location for next year's general meeting. . . . Jacob was bored. He was silent. He knew it did not matter. He was not listening. The chatter receded. After a while, it went away altogether.

* * *

The young waitress brought him a fresh tumbler of ice water. It stood before him on the table. A ray of the sun was caught in it. Refracted in brilliant stars, it burst from the ornamental edges of the glass. Cubes of clear ice were floating in the water. They were transparent like the water, but along the fine demarcation lines indicating the shape of each cube gleamed the iridescent fire of the spectrum. Jacob watched it in mesmerized wonder.

A chalice ablaze with light.

The table below it disappeared, the faces surrounding it, the room, the world—it was suspended in space—alone in the universe but for the eyes that saw it, the mind that kindling from its blaze comprehended with the fire of sudden hope at last withering the senseless lacunae, the bottomless disgust, the eternal despair. Fresh vigour driven through his arteries in these new seconds—millennia—eternities—Columbus seeing land, Hillary within grasp of the summit, a tapping on the eggshell—from inside: Jacob Harald about to reclaim his life, suddenly knowing that the torment in himself was not invincible—staring at chaos and in this instant seeing there an exalted order—a crescendo of sounds melting suddenly into music—life was his once again to love, to savour, to be bathed in—to swim in—forward—outward—into the sun—

It was, after all, so simple. So very simple. Not in terms of one's own activities, of course—far from it—but perhaps in terms of why one had, in one's efforts on the side of life, the great imprimatur. Jacob tried hard to channel this commotion into language.

The ice cubes were of the same stuff as the water. No doubt about this. Water had brought them forth, had formed them from its own H_2O. And yet, they were not the same as the water. Ice had properties different from water. Very different properties, even though it retained the same hydrogen, the same oxygen. Ice could produce beautiful forms, but it could also be shattered into fragments jagged with edges and points, could pierce and cut and lacerate. . . .

It was all so clear. A sudden freedom: Originating Existence had brought forth the universe. But in Jacob's new perspective, this no longer had to mean that creation with all its abysmal horror was wholly at one with Originating Existence, the Creator. Fashioned from the Primary, the universe was ablaze with the primal creative fire, yes; but it was in another state of being now, had become different from the Primary. It was concretized, in splinters individualized, altered, open to dangers, to who knows what accidental difficulties.

At this moment, Jacob's only clarity was the cognition that though there was oneness, there could still be difference. And he needed this knowledge, for without it, all hope was blighted and any struggle save those of the most obvious utility had become meaningless. In the duality Jacob now saw, it was possible to say, yes, creation flows from the Originating Existence, but creation and the Source are not the same, and the destructiveness, the evil that infects creation, has no part in the Source. At this moment, Jacob did not know what logical proof he could offer for this idea, save that destructiveness can have no being in the essentially creative Impulse. Nor did he know where the arguments that passed through his mind like dim premonitions would eventually lead him. But there was in him a misty certitude that a path was now open. He was emerging from the cave. It was only a matter of time.

He took a deep, liberated breath. The pain had disappeared. His understanding of reality was transformed utterly.

*   *   *

Somewhat later, when the Elbtrees and the Jamiesons had gone to their rooms to dress for their convention banquet, Eve bought a stack of postcards at the hotel store, something she had meant to do for a long time, and she settled down in a pleasant corner of the lobby where they could write. But Jacob said he would go for a walk.

He hurried most of the way: down Botta Street and down Shamma toward the Jaffa Gate, the Tower of David, the old Jewish quarter, where the architecture of rebuilt *yeshivot* seemed to have distilled the past into a serene, confident future—he did not see anything, he did not see anyone, quickly through the military checkpoint—down to the bright, open, welcoming plaza and across it to the Western Wall. He stood close and looked up. Its majesty rose above him, drenched in sun. He felt its presence as he had never felt it before. The dark fissures of time in the worn rock, and life, life in the greening leaves emerging high up from the shelter of its crevices. Jacob's lips formed the words of the Kaddish, the ancient prayer for the dead, which does not mention death. *Yitgadal veyitkadash.* . . . It rises in jubilant affirmation: *Let the glory of God be extolled.* . . . It was a return. Here was the home of a great reaching out toward the creative Essence. And in a storm-flood of gratitude, his lips touched the stone. It was warm, like a living thing.

He climbed up the mount where the Temple had stood in the days of Solomon, in the days of Judaea. Up here—what was it in the air? So pure, so still, so luminous. And swallows gliding in and out of trees. Were they descended from the swallows who nested here millennia ago in the Sanctuary of the Temple? The Sanctuary had survived. He was looking deep into the vast clarity of the sky. Intensity. A brightness in heart and mind. Never had there been such sunlight. *Shema.* . . . *Shema.* . . .

At The Foot of The Mountains
on The Shore of The Sea

VII

"Nature is deeply misunderstood when life and death are considered to be equal components in the natural process. We must attempt to look in a fresh and different way at the familiar cycle of building and destruction."

It had taken Jacob a very long time before, finally, he had begun to formulate his thoughts in this manner. For two years, he had quietly and methodically pursued his ideas, but it was only now, while they were visiting Susan and Ron in their new Vancouver home, that he found the inner quietude to let it all drift into place. The pattern assumed clarity of outline.

It must have something to do with the place. In the past, this region of mountain forests above wide stretches of salt-water driven in by the tides of the Pacific had inspired him to do bold things. To make decisions. One couldn't be quite sure how the landscape insinuated itself into the chemistry. It could make one afraid. But then again it awakened a lust for the things one might do, provided the scope was right and one's foresight sharpened so that one could distinguish between the inexorable and the manageable.

The waves were tamed by the gigantic buffer island out there beyond the Straits. It blocked the crashing breakers of the ocean but left the water strong enough to be your master if you didn't have enough respect for it. It could be treacherous and no less a danger than the cougars which made occasional appearances in the bush beyond the North shore bungalows. On a windy day, a man swimming out too far from the shallows of Kitsilano could be carried with astonishing speed into the bay where the current hurried the waves toward Siwash Rock. Jacob remembered climbers who had gone for an afternoon up Mount Seymour to look at the city below and at the white mirage of Mount Baker far in Washington; and they never returned from the mountain—not alive, at any rate. It was a region that demanded the wooing of a respectful lover, but at the same time, it wakened something in you, something not quite definable that you hadn't known about. The great city that spilled south to the estuary of the Fraser and struggled up the northern mountain slopes across the inlet and extended its groomed fingers into the sky was clearly an incongruence. Jacob loved to tell the story how one day he had spent a couple of hours at an art gallery in downtown Vancouver, and how afterwards, only a short drive away, when he visited a friend in the West Vancouver suburb, they met a black bear in a berry patch just a short stroll from the friend's back yard. People invariably asked: "What did you do?!" And Jacob was fond of replying with nonchalance, "Well, that bear minded *his* business and we minded ours. Except that we had to adjust a little the nature of our business. Instead of picking blueberries, we got ourselves out of sight, slowly and carefully, and then walked home—on the double." It was many years since Jacob had visited Vancouver, but he still thought the city was an incongruence—like a computer chip working away, processing messages inside the nest of an eagle.

For him and Eve, this was a special kind of homecoming. It was not, of course, without disappointments. They had longed to be with their Sharon, their grandchild, but the little girl was overly shy with them; well brought up and polite, but oh, so shy. They had hoped for a granddaughter who was outgoing and curious. They wanted to experience her life; give her things that would astonish her; take her to places she had never seen before. But there seemed to be no toy that would impress her: she had so many spectacular ones. And there was no place in the vicinity they could think of where she had not been.

It was no wonder. Her father, an executive with a computer firm, was negotiating the hairpin curves on his way up toward the top of the corporate pyramid and earning a more substantial salary now in his thirties than Jacob had earned at the height of his career. This demanded a readjusting of one's sensibilities, paternal and economic, a certain push toward vicarious pleasure. Ron came from Colorado, a man with most friendly, easy-going manners, and thoroughly likeable. One really couldn't blame him for being perhaps a trifle too proud when he was showing his in-laws around the new split-level home with the cut-stone front, the Thunderbird and the red sports car in the garage, and the expertly landscaped rock plantings in the garden. One could not even feel envy, for he was confident like a little boy that others would share his pride, especially when he showed off his newest acquisition, a neat little cabin cruiser called *Sharon.* Their son-in-law had grown up so far from the ocean, he had to make up for the deprivation; and he adored boats: rowboats, sailboats, any old boat. The *Sharon,* however, was by no means old. Her teak polished to a sleek perfection and her flawless paint and furnishings looked as if she had only just left the boat-yard (which, indeed, she had).

Ron was a Quaker. When Susan had first brought him to meet them, the Haralds had their quiet misgivings, but these quickly disappeared. Ron had no objections if his children were brought up Jewish. He said his values could be expressed in many different ways, and that God's grace was universal. "You have to understand," Eve said in reply, "that we don't deny this at all. We respect your religion as you respect ours. It's just that we belong to a tribe that in the old days—how shall I say it—has articulated its awareness of God in a certain way, and it has created—I suppose you would call them 'traditions', atti-tudes, and some of them have become very dear to us. I'm afraid we aren't even very observant Jews. But we don't want our ways to disappear from the earth. And there is a real danger. We want to keep it alive. Do you understand that?" Ron said he understood. Nowadays, the Haralds confessed—strictly to themselves, never to each other—that they liked their son-in-law better than their own daughter, whom they suspected (to some extent unjustly) of a certain shallowness of emotion. It did not make them love her less devotedly, of course. They would have sacrificed their lives for her. Liking was another matter. They only prayed her husband might never find her out. Luckily, there was no immediate danger of this at present. Susan was exceedingly decorative and very efficient. She was a credit to him in the ceaseless turbulence of his professional and social obligations. And she had even surprised and delighted and impressed them all by enrolling in a course that would enable her to take full command of the *Sharon*. And Ronny appreciated it. He said this would give him a few hours of pure vacation when they were taking the boat around the coastal islands of the Sound and into Indian Arm.

This kind of initiative soothed Eve's tautly stressed nerves, making up to some extent even for the contemptuous way in which Susan dismissed her mother's taste in fashion and views on child rearing. There were tensions over trivial matters.

*   *   *

And one of them turned out to be not so trivial. Every Thursday, Susan attended meetings of a women's club where invited speakers gave talks ranging from literature, physical fitness, fashions, and travel to investment advice, attitudinal changes for businesswomen, international affairs, and women's rights. One Thursday after lunch when, as usual, a mildly protesting Sharon had been put to bed for an hour, they were sitting in the living room by the large fireplace, a showpiece of irregularly shaped slabs of granite that reached the ceiling. The Haralds were comfortable on the deep and puffy white leather settee, and Susan, in a pale yellow jump suit, was lounging across from them, the yellow of her cotton matching streaks in the upholstery of her chair, soft cushions all covered with flowers, pink and white and pale yellow and fuchsia and pale blue. She rested her feet on a pink leather ottoman. On the glass top of the coffee table, which allowed one to see the silvery grey carpet and carvings adorning the trestles of satiny walnut underneath, a solitary, low vase displayed boldly curving lines in modern French crystal. It held a single spray of dogwood in full flower and some fresh mimosa. "You look like something out of *Vogue*," said Eve admiringly taking in the whole scene.

"I wish I didn't have to go to that damn lecture tonight," said Susan.

"Then don't go," said Eve.

"If I did that every time I don't feel like going, I'd probably stay home half the time."

"So? Do you *have* to go?"

Susan looked at her mother defiantly, the way she had looked at her as a teenager just before saying something to outrage her.

"Yes, it's important. Ron is playing squash every Tuesday night. There has to be some balance; otherwise, after awhile, he'll think I'm the little woman who's expected to sit at home waiting for him."

"But Ron needs the exercise!" said Eve, barely controlling her disgust. "You would rather do something you don't really enjoy just to show him?!"

Susan parried. Having achieved a vague purpose, she was quite calm. "Don't get excited, Mother. He understands that I can't be here every night of the week. Alice says it's necessary for women to be vigilant if they want to maintain status. It's no less important in the home than in the workplace."

A hyper-sensitivity had told Susan that her mother disliked her dearest friend. Now it was not conscious, not premeditated—just that something in Susan was urging her to bring it out into the open. And Eve took the bait, bursting out, "That stupid bitch only comes in contact with marriages that are rotten, dead, the dregs! What does she know?"

It was what Susan had suspected. Her mother's insult stung her badly. She was proud of her friendship with Alice Lombard, a prominent lawyer. Currently, Alice was representing a secretary whose boss, a senior member of the city administration, had allegedly been guilty of sexually harassing her, and the media loved this case. Together with her client, Alice had been on television, and photographs of them had appeared in the press. She had been interviewed on radio. Alice Lombard was always aggressively critical of men and habitually spoke of them as if they were congenitally hostile to women. People quoted her. And Susan was dazzled by her success.

She said, "Alice sees a lot of broken marriages. That's why she knows what men are capable of when the chips are down. That's why her advice is valuable. Women have to protect themselves. You never know what may happen. Alice says no one can foresee all eventualities. A man may be all sweetness today—"

Jacob usually avoided mixing in when Susan and her mother disagreed, but this was serious: "You don't know what may happen?! Has Ron given you any cause. . . .?"

"Of course not, Daddy! Ron and I are very happy. But a woman has to keep her eyes open. Who knows what may happen down the road. Alice was appalled when I told her Ron and I didn't make a contract before we got married—"

"To protect your dowry?" shouted Eve. "To make sure he doesn't run off with the five pots and three tablecloths you brought with you?!"

Eve didn't know whether to laugh or weep.

"Mother! You'll wake Sharon. Alice believes she can still get me something like a marriage contract. If Ron should ever want a second mortgage on the house to invest or maybe to get us a cottage, he'd need my signature. That'd be a good opportunity to widen the negotiations a bit. She thinks she could work in some concessions. . . ."

They both stared at Susan. "Concessions?! You are talking as if Ron were an adversary whom you have to outwit! Don't you have any trust, any loyalty?" asked Jacob.

"Women have always trusted men. . . ."

"Men?! Men?! Don't you think your father deserves to be trusted?! Blindly?! Absolutely?!" Eve reached for Jacob's arm as if to defend him against a posse of irate feminists. (She was unaware of his half-suppressed, amused smile.) When she heard such generalizations, she felt that he, too, was under attack, and it offended her painfully.

"Daddy is different," Susan conceded.

"Different? From whom? What right do you have to suspect Ron—a kind and wonderful and honourable boy if I've ever met one!"

"I don't suspect him of anything," Susan insisted. "It's just that things are different today. Alice says in case of a divorce, there should always be provisions—about custody and financial—" Susan saw the way her parents looked at her, and their astonished silence made her uncomfortable. She began to tone it down. "Well, my chief aim would be to make sure Ron doesn't object if I want to open my own interior decorator's business later on, and—"

"Surely, Ron isn't the man who would ever hinder you." Susan heard a note of real distress in her father's interjection.

"And I also think I should have it in writing that he'll be more helpful in the kitchen when I start work," she added.

Eve laughed out loud: "And you think a contract will give you that assurance?!"

"Maybe not," said Susan. "Alice told me the courts would never enforce such a provision, but having it in writing would give me a bit more clout, she says. She thinks it would be irresponsible if I could get a contract and didn't jump at the opportunity."

"Clout?! Jump at the opportunity? You jump! You do just that, and I guarantee you the day will come when you'll be looking for Ron. . . ."

"Where do we jump?" asked Sharon from the stairs. She was in her pajamas, and she carried the white teddy bear with the pale blue silky bow. She tried to tickle him by passing her loose auburn curls across his nose. "Mommy has a jump suit."

"Put on your dungarees, Pussycat, and skip down to the garden," said Susan. "I want you to pick a nice little bunch of parsley for your daddy's dinner."

Eve turned to Susan. "Little One," she said, reverting to the pet name of long ago, "Ron doesn't look like a man who would burden the homestead unless he has to, but if the time ever comes and he needs your signature. . . Little One. . . some times we say or do things or have a way with things that seems very right at the time, and afterwards it doesn't seem so right. We don't want you to have regrets for the rest of your life. . . ."

Jacob wondered: does she, too, still think of that last weekend with Pierre? Is she haunted by the same helpless, inveterate regret? He placed a reassuring arm around her shoulders. He shared her fear about Susan, and he understood her anger. Her disappointment metamorphosed her into a wild thing defending its cub. More and more he knew that Susan, with all her advantages, would never comprehend their ultimate oneness. But Eve could never admit that, for it spelled danger, and Eve could never, not ever, give up on her child. So she blamed the new forces for repressing in Susan a talent and a will that perhaps she had never possessed. She blamed the Alice Lombards and the media that gave them space and galvanized their dogmas.

In spite of all sorts of irritation, however, the Haralds had a fine time, especially when Berni came down for a few days to join them. He flew in from the North, where he was teaching mentally handicapped children. A young man with a beard. They said they could barely recognize him, but in truth, he had not changed a great deal, neither in looks nor conduct. He steadfastly, and without allowing himself to be snared by arguments, refused to wear anything but jeans and an open-necked shirt even when—or perhaps especially when— important guests came in for cocktails. And he was kind but distant with his parents, as he had always been. They had never understood why their love and interest and support could not penetrate more deeply, make him open up, discuss with them the things that truly moved him. They had given up trying a long time ago. Now they were content to hear him speak knowledgeably, even animatedly, about his new job. They no longer thought that he would ever have the brilliant career they had expected; but it didn't matter now, as long as he was in tune with what he demanded of himself.

After so many years, they enjoyed having their entire family under one roof. They were pleased when they noticed how cordial the two young men were with each other. It was due mainly—they were convinced of that—to Ron's pleasant personality, his openness and sincere efforts to make his brother-in-law welcome. But even so, it was good to see.

At the dinner table they looked from one face to the other, and they felt none of these minor sorrows. They were content. Eve had produced Sharon's favourite dessert, and now she cut the crisp, sugary crust and put it on a plate with moist raspberries and a small tuft of whipped cream. She served Sharon first. The little girl had got up from her chair so that she could watch better this important procedure, her large, dark eyes devouring the pretty mixture of pink and white and shades of golden brown, her little tongue showing for an instant like the tongue of a kitten. She took the plate in both hands and then, without anyone prompting her, turned around and offered it to Jacob. Here was a moment of unalloyed bliss.

*   *   *

But when they left the elegant house with the cut-stone front, they went in search of the city they remembered. It was transformed now, bold, a throbbing apparition in glass—pink and black and green with silvery girdings and golden lights, jubilant at its centre with wide flights of stairs and waterfalls; with myriad balconies and lookouts; houseboats and gleaming marinas and markets and parks; big, white cruise ships moored alongside elevated promenades; plantings glowing in the interior of skyscrapers among stone and deep carpeting and spilling over terraces onto flowerbeds; a sweeping pattern of daring geometries coming into view, fascinating like a human being that constantly surprises with ideas and sparkle and spirit. And always the mountains. And always the sea.

On the University of British Columbia campus, where Jacob had taught as an assistant professor, they had to ask for direction. Several times on their walks, the Haralds lost their way. Where the old army huts, ramshackle and austere, had provided offices and classrooms, a disconcerting maze of solid structures had sprung into being, and there were signs of more building activity here and there. Of course, many more students now populated the campus, a multiracial throng reflecting the life in the streets of downtown Vancouver. The faculty had become huge; Jacob didn't even know how many people were teaching in the English Department. But some things were familiar still. Up on the point, beyond the stately trees of the Main Mall, where it joins Crescent Road and the prospect suddenly opens toward north and west, the flag was blowing in a wind that carried salt and the scent of April flowers, welcoming the deep-sea freighters down below as they came in from the Straits and slowly passed Howe Sound to enter Burrard Inlet. Beyond the Sound, the crown of the coastal mountains, ridges, peaks, and crags made one ache with a joy too fundamental ever to go away altogether from one's consciousness.

*   *   *

In a desk drawer, at home, Jacob still kept the lines on Vancouver that Eve Kaplansky had written for him as part of a free-ranging assignment. It was after he had spoken to the class on the role of place in the Romantic imagination:

> Some writers and painters have immortalized the cities in which they lived, and people who visit those places feel that they share in the lives of the great. Some old house or park, some indifferent street becomes dear to people because they have seen a painting of it, or read about it, or heard it praised in a song.
>
> But Vancouver is different. It will not become the city which is visited for the sake of someone else's experience, the city which assumes the atmosphere, the scent of another man's life. Vancouver is a place each has to experience on his own. It is a personal thing between each human being and the landscape. No one, however famous or beloved, will transform it into a reflection of himself. No one will ever leave here the stamp of his own personality. People don't make the essence of Vancouver. The essence of Vancouver makes people: it makes their innermost self rise to the surface and look at the world.
>
> Some people are deaf to Vancouver. They come and they leave, and what they remember is that place with a bridge proudly emerging from the forest, or the place where the fat seagulls were standing around in the dirty snow on Victory Square; or the place where they fed penguins in a deluxe concrete pool and bears in miserable cages. Even some of the natives are deaf to the city, except when the weather is fine and they can toast marshmallows on the sand of Spanish Banks; and some of the long-time residents dream of other places where they have been

happy: England or Kingston, Jamaica, where the laburnum trees with their cascades of brilliant yellow, so they say, grow much taller and produce more blossoms. But it is not a matter of people who are deaf to the language of Vancouver. The city has no dealings with them. They are mere flotsam which is incidental to the environment. Vancouver leaves its mark only on those who listen.

After reading these lines, he had first noticed Eve, and a short time afterwards, he asked her to have lunch with him. Not in the cafeteria. In the faculty club, no less. She looked different from the other campus girls with her thick, dark braid. It was no longer so dark now, and it no longer fell down her back, but she still wore the braid—in spite of admonitions from her daughter and from cropped, curly-haired acquaintances, who advised her to have it cut and to get a perm.

Often they had stood by the flagstaff on Point Grey, looking into the Sound, longing for the mountains, for their favourite mountain, the incomparable one in the West, beyond Bowen Island. They asked so many people, but no one could tell them the name, and no one knew the trail that led to its long, snow-covered grade. Eve said it was waiting as it lay there, flung open to the sky. . . .

* * *

He thought she had come to him from the sea.

It seemed to him that the graceful strength of her love echoed in the way her eyes were straining toward the landscape, and that her passion for the sea and the mountains expressed itself in the way her body responded to his. And he felt that only now had he discovered the sun and the forest, the scent of the shore, and the glittering city.

* * *

And then, one day on their walk, he found her remarkably taciturn; and he was afraid the stress was becoming too much for her. She was, after all, a student in his class, and there were certain codes, a well-understood, unwritten discipline regardless of what one might think or feel. They both knew the risk. The relationship had already gone far beyond where danger was a mere hypothesis.

He asked her what it was. "Why are you so quiet? Is anything the matter?" Her only reply was an ill-humoured shake of the head. There was an embarrassing suspicion suddenly uppermost and crowding out all other possibilities. Is she beginning to see our relationship the way others would see it if they knew about it? he asked himself with an uncomfortable realization that he was, after all, not so far above the whisper and prattle of conventional propriety as he had thought. If there is any doubt in Eve's mind that our relationship is different from all others, untouchable, then I have lost her, he thought with a fear that was mixed with anger. He looked at her, questioningly and waiting, but she did not react.

They were walking along the edge of the water from the university toward English Bay. A rather terrifying thought occurred to him. Supposing someone had actually made a remark. Maybe someone had seen her enter the apartment building on Fourth Avenue where he rented. They were very careful about her coming and leaving, but one never could be sure. A passing car. Someone on a bus. It could have been a student; but then, students would hardly know where he lived. So it was worse. It would have been a colleague. And this was serious. Truly serious. There were only five other apartments in the building, and they all belonged to very elderly people. If a colleague of his knew Eve and also had some contact in that building, it would be easy to figure out whom she went to see there. They had been together openly in too many places. Far-fetched as this was, he knew now that he should have been more careful.

He suddenly had a horrid vision of Sondra Boyd (who tacitly seemed to disapprove of him professionally and altogether) saying something snide to Eve. Sondra had taught Eve during the previous session and there had been a mutual dislike. And it was Sondra who had passed them the other night as they were leaving a movie house at ten thirty. He had simply ignored the encounter, assuming Sondra had not been aware that he and Eve were together. A group of young people walking alongside could have been her obvious companions. But maybe he should have said something to Sondra on Monday; something about a new scheme of taking exceptional students individually to see films and plays which were discussed afterwards in a café to sharpen the student's critical faculties and a sense of his or her own importance within the system. An experiment. . . . But no. Such a lie would have been even worse. *Qui s'excuse s'accuse.* And it would have tainted something that was infinitely good.

Again he looked at Eve. She was walking at his side, silent and serious. He dared not say anything. The suspicion and embarrassment deprived him of all possibility to make normal conversation.

Sondra Boyd was a tenured full professor. She had enormous influence in the department and liked the weight of her opinions. There was no doubt she would let the chairman know —and even the dean if the opportunity arose. . . .

They made their way till they reached the club where sailboats were hoisted on shore waiting to be painted later in the spring. There they turned and walked back, climbing over rocks, jumping over tidal puddles, all without a word or a smile. Though she did not show it, Eve became increasingly disheartened. It was callous of him not to find out why she suffered. True, he had asked. But it had sounded casual. Also, it was too complicated. He would probably not see the connection, not understand why it bothered her so; and she didn't want to become obvious in her expectations. . . . If he asked her again, if he put his arms around her, she could say it; but he was cold and silent. Just because she wasn't her normal, affectionate, happy self, he punished her, repaying silence with silence. Obviously this was a contest of wills. Who is going to speak first? She couldn't do it now, and she wouldn't. She wanted him to coax it out of her. She would be able to say it if she was assured of his love; but like this. . . ?

They were walking for hours, not touching and completely silent. The longer it lasted, the more certain it appeared to Jacob that his worst suspicions were justified, and he feared if he made her speak, the horrid facts would come down on his head. Sondra knew. She had poisoned Eve's mind. And she wasn't going to stop there. And would it not be the most grotesque irony if he, Jacob Harald, were to be hauled before the chairman, perhaps before an ethics committee—he, Jacob Harald, who had led a completely celibate life until quite recently, preferring all that suffering and all those excited dreams with their wet endings to a turn with a prostitute who might carry a contagion? This, of course, had been the true reason for his abstinence. No condom could shield him from the revulsion. It was insurmountable. Nevertheless, he had always felt morally superior to his friends and acquaintances who, as teenagers, had urged him to prove himself with purchases of this kind, and later on had good-naturedly steered the occasional classy lady in his direction. Not all prostitutes are alike, Jimmy had assured him. It could all be safe and discreet. But not for him, Jacob Harald. Not for him. And stubbornly he had evaded all serious entanglements with so-called good women who might have been willing to go to bed with him. He feared the trap, the emotional pressure, dreaded being stuck with someone he didn't really want. And after all this, would it not be intolerable if his career were damaged, if maybe he was to lose his job because he had gone to bed with a student of his—he, whose life had always been above reproach?! He could just imagine the tittle-tattle and snickering. If Sondra had opened her mouth, his reputation was beyond repair.

Eve was thinking, if he loved me, he would talk to me. He would want to know why I am so unhappy. Her sneaker was rubbing the back of her heel. She stopped and took off the shoe and plaintively looked at the blister. "Shall I get the car?" he asked. She walked ahead without a reply, the right shoe in her hand.

Jacob was furious. He didn't want Sondra's imagination to soil a relationship that in his mind was pure and perfect. When Eve had appeared on his horizon, all considerations, reservations, prudencies, justified or unjustified, had vanished. He was responding passionately to her passionate responses, and it was as natural to take her as taking breath.

Yes, absolutely natural, he told himself. He had despised Jimmy's warnings when he threatened him with the common folklore that a man without previous experience was sure to make a sorry fool of himself and cause pain and embarrassment if eventually he took on a virgin girl. Jimmy had merely rationalized his promiscuity, and Jacob wished he could tell him so now: See, Jimmy, old high school chum? It's me, Jacob, Jacob the wise! Every little cat knows what to do, doesn't he? There had been no difficulty. From the first it had been obliteration of all otherness, a melting of selves into the long rush of gathering light. . . .

And now she was walking here beside him, not speaking. Why was she sulking? He didn't want to know. He was distraught. He didn't want it to come crashing on his head.

*   *   *

The day was declining. So he won't ask me, Eve thought, feeling chilly and miserable. If he cared for me, he would ask. She put on her shoe and was limping, and it hurt badly.

"I'll take you home," he said. He walked with her up to the doorstep of the old-fashioned frame house where Eve lived with her mother, a lady with vague ambitions as an actress—she sometimes talked about founding a company of her own—and strong leftist leanings. For eleven years she had been married to the owner of a successful car dealership in Toronto, a man who believed that politics should be *left*—to politicians, especially as people of diverse political hues were among his clientele. It was a view shared unreservedly by his present wife, a corpulent, exceedingly well groomed woman who disliked Eve.

Jacob didn't feel quite himself whenever the first Mrs. Kaplansky scrutinized him, and today he didn't want to meet her at all. He said goodnight and walked away.

Eve thought, I can't. Speaking now would be too humiliating. It would mean I am giving in. But she didn't care any more if he won this contest of wills. She couldn't let him go like this. She was late for supper, but she ran after him and caught his arm, and they held each other close right there in the street.

And it came out with all her fear and anger: her sociology class had a visiting professor this morning, a man of considerable repute. At one point he told the class: "people expect way too much. This is what makes marriages go wrong. They think there can be an eternal honeymoon. So, naturally, they get disappointed." Eve was bitter and reproachful—as if Jacob had already betrayed her, as if he had already been guilty of destroying her aspirations and dreams. Her voice was shaky. Jacob had never before seen tears in her eyes. The professor said: "People have to understand that no honeymoon can last forever!"

*   *   *

Jacob suppressed a heart-felt laugh. In his mind flashed memories of his parents' household. He couldn't remember a quarrel between them—not a real quarrel, at any rate. Worried and overworked, they had occasionally snapped at each other impatiently, but it was gone in an instant. And whenever one of them had been in a grouchy mood and difficult, the other automatically had assumed an air of benevolent superiority, like a parent who calms a cranky child. And there was that rule of thumb, famous in his family: it's easier to forgo something one likes than to put up with a thing one dislikes. Accordingly, when one of them, for instance, was charmed by a rug that seemed just perfectly suited to replace the old bedroom carpeting, and the other couldn't stand the look of that rug, the rule of thumb was applied, and that rug didn't get bought. . . . But this was not all that flashed through Jacob's mind.

He could feel a roguish expression on his face. He wanted to say, "Of course, honeymoons can't last forever: afterwards it gets even better. Only those imbeciles don't tell you that." But he refrained. He didn't say it because he was afraid Eve would think he didn't take it seriously, and he could see how upset she was.

So he just said, "Honeymoons can't last forever? Don't believe that hackneyed old lie."

They decide to meet again after supper, and later that evening, he asked her to marry him. She was eight years younger than he and in her sophomore year.

*   *   *

They often walked along the edge of the water, and in some undefined, metaphysical sense, elements of the landscape entered their being and found a permanent home there.

Mountain peaks brilliantly white against cloudless blue—and sunlight in dazzling radiance on icy summits—and storm of spring ablaze with light and blowing from the sunny snow of the mountains, blowing in sunlight across blue-green water, making the waves rush toward the shore and the spray dance and glitter, white like the sunny snow. . . . it reached into their future—it was in them still.

* * *

And now—after how many decades?—they were walking again along the familiar shore toward the city.

Eve asked, "Why do you say that nature is deeply misunderstood? Don't most people believe nature needs both life and death in order to function? Equal components—aren't they?"

Jacob said, "I, for one, don't. I think life and death are most unequal components. I'm not asking just now whether nature could function without death. I merely ask: Is nature 'impartial' in this? And I maintain that nature is by no means impartial. I argue that nature's tendencies show—how shall I put it?—*abhorrence* of death, of disintegration, of not being. Nature *favours* creativity, becoming, vitality. I argue that from the very Source, from the Originating Existence rises an essential preference for life, a thrust toward consciousness."

Jacob felt that at last he could speak to her about this. He wanted to put his ideas to the test, let them make their way. Eve sat down on a log that the waves had left on the sand, and he stood before her. She looked at him critically for a moment: "If I remember rightly what I learned in biology class—and I was very good at it, exceptionally good—nature doesn't favour and abhor. You sound as if you believed nature had intentions and feelings about things. Surely . . . I never thought. . . ."

There he was—in the greatest lecture hall on earth, and she was all the audiences he had ever loved, and he had started out wrong. "Just a minute! Please—wait," he said. "These words need a bit of explanation. They aren't meant in the ordinary sense."

She gave a barely perceptible nod and waited with a quiet expectancy that made him grateful. So he continued.

"When I say 'abhorrence' and 'favour', I mean that nature, in its very atoms, even in the subatomic particles, has certain qualities and tendencies, which in conscious beings then manifest themselves as abhorring or favouring."

"But isn't this rather controversial?" she interrupted. "I read the other day that many scientists believe we shouldn't expect subatomic particles to contain a kind of blueprint for what develops in the cosmos. They say, 'Look at pieces of lumber. You can assemble them and make a fence or a pyramid or a box. But this doesn't mean that the pieces have already in them some fencishness or pyramidishness or boxishness. That's how it is with nature."

"With this I can agree only up to a point," he said. "There would be no fence if the lumber didn't have certain qualities—a proper stiffness, for instance. To some extent, that from which a thing is made does predetermine what is being produced. You can't make an anvil from an egg. So when it comes to consciousness, I say the atoms from which a living being is made must possess a quality that makes them *fit* material; and in turn, the subatomic particles, which constitute the atoms, must be *fit* to become conscious.

"Some say life and consciousness sprang into being because, by chance, the right atoms combined in the right way. Yet, this alone would not have been enough. I believe that what took place was an unlocking of a ubiquitous talent. No combination of atoms could have brought about life and consciousness if the subatomic particles (the quarks and electrons which form *all* atoms) were not *the way they are,* namely, capable of being alive and conscious. I go further still: the particles could not have this capability if the potential for it were not a quality of cosmic power, of the Originating Existence, which produces the subatomic world." Jacob waited for a moment. "Maybe you feel that I am stating the obvious. I try to be systematic."

"None of which convinces me that nature 'abhors' death,"

said Eve. Her laconic interruption brought a smile to his face, so that at first she wasn't quite sure whether he seriously meant what he was now proposing: "Isn't this abhorrence of death obvious from pole to pole? Nature is permeated with craving for prosperity. Eating is pleasure. The creative moment brings ecstasy. Nurturing the young is essentially joyful.

"And injurious conditions produce suffering, don't they. When there is pain, a conscious organism feels the necessity to recoil and seek conditions that are likely to prolong life.

"In the pain that accompanies destruction, there is an intrinsic crying out against a reversal of the building trend. In the joy that emerges from creative activities, there is an unmistakable acceptance. This suffering and abhorrence at injury and destruction and the feelings of well-being and joy when there is life and health appear to be basic characteristics of all conscious matter. And this tells me something about subatomic particles. Consciousness could not be endowed with these characteristics if the particles were not of the right quality to produce them. Ultimately, we can only possess a consciousness that abhors death and loves life because Originating Existence, the power that forms the subatomic particles, is such that it brings forth a consciousness with these traits. The ethic that hates death and loves life is therefore deeply rooted in our original Parent.

"Clearly, then, we *do* have an objective standard telling us what is evil and what is good. The commandments that seek to prevent pain and death and to further life and health—Love your neighbour . . . You shall not murder—are not mere arbitrary human inventions (as so many will have it). They translate into human language the powerful signals rising from the depth of the cosmos, from the nature of Originating Existence."

*   *   *

She wanted to believe it but couldn't quite find the chord that would bring her into harmony with his thinking. She saw an array of objections that couldn't be ignored. "An organism that would hate life and love its own destruction couldn't very well survive, could it?" she remarked with an eagerness that pleased him. "So the only consciousness that could make it was the life-loving one. But this doesn't mean that Originating Existence couldn't have brought both into being. The life-hating one just didn't survive."

"Which only means," said Jacob, "that the intrinsic logic of natural law, which is the law of the Originating Existence, made it possible only for a life-affirming consciousness to develop into higher organisms. What is important is that nature establishes this clear preference. Personally, I cannot think that a consciousness basically in favour of its own destruction ever made an appearance."

She weighed what he said but obviously was still quite uneasy about it. "Nature doesn't always put pain and disintegration together," she said. "Far from it. There are so many exceptions. Childbirth hurts. Remember?"

"You know as well as I do why that is. We've been degenerating with too much food and too little exercise, and so have our poor domestic animals." His smugness amused her. His expertise in this, after all, couldn't rival what she knew about the subject. "But it's still a creative activity, and believe me, it's painful," she insisted. He was adamant: "You would admit, though, that the original trend in nature was birth without pain. A she-bear manages very nicely," he said.

"Yes, I do admit that. But sometimes there is destruction and things go terribly wrong, and the outcry is not there. Pain does not appear. Diseases go undetected until it is too late. And operations can be very painful, and yet they contribute to life. How do you explain that?"

Jacob replied, "I don't think this invalidates what I am saying. The brain may fail to register pain because of chance conditions. It may be blocked off from the distressed part by the illness itself. As to operations—we feel pain at the place of incision and wherever cells are destroyed or under stress. When there is healing, there is well-being."

It seemed to satisfy her. "But there is something else," she said. "I know you don't like the idea, but what can we say ultimately when people are convinced that pain should be accepted because it can bring out nobility and heroism and selflessness —all sorts of marvellous qualities."

It was a point of view that had roused Jacob's ire on another occasion. "I know what you're thinking of," he said. "I remember that insufferable man on the *Christophoro Colombo* while we were anchored off Gibraltar; how he gave us his little speech about war, how he wished we didn't consider it just a horrible affliction because suffering, after all, brought out the best in some people and led to so many important inventions. . . . He might as well have said that polio was valuable because it gave Dr. Salk an opportunity to show how clever he was. Heroism, selflessness, inventiveness—these are the medication designed to do away with the suffering. People who romanticize suffering itself because it brings about this 'medication' are confusing things. They value the disease because it makes medications appear."

"But what if people feel that they derive some good from death? When there is an accident and the kidney of the victim is used to save a life, won't the recipient be happy?"

Jacob's head jerked in vehement denial. "Naturally, a patient will rejoice when he recovers. But no one can rightly feel that the accident was a good thing. What is good here is the human ingenuity that is able to wrest life from death—how, from the depth of destruction, life is extricating itself."

He suddenly noticed a particular deliberateness in Eve's tone, and perhaps there was something else in it, too.

"Supposing . . . supposing a man commits adultery, and the wife can't possibly find out about it. According to your theory, this is perfectly all right, then, because there is no pain, and probably a lot of pleasure, and no visible harm is done anywhere."

He took her firmly by the shoulders and slowly turned her to face him. His lips were narrowed, and he looked straight into her eyes. "When one breaks a trust, there is destruction of something that nurtures life, and when one begins to make peace with this kind of attitude, one is paving the way, and sooner or later, there'll be general acceptance of it. Somewhere, in some circumstances, pain will eventually follow, you can depend on it." He let her go.

More than his words, an undertone of annoyance in his voice mollified her. But he wasn't going to let her off that easily: What?! Imputing things? To him?! He said, "I think you would agree, though, that one has to judge each case on its merits. Supposing a man is in a mental hospital, and there is no prospect at all that he will ever come home to his wife. If she commits adultery to salvage her life, isn't it better, perhaps, than getting a divorce and formally abandoning him?"

He knew very well that she didn't like thinking about such contingencies, even in theory, even when they referred to some hypothetical stranger. She looked very unhappy and didn't reply. He relished her retreat.

*   *   *

"I can still see some difficulties," she mused. "What about drugs? They're pretty destructive and they produce pleasure, in spite of it. How come?"

"Yes, yes, I can see the difficulty there, but I don't think it scuttles my theory," he said. "If I put my finger into a flame, I know at once that it is destructive. That there is danger in the contact with certain other substances, like drugs, or that there is danger in certain complex situations, like adultery, takes longer to register. It's probably a coincidence that the chemistry of a harmful drug is able to stimulate the brain, fool it to register a temporary semblance of well-being. But taking drugs for pleasure is a quirk. Normally, the brain has no contact with drugs.

Evolution hasn't prepared it. When actual deterioration begins, there *is* distress. In any case, you are talking about exceptions.

"*I* am arguing that pain and well-being tell us in the plainest possible language what nature experiences as desirable and good and what is abhorrent. They are so strong that they define an act even beyond themselves: an injurious act is evil even when the victim is oblivious. They are witness to the absolute.

"If a man comes to me and philosophizes about the relativity of good and evil, and how it all depends on one's social environment and upbringing and on one's personal point of view, and I punch him in the nose, he will *know* beyond all sophistication and quibbling that what I have done is evil."

"Unless he happens to be a masochist," retorted Eve.

"Precisely," said Jacob. "There *are* exceptional reactions. Deviations from the norm. But it is the norm which tells us what is characteristic of the species, not the oddity. If you see a malformed apple, do you assume that this is characteristic of apples? No. You assume that something happened to go wrong. Surely, it is only from the norm that we deduce what nature's standards are.

"Destruction, disintegration, death are *normally* accompanied by discomforts and pain, physical and intellectual, and conscious beings learn to shun them as much as they possibly can, whereas creative action, love, they seek to the utmost of their energy. Even an amoeba tries to remove itself when poked and to exert itself when there's something edible around. And evolution makes this essential characteristic of consciousness more and more evident: the more we advance, the more elaborate our efforts to survive. It generates our most vehement feelings and our most desperate ingenuity. This is the norm. This tells me what is essential to nature. And from this compelling evidence, I draw conclusions concerning the Originating Existence."

He needed her approval. It was of immense importance to him. He watched her but could not fathom what her reaction would be and added what so often he had said to himself: "From that Source rises all the power raging toward creativity and all the effort we employ to overcome disintegration."

*   *   *

Eve looked at him intently and hesitated. "You are saying that feelings of pain—*articulate* . . . intrinsically . . . a cosmic suffering . . . at disintegration. And with it . . . an intrinsic revulsion."

Jacob nodded. "This is what I mean."

"I understand," she said. She paused. And in her own way she understood that at the heart of it all was a pure Strength propelling toward life, and that in our suffering, we were not alone because everything that made us suffer was an injury and an obstacle to that great Strength from whom we are formed, so that our suffering was in the totality of it. And dimly she knew that struggling free, or even in just struggling against the obstacles, we were scooped into an advanced thrust of that Strength blazing toward the future.

She got up and ran to the water's edge and stood there as if to tell it, call out, shout it across the wide waters to the North Shore: "But this is it!" And she turned and called out to Jacob: "This is it! Don't you see? Don't you see?" And she came back and put her arms around him. "Isn't this exactly what Pierre needed to know? You must tell him if—"

"If he ever comes back." The old torment parched his lips.

"But he will! He must." she tried with her eyes to pour into him her confidence; and he knew that at this moment she knew where he had been.

*   *   *

There was in him turmoil and liberation. He tried to control it, and he spoke slowly, in a low voice: "I wish I had been ready when Pierre asked us that—that question. Now it has become clear to me. *The depth and the extent of that ultimate, unimaginable suffering that was caused in the* Shoah *indicate the measure of nature's intrinsic abhorrence and, therefore, also God's intrinsic abhorrence of those deeds. In the victims' longing for life—to their final gasp for breath—THERE was the affirmation of the Originating Existence. THERE was the will of God.*

"I know it now; this is what I should have said to Pierre."

* * *

For a while they were very quiet.

"Look at the boats," she said, motioning toward the white sails far out in the bay.

And after a long silence: "But if we are all made from the Originating Existence, whose nature is love of life and hatred of disintegration, how can things go wrong? Why do things cause pain. . . . ? *Why* does evil exist? *Why?!*"

They walked against the breeze, and then they were sitting on another huge log which had come to rest on the shore. Driftwood was piled up along most of the beach. Dull bluish clouds all but covered the sky, and the tall, slim towers of the city across English Bay were outlined against an opaque, blue mountain range. But in the west, luminous, transparent shafts of sun had broken through the sombre cumuli, and in a great semicircle, they touched the mountains and the sea. There was a glow verdant on the forested slopes and a pool of dazzling brightness on the water. Eve discovered it first: "As if the sky were reaching down to gather up the world in its arms of light." Her head touched Jacob's shoulder. They were alone on the beach. They kissed like young lovers; only it was more wonderful now because fear and frenzies and worry and jobs and struggle that so often had impinged upon their happiness had receded and paled in their consciousness.

* * *

"Why is there evil? Some of the mystics believed that the substance of the world was flowing from the Godhood, and the farther away it flowed, the weaker the influence of the Divine. I shouldn't want to put it quite in these terms, of course," said Jacob, "but basically, perhaps they had the right understanding. Today we know that particles are 'condensed' energy, that our world seems to 'freeze' out of what scientists call 'space-time', and beyond it, perhaps, out of the absolute vacuum, out of 'nothing'; and in the process from 'No-Thingness,' or from some other at present unknown generating Source, to particle, a change occurs. The particle, though it comes into being out of this mysterious Originating Existence, is different from its Source. It has become an *otherness.*"

"How can we know it is an otherness when we can't really know the nature of the Originating Existence?" asked Eve. She was in a bad mood because today she would have preferred to remain in complete harmony.

Jacob gave her a pensive glance. Maybe it was a dutiful effort of hers to keep the dialectics going. But no, not this time. He recognized skepticism, deep and true. Something that called for assertion on his part. He was casting about for words that would leave no doubt how it was meant.

"To begin with, the very fact that we do not perceive the actual nature of the Originating Existence in any scientific sense, whereas we can observe matter and make all sorts of measurements and predictions about it, proves that there is a very profound difference."

He hesitated. "Part of what I am going to say is probably intuitive speculation, but I trust it is not just that. We have logic on our side when we assume that the Primary Source is creative power. Its offspring, matter, retains its divine heritage, an elemental capacity to produce meaningful entities, the urgency to create, a straining that leads to life. To this extent, matter is not an otherness. But matter is plagued with evils that, to a large extent, appear to be *accidents* or a *malfunctioning*. They pertain to the 'frozen' condition which is matter and do not seem to be components of essential nature."

"Accident...." She felt very definite dissatisfaction with an explanation so simple for a thing so terrible as the world's suffering. "Accident....?"

"Let me give you a well-known example," replied Jacob.

"Frozen water has the innate characteristic to crystallize in a beautiful, symmetric, hexagonal pattern. But when you look at a snowflake, most often some inimical, accidental conditions have mutilated its shape. This observation can be applied to matter in general. When nothing interferes with the essential heritage, there is order, health, well-being."

"Could it be," said Eve, "that a true prayer is really—how shall I put it?—a straining toward the fundamental Power, so that the essential, unalloyed pattern in us is made more strong —so that it can function to the best of its potential?"

Fleetingly, it came to Jacob that in the happiest moments of his entire teaching career, there had been students who not only understood but suddenly could proceed on their own, sailing away, navigating in a new direction. "Thank you."

Even years later, she could still remember the expression on his face when he said this.

*   *   *

Still, his argument was open. It didn't satisfy her at all. Why could nature not function without accident?

He tried to formulate it as best he could: "Matter is constantly in such a teeming, seething turmoil, and zillions of normal, harmless processes constantly develop in countless directions. Sometimes, by coincidence, there are 'collisions', and then, if conscious beings are involved, there is pain."

"You mean—geological process which forms a narrow

valley with steep cliffs in itself is not harmful. A flood in itself is not harmful. Migrations of human beings as such are not harmful. But when these three circumstances happen to meet, an accident occurs. People drown. There is suffering, and we become conscious of evil."

"Exactly. Only, of course, the role accident plays isn't always that obvious," he said.

"In genetic flaws, for instance."

"Exactly," Jacob said. "Most people have some inkling by now that toxins and radiation can cause mutations. What is usually not so clear to people is that the possibility of accidental mutation is always there. Today we are told that subatomic particles, the quanta, are not really solid packets of matter but exuberant, minute patterns of concentrated strength, which are in constant motion. The quantum physicists tell us that, on the basis of statistics, one can predict what the broad multitude of quanta will probably do, but that it's impossible to foretell with any certainty what an individual particle will do next. Particles can spontaneously link up at random in some unforeseen place and cause new developments to start up. And when this happens in the DNA of a gene, then mutation can occur."

"As every good little evolutionist knows, that's a very beneficial thing." said Eve. "Without it, there would be no new forms of life. *We* wouldn't be here." She didn't want him to think her ignorance extended to basics of this kind.

"I agree," he said, "but sometimes when a particle leaves the mainstream and randomly hooks up somewhere else, it can by chance be in a place where its presence causes havoc. And then we see a fruit fly that has sprouted an extra leg in the wrong place. Or suddenly an organism is born without a stomach. And then we become conscious of evil because there is injury to life."

*   *   *

Eve mulled over this for a moment. "What about carnivores?" she asked. "They cause suffering, but can nature function without them? If creatures didn't get eaten, wouldn't they carpet the earth and starve to death? Can this fit into your theory that nature abhors suffering, and that evil is caused simply by accident or a malfunctioning?"

"Yes, even this," replied Jacob, ignoring the defiance in her voice. "I am convinced this perpetual killing is not an inexorable characteristic of nature. When locusts get too crowded, their hormones change, and then there are few offspring and the swarms disappear. It's not unreasonable to think that without carnivores, regulating mechanisms could evolve that would limit breeding. Essentially, the system doesn't *have* to include violent attack upon conscious life—neither to avoid overcrowding nor to appease hunger. Nature has the talent to function very well without it."

"Yes, but how? Don't you have any feelings for carrots and cabbages?" Eve demanded. Her face was perfectly straight, and he couldn't tell for certain whether or not she was joking.

"Plants lack a highly developed central nervous system, so I think we may suppose they aren't conscious of pain." He had learned over the years to treat such questions with respect. "The absence of pain when plants are eaten and transformed into conscious organisms I take as an indication that this kind of nourishment isn't objectionable in nature," he said.

"Then I take it you are going to give a public lecture soon—for spiders, eagles, tigers . . . teach them to be vegetarians? You know what their reaction will be!" She did as if she were going to swallow Jacob in one ferocious gulp.

"No, I am serious."

"And what about the tiger who eats a lamb?!" cried Eve, still teasing, though her skepticism was honest enough. "You said that constructive actions cause pleasure—nature's normal reaction. I'm sure a tiger is very pleased when he eats. He's building tigers. But at the same time, he is cruelly destructive, too. So it seems to me this is all very confusing. . . ." For a moment she was afraid she had cornered him.

But he was far from disconcerted. "To begin with," he said, "the tiger is not cruel: He can't appreciate the character of his action. Yes, the tiger has pleasure when he kills, but the pleasure doesn't stem from the killing as such. It comes from a constructive urge, from the stilling of hunger. And the hunger could be stilled harmlessly, if ancestors of the tiger had not been misdirected by accident."

*   *   *

Now she was angry and impatient. She didn't want to destroy his theory, but then again, she felt that feigning agreement was unworthy of them. "How can you say a tiger is misdirected when he feeds?! That's how nature made him. Right?"

"Look," he said, "all life is endowed with this overwhelming desire to remain alive. When a mutation produces sharp claws, sooner or later the animal will find out by chance that other creatures are weaker and edible and that the claws can be used to make a meal of them. Young tigers inherit the claws and imitate their parents. Feeding habits are encoded. Voilà—a carnivore! You can see, it starts with random mutation and chance opportunities. In the ancestors of the plague bacterium and the tiger, the normal will to survive was channelled by accident so that they embarked on a parasitic career. But their life-style is not an expression of essential nature.

"Against this, I think of the pain that results from the feeding habits of the carnivore. The ability to feel pain is part of consciousness, and as such, it rises from the fundamental power of the cosmos. Its language is unmistakable. The outraged outcry: *No! Stop! Don't do this to me!* which is implicit in all pain tells me that I am witnessing something that nature in its essence rejects."

Jacob had thought about this long. Always probing. And he added what had recently suggested itself to him: "When an organism mutilates itself, we don't consider this normal. When a bird plucks its own feathers or when a person deliberately bangs his head against the wall, we know there is sickness of some kind. The material universe, as we now know, is *one* organism. So when it develops an accidental feature that causes suffering in another part of itself, we may, I think, suspect that something is wrong. Those who say with Darwin that nature is 'red in tooth and claw' are talking about its pathology."

"But if there is no cure. . . ." The age-old bitterness was in Eve's voice.

"A cure? . . . A cure. Not for everything. Certainly not at present," he said. "I don't think nature can eliminate disastrous coincidences. But then, as you yourself pointed out, this randomness in mutation can also be helpful."

"Yes," she said. "The skunk has evolved its odour and the fawn has its protective colouring. . . . But all the same, they get eaten. And look at us! We don't even have that."

"We do a lot better," he said confidently. "WE have the mightiest of all defence mechanisms." And he added (somewhat grandiosely, she thought): "We have reasoning power."

Eve answered with a hysterical laugh: "Our reasoning power! Now, that's really something to brag about!"

He cast about for arguments: "I'm not saying that reason doesn't make wrong judgements. Often it's misinformed, starts with the wrong premise by accident or through some malfunctioning down the line. Sometimes the problems it is up against are so complex, it's difficult to sort out what action—"

Eve broke in with rare sardonic mirth: "This defence mechanism is finally going to blow us all to smithereens! At least the stink of a skunk can be relied on always to work in the right direction. A skunk doesn't pollute itself, I don't think."

Jacob wasn't in the mood for drollery, but he was drawn to answer her angry banter. "Our reasoning power is a caterpillar," he said. "Ravenous and unready. It always tries to get satisfied: with food, with love, with power, with fame. Even when it's reaching to the stars, it's to satisfy its curiosity. But it hasn't reached its higher form. Remember how clumsy and stupid we were at age three?" he said. "And look at us now! So if mankind as a whole can hang on long enough to age and mature, maybe more people will start thinking like you and me!" He expected her to laugh.

"Just maybe," she said moodily. "Just maybe."

He watched her face intently. It was vital for him to have her as an ally in this. And it was so difficult to express, and so important, and so easy to convey it wrongly.

*   *   *

"There is something important here," he said. Reason isn't of the same order as the spotted coat of a young buck, which has come about through chance combination of particles and natural selection and has turned out to be a protection through accidental circumstances. Reason, like feelings of pain and joy, is a talent integral to consciousness, which evolution unlocks from an innate quality of the particles. It's an inheritance from Originating Existence. And it's here that nature's preference for life is most evident: through reason, consciousness is *deliberately* trying to protect itself."

"I don't dispute it's *trying,* " she scowled.

"And as it unfolds toward its full potential, it slowly begins to be coloured by compassion," he said. "In its more advanced form, it is squarely pitted against evil."

She had been listening patiently. Now her face suddenly changed. "You really believe this? Mankind is becoming compassionate? You astound me." She gave an exasperated laugh, which ended in a coughing fit. "Don't talk to me about compassion," she managed to say amidst more nervous coughs. "People haven't enough imagination for that. They just have weak nerves, and that sometimes masquerades as compassion. . . ." More coughs.

It startled him, this biting denial. It seemed so out of character. An eruption like this needed a period of incubation. He wondered whether she suffered in ways he didn't know. Perhaps she had kept from him disgust and rages, who knows what disturbances, in order to protect him. "But Eve," he pleaded, "I didn't say mankind *is* compassionate. It *can* be. It *will* be if we have enough time to evolve. It's on the way. Even in some animals, we get glimpses of it. Cats and dogs, they say, sometimes try to comfort their owners. And there are those tales of dolphins who come to the aid of creatures in distress."

"Maybe dolphins . . . " she said. "Yes, maybe dolphins. . . ."

"For us, it begins . . . very slowly." He wanted her to share this and wasn't sure now how far this was possible. "Our first records of it, after all, they are not even four thousand years old. In Genesis we read of Abraham on Mount Moriah, how he is about to sacrifice his son—and cannot. We are told an angel from God stays his hand as it is poised to kill. That angel was the dawn of compassion, the enlightenment in Abraham's mind."

"You think that's historical?"

"It doesn't matter. Maybe Abraham was a real person. Maybe he's the symbol of a generation. *Someone* did have a revelation; someone's mind had evolved to the stage where it could begin to understand and feel more clearly—I mean more in harmony with the Originating Existence. That's what revelation is. We take a long time, but slowly—I grant you, very slowly—compassion begins to spread."

Eve said, "In isolated cases. But otherwise, it hasn't really worked, has it."

"But it *is* gaining ground." He was not giving up. "From the

Poles who were hiding Jews and were hanged for it by the Nazis in a public square to that man who suspended himself from a helicopter and snatched up a dog—you remember that dog running around lost on an ice floe out at sea—there is much compassion, even now. If you want to see progress, you've got to look at the kind of justice even so-called civilized nations were dispensing barely a century ago. Today, by and large, the world judges the degree of a people's civilization by the compassion it shows in its judicial system. . . ."

But she only shook her head wearily. "Look at Nietzsche," she said. "There's a passage where he calls compassion 'unnatural'! He argues that compassion is best avoided because it prevents the weeding out of weak individuals and becomes an impediment to the evolution of a strong species. Of course, he was insane. But look how many people still admire him, and not just Nazis.

"Most people who admire him probably never came across that absurd passage. A colossal error," Jacob said. "Even the most hard-nosed Darwinian would have to disagree with him. If only robust, healthy individuals were allowed to procreate, we'd be deprived of an irreplaceable pool of genes. Compassion represents the most advanced stage evolution has reached on this planet."

She visibly rallied, and he felt the excitement of being able to take her with him. There were animation and warmth in his voice now. And he went on: "As consciousness becomes more and more keen, it feels pain more and more clearly, doesn't it? At least, we think an ape can suffer more acutely than a flea. Compassion, then, is an extension of pain, and as a phenomenon of consciousness, it too stems from a primordial quality in the nature of the cosmos. Only now it is no longer the point of impact alone that hurts. Now we can experience injury even when it occurs at a distance, and we are prompted to fight what causes injury even when it's inflicted on someone unrelated to us. I see here the evolution of a most powerful antidote against evil. It's as if humanity were becoming sensitized to the oneness of the universe."

"Except that vast numbers are lagging behind, or they're drowning it out," she said. "Like a fool. A fool with a thorn in his toe. He'd rather swallow a painkiller than stoop and pull out the thorn. I wish I had your optimism."

*   *   *

He badly wanted to lash out and tell her what he had often thought: There are two clichés in the language I particularly detest. The word 'optimism' is habitually linked with 'shallow.' It is good form to be angry at shallow optimists. Pessimism, on the other hand, is 'profound.' It produces a kind of grim solidarity among some people, almost a kind of catharsis. Like a swamp, it can give off a certain shimmering, seductive poetry. And yet, Jacob thought, and yet, when I think of that lad I saw the other day, it seems to me that the shallows are not such a bad place to wade in. And then he remembered that he had neglected to tell Eve about this lad.

"You remember the other day when we went to Stanley Park?" Jacob said. "You remember I decided to sit on the lawn while you and the kids were taking Sharon to see the deer. There were two boys there kicking an empty plastic bottle around as if it were a football. They could have been ten years old, maybe eleven. And suddenly one of them stopped and called out to the other, 'Look at this ugly bug!' And the other came running to see what was in the grass. He said, 'Sure is ugly.' And the first said, 'I'm going to squash it!' And the second boy shouted, 'No!' and they started jostling each other. And the first one yelled, 'My mom squashes them all the time. My old man too.' And then suddenly the second one was almost crying. He shouted, 'I don't want this bug dead!' and he kicked the bottle as far as he could, and they were running after it. So there it was: That boy had overcome the ancestral shudder—vertebrate against invertebrate: Watch out for that arthropod! Kill or become somebody else's meal."

Eve listened in silence.

"That such an evolution is possible at all—I think there is a triumph in this," Jacob said. "That for some human beings it's no longer just 'I don't want to be dead', it's 'I don't want that bug to be dead'; there's an unfolding in this of the fundamental imperative. . . ."

She did not reply.

*   *   *

They were watching a tug boat coming in. It was towing a long scow with lumber. Two small motor boats were playing alongside, and a third one was racing in for a closer look. Feisty little tug! Pulling that giant barge at full speed. And in the opposite direction, the grey bulk of a dilapidated freighter chuffing toward the ocean . . . .

She had slid down from the log. She sat on the sand, leaning her back against it, and he took off his coat and made a pad against the log. For a brief moment she closed her eyes to feel more intensely on her face and limbs the flutter and brush of the constant coastal breeze. Something was worrying her terribly. When he looked again, her mood had clouded over.

"Accident, is it?" she said. "I don't believe all evil is accident. Drowning out compassion in oneself—that's no accident."

"I never said it was, entirely." He recognized a flickering of storm and knew it wouldn't stay beyond the horizon. He got up and walked the length of their log and then behind it passed the cliff where trees and bushes in young leaf gripped the scant earth. A tangle of rugged branches was reaching down to him, and as he walked, he reached up to them, feeling agreeably the stretch and pull of his muscles. He had anticipated her objection, had in a sense waited for it, knowing that they were inevitably nearing a moment of crisis, in which they had to confront squarely the evil that had sent him on his long, uncharted voyage. He pushed himself to deal with it. When he returned to her, he was able to face it.

"As I told you—matter, I believe, can malfunction, get out of control; and for this, there can be many coincidental causes. Individual strands in our consciousness can gain excessive momentum. I say 'excessive' because when it happens—pain appears; a sure sign that there is an affront to essential nature."

"I don't understand what you're saying."

"Hunger becomes gluttony; the normal urge to gather supply becomes greed; the desire for sex turns into destructive frenzy. Or take alertness: such a beneficial trait. In its decadent form, it becomes irrational fear—paranoia—the arms race."

"This is too cold," said Eve. "Maybe it's a way of getting at it. But it's too cold."

"We can't understand it when the mind is hot," he said. "And I *am* trying to understand it. The old mythologies said it in *their* own way, but people can't believe them anymore, though much of it is the truth. I've got to translate it. For *my* own day. In the old legend that Milton used in *Paradise Lost*, the angels fell because they rebelled against God, and as a result, they turned into fiends and became the stuff hell is made of. Angelos—the messenger from God. In a way, I think of those phenomena in our consciousness as messengers from the Originating Existence. Hunger, alertness. . . . they help us to live . . . and in their 'fallen' state, distorted, when they're over-blown—aren't they at the bottom of every evil perpetrated by man?"

"I remember that passage—the fallen angels in the burning lake," she said. "It's a beautiful passage. Poetry makes evil look attractive. But it's lying. Evil is nothing but ugliness."

"When it's great art, the truth is there in spite of the lie," he said. "Do you remember Lucifer, the brightest of all the angels, and how he fell because of his excessive pride and turned into—Satan?"

"I remember."

He was near the secret, the explanation or at least, perhaps, the penultimate veil beneath which the final abomination could be discovered. He did not want to lift this veil now. Especially not today. Not here. Not ever again, if at all possible. But he knew this was useless.

She sensed what he was going to talk about and felt the tension. She climbed back onto the log, apprehensive and resentful because, in this place of beauty and grandeur, before these waves and these mountains, to probe the final obscenity was like a desecration. And yet, she knew the necessity. They couldn't turn back.

His voice reflected the strain. "I don't think there is much in our experience more wonderful than the feeling we get when we have achieved. Some of it must be in the cat when she brings us her kitten. I'm sure it's in a dog when he retrieves a stick and wags his tail. It's in every one of us when we feel preened and strong—it's a joy in ourselves—it's pride. Healthy pride isn't hostile to anyone. It's just self-confidence, security. But when it's overly fed, or when it's frustrated and defends itself with counterpressure, it grows, and then it can become exaggerated. That's the first stage of deterioration. It begins to overcompensate, just to make sure it's safe. Only sometimes it keeps on rolling. It doesn't stop. Then it shows itself as arrogance toward others, even when those others don't represent a danger that has to be countered with self-assurance. In the last stage of degeneration, it eventually insists on the subjugation of others. In its runaway form, self-confidence has turned into the very worst of evils, into a lust for power."

As she listened to him, her gloom gathered rapidly. "Your

explanation, then, for the worst?" she asked.

"It is," he said. "For me, it is."

"There *was* a lot of frustrated pride there," she said, musing. "After the defeat in the First World War. I suppose it explains why the Germans told each other they were better than anyone else—a master race. From school kids to university rector, they revelled in it, didn't they?"

"To be masters, they needed slaves. And what easier target? Jews and Gypsies in their midst—small minorities, unarmed, scattered, with nowhere to go to make a stand."

"But there were other factors, too. There were many." She could recall reports, editorial analyses, numberless debates.

"Sure, there were," he said. "But when they dragged people into the gas, it wasn't the age-old inveterate fear of the neighbour who is different. Their victims were already isolated and had no power whatever. And it wasn't even greed. They had already taken away from them all their possessions and their jobs. Some say it can't be explained. But I believe it was pride at the nadir. The revelling in power . . . I remember—"

"In 1937? When you stayed with your poor Aunt Lilly in Leipzig?"

"Yes. Every time there was a new restriction to what Jews were allowed to do or where they were allowed to go, there was this gleeful excitement. People really enjoyed it. Every sensational humiliation. You could feel it everywhere, even in the railway station. I remember. Even in the waiting room—those loud, provocative voices: 'the Jews . . . the Jews . . .' One could see the fear on Aunt Lilly's face. That's what they wanted: fear, desperation. Every time Hitler gave a speech, and it was broadcast over the radio—those gleeful screams of approval, like from a hundred thousand throats. Seemed they couldn't get enough of his attacks on Jews. When people hate those who have wronged them, they hate with pain. When people hate others who have done them no harm, they hate with glee. You never noticed this?"

"Frequently," she said.

"That's the beginning of the final stage of decay. Murder is the end. Maybe, if we go deep enough, if we analyse closely enough, we shall find that degenerate pride is a major component in every murder: it turns into a lust that seeks final subjugation; it thrives on killing."

*   *   *

She could feel for how long a time he had wanted to share his thoughts. And she was thinking of Pierre. And she was thinking of Sala's mother and poor Aunt Lilly, who hadn't tried to leave Germany when it was still possible because her husband, who had owned a small candy factory, was in Dachau, and she wanted to get him out. Their exact fate wasn't known, but neither had returned from the camps. . . . And she was thinking of a grey, featureless, ghostly throng of people who had been like her, feeling and loving and wanting to live. A large wave had fanned out from the wake of an incoming ship and splashed against a nearby chunk of cement. If it could wash it all away, Eve thought. To undo it. . . . She attempted to deal with an undercurrent worry that became increasingly bothersome, and suddenly it precipitated itself into a wild, extremely repugnant thought. Jacob could not recall ever having seen such anger in her eyes.

She started not quite knowing how to spit it out, but it came quickly. "So there we have it! It's a defect in the psyche, then!" she started accusingly, her agitation mounting. "People's pride is injured, they overcompensate, and—zoom!—it starts rolling, and they don't know when enough is enough! It's like a sickness, then! People aren't to blame. . . . ."

"You forget, people do have antidotes," he said as quietly as possible, not entirely sure where she was heading.

She stood there aflame. "Yes? But what if the antidotes aren't available? What if someone's intelligence is closer to the apes than to a really human being? Not enough intelligence. No reasoning power. What if someone's too backward for compassion? Don't we have to pity him rather than execrate him—the way we pity a rabid dog?" Jacob made an effort to interrupt, but she didn't even take it in. "There's no need for hate anywhere, then!" She raised her voice even more and no longer tried to hold back the tears. "This should be a relief, I suppose. But it isn't!—Sorry," she added, "but I'm not ready for this at all. Especially not when I think of the *Shoah*. This is too cold for me!" It was like a solemn declaration. An oath of allegiance. A forging in fire. "If I couldn't hate the man who murdered Sala's mother, I should hate myself! I should despise myself. My body would revolt, I should get ill. When you think it to the end, your theory absolves every criminal of responsibility."

"No!" Jacob felt an unpleasant shudder going down his spine. He said, "I understand why you are afraid: a handy excuse—for everybody! But this is not how I see it. Some very penetrating minds have taken this position. But it is not mine." Her accusation was injurious. "It can never be mine. Never."

She waited silently. She deeply wanted to be rescued.

"There are differences," Jacob said firmly, precluding interruption. "Is an elephant guilty when he flees from a rifle shot and tramples a child? If a man grew up, let us say, among headhunters and had no outside influence at all, can I hate him when he attacks and murders someone? I'd look upon him with horror but also with pity; as I regard a rabid dog. Some people are born unable to feel for others. Sometimes a brutal environment makes them emotional cripples. Such people I cannot hate. That's accident, coincidental circumstances. But at the other end of the scale, when someone had the advantages—Leviticus: 'Love thy neighbour', table manners, Enlightenment, bathtubs, democracy—and demonstrates that in daily life he is quite capable of civilized behaviour, even with strangers, even with his dog; when neither hunger nor a gun at his throat forces his action; when he shows that he can make sophisticated decisions and is rational in every other way; when such a one goes out and indulges in fiendishness, I cannot but believe that he has at least a measure of choice. We call it 'free will.' And so, I do hold the Nazis and other such types responsible for what they did." Jacob took a deep breath. He had weathered her accusation. He wanted to relax. But she was flushed and still anguished. What is wrong now? he wondered impatiently.

"If there is free will and guilt, then there ought to be punishment," she said with hostility. "I suspect there isn't any of this in your theory, is there! Does nature care about justice? And the Originating Existence?"

"Justice," Jacob murmured, disconcerted and worried, "Justice. . . . Yes, I do think there is justice. When people overeat they get sick. And nature does bring about justice through the human brain. We make laws to restrain criminals."

"Restrain a murderer?" Tears made wet streaks on her face. "Restrain him? This is justice? I think it's an affront to the victim!" Her anger was taking hold of her altogether. "I don't care if what I want is called 'revenge'! I don't care!" she cried. "Christians at least can believe in hell. I wish I could believe there is a hell! If there can't be any justice. . . ." It had never hit her with such ferocity.

Jacob kept his voice low on purpose; and it wasn't just to calm Eve but for himself, too. He needed a tight reign on his own emotions. "I agree with you," he said. "For the worst kind of murder, the perpetrator deserves to die. I have no doubt of this at all. It's only that absolutely nothing can ever atone for the murder of innocent life."

"So we just sit back—"

"What will you have? Shall we allow a damned scoundrel to contaminate us with his crime?" Jacob asked. "Let him make us killers also, when we don't have the one valid excuse that we are killing in immediate defence of life?"

"So, in your opinion, we just have to sit back and make peace with the fact that the victim got the short end of the stick! 'Too bad, chum! You've had it!'" She was trembling. Outraged.

This was the most difficult thing. It was important. Jacob straightened his back and felt professorial. One had in oneself the responsibility of judge and jury—even here in private conversation. One spoke on behalf of the victims, and ultimately, an integrity in remembering them could be served only if one judged nobly, with a cold, unswerving objectivity that looked beyond the crime without and the emotions within.

He said: "In lands where there is capital punishment and murderers are executed, sooner or later—even with the best judiciary on the planet, even with the most advanced and careful screening by state-of-the-art technology and the most conscientiously designed safeguards—as surely as I am speaking to you now—sooner or later in such lands, a mistake will be made and an innocent person will be executed, murdered by the law. It's inevitable. And then, whoever accepted the risk is no better than a murderer. The risk that an innocent person will be executed *cannot* be eliminated."

"I do understand this, I do agree. . . ." She was sobbing now and choked with her dilemma. It was descending on her, the ghastly realization that if Jacob was right—and she knew he was: completely, hopelessly right—then justice was impossible; then the most outrageous murder could never be avenged, the universe could never be returned to something like an equilibrium. The entire cosmos was forever out of balance.

* * *

She didn't know where these thoughts came from or why she had them. It was just as if all of her had suddenly been burdened intolerably. Killers—in jail for a while, drinking their coffee, talking to psychiatrists, watching TV, and off they go—laughing maybe. And sometimes even this miserable semblance of punishment doesn't catch up with them. And their victims—defeated, deprived of their moment of sky forever. Forever. . . . "I wish I could believe in hell!" she screamed, helpless now in her fury. It was as if a swirling, menacing darkness, a triumphant evil were sweeping over her. And as Jacob was bending toward her, alarmed, she buried her head against his neck, and for a moment remembered a woman she had met on a bus, a woman from Kansas who told her the way to protect yourself in the path of a tornado was to press your body into a hollow of the earth . . . and she pressed her face into the hollow under his chin, not caring at all though some young people were strolling by at no great distance and could see them there sitting on the log in an embrace. "I can't be without justice," she whispered. "I can't . . . I can't . . . I can't. . . ."

Jacob held her to himself. His own speculation had not reached this far, had not, ultimately, included this issue. Now he asked himself whether, perhaps, he had shied away from the question of justice because in him, too, resided this offended craving for it, and it was difficult to imagine how in the universe, as he saw it, there could be adequate retribution for the murder of innocent life.

He understood her and pitied her, and as he held her, wanted to enfold her, make a shell for her—and found that he was recalling something—like a faint streak of light from his youth or a liberating dream that had survived into the morning and had taken on concrete shape.

"If someone has committed a heinous crime and has not made up for it—and murder, of course, is a crime for which compensation is impossible—for such a one there is punishment quite apart from human laws."

She looked up—questioning and extricating herself from his

arms. He let her go. He was looking ahead now, speaking more to the air and the steel-blue waves and the North Shore bungalows on the mountain slopes across Burrard Inlet, speaking as if he wanted his explanation (definition? statement? message?) to reach a world gone, and a world formed and forming itself at this moment, and a world yet unborn, and speaking as in a ground swell to rid himself of the pain that was her pain, too.

"When people give in to their lust for power, they want to grind their fellow beings into the dust. They want to be elevated through the debasement of others. But retribution is built into their action; for, in truth, the action debases, and in the case of murder, debases beyond all cosmic dimension. To murder is to be in total opposition to Originating Existence. And this is true death, invalidated being. This is ultimate, perpetual dishonour . . . ."

She looked puzzled, "Perpetual?"

"Yes, perpetual, forever," said Jacob. "When I was an undergraduate, there was an old philosophy professor, a Russian by the name of Maslow, who told us of Parmenides and his theory that nothing ever moves or changes. And I couldn't understand this, and I plagued him with questions. And at last he said, 'Imagine you are looking at a film. Everything moves, everything changes all the time. But you could take the film out of the projector and put it flat on the table, and then you would have a lot of unchanging individual pictures. If you imagine a mind looking at the universe from the outside, you can imagine such a mind could observe each moment, each infinitesimal segment of events as a separate entity which can never be changed.'"

There was a slight tremor in his voice, and instinctively, she was reaching to hold him, but he moved free and stood up.

"I go on from this: Real murder can never be erased, and there can't be anything to balance it, as there might be with other actions that can be atoned for. The body of the murderer, the form that has destroyed its divine heritage, dissolves, and the particles are free again of its taint; like a rotting branch that has fallen off the tree and turns again into wholesome soil. But the fact of its degradation, the loathsomeness of it, the squandering of selfhood, the limitless failure—this will be always be there, a permanent component of reality."

He paused. Her eyes told him: I understand. I accept.

"And maybe," he continued, "maybe there will come a time when humanity will be sensitized to the profundity of this shame and see in it the incommutable punishment that it truly is."

She doubted such a time would ever come; but she was calm now. The tornado had disintegrated.

And Jacob felt as if a great calm were spreading through every artery and every vein and every tiny vessel of his body.

*   *   *

Eve picked up his jacket from the sand and shook it out and handed it to him. Then she touched the braid that was fastened in a twist at the back of her head. In Jacob's arms it had come loose, and she took out the hairpins and put them in a pocket of her denim skirt, and with a few swift motions of her hands undid the braid, knowing that he liked it when the freedom and fullness of her long hair were allowed to frame her face. Then she got up. Resolutely.

They resumed their walk, and she was trying to make up her mind about some of the things he had said to her, but it was leading her into her own thoughts. She stopped, and they were facing each other and reaching toward each other with a new completeness.

"We Jews have always believed God is all-powerful," she said, and before Jacob could reply, she took his hands and as she spoke sought agreement in his eyes. "Nature fights what opposes its creativity," she said. "Isn't that so? Plagues are conquered. Tyrannies disintegrate. The combat continues. When we say God is all-powerful, we are expressing the trust that the Originating Existence will be triumphant in the end. Don't you agree?"

*   *   *

They walked briskly now, and he was holding her close, his right arm around her shoulders.

"My eloquent darling."

She laughed: "Being married for decades to Professor Harald. That's what it does to one."

The shore wind, coming up strong now, was blowing her long, softly greying hair. A vacationing couple from Dawson, who perched on the trunk of an uprooted, sun-bleached elm, thought she looked eccentric, but when they noticed how the man at her side glanced down at her and smiled, they decided there had to be more to the woman than met the eye. And the sight of the two strangers passing them on the beach suddenly made them look at each other.

VIII

It was remarkable that during the speculations, musings, and gropings of recent months, Jacob had not been thinking of Pierre at all. Now that he knew what it was he ought to have told him, the old aching memory of that long-ago weekend returned. Usually, to be exact, it was no longer the same remorseful pain. He knew he did not have, then, the clear conviction of the present. His brusqueness had resulted mostly from his own helplessness. So the aching regret was replaced by a persistent longing for another chance. Only sometimes, rarely, out of a dreaded abyss, a faint voice asked: couldn't you have *talked* to him? Even ignorantly?

He searched for Pierre in the Vancouver telephone directory; and in Victoria, where they had gone for a few days to explore the island, he found Eve with the local directory open. She was looking at the names under "R." Wherever they went, they never forgot to check. One could never tell. Pierre could have settled down in some outlying community. They might find him as a store clerk in Port Alberni or in Campbell River. And they did not confess, even to themselves, how unlikely that was.

* * *

The Haralds had decided to enjoy the spring and early summer of the coast. They were renting a small, furnished apartment in the Kitsilano district, not very far from the waterfront, so that they had adequate privacy and yet could be in easy contact with the children. Above all, they wanted Sharon to get to know them better. There was in them a certain jealous anxiety that she might come to feel closer to Ronny's parents, who were planning a two-month visit later in the year.

Susan was pregnant, and this proved to have a beneficial influence on the timbre of their relationship. There was a truce between Susan and her mother, brought about mainly by a determined forbearance on Eve's part. Susan certainly had all the jargon currently in vogue, and occasionally Eve had to hold on tight to prevent herself from flaring up again.

Sometimes it required superhuman efforts; as for instance when Susan reported reading in a magazine that feminist groups were circulating memos among female teachers and university professors, demanding that they refrain from using words like "seminal" and "emasculate" because such expressions implied masculine superiority. Susan seemed genuinely hurt when her father answered this juicy tidbit of information with nothing but a loud guffaw. Ronny, mercifully, was not present at the time. Perhaps her goading was a show of loyalty to her friends. Quite possibly it was a quirky symptom of the confused fears Alice had wakened in her, a frame of mind that regarded assertiveness as a duty, even when there seemed to be no special need for it. Her parents wondered but knew of no magic to counter the spell and felt inadequate. In another climate, Susan might have found all the solutions in Ron's arms. But the climate of now was not propitious, and hypnotised by a phantom problem, she seemed to be hurling herself right into its maw, causing it to become real.

Only once Eve "fell off the wagon," as she later apologetically said to Jacob, contrite over the collapse of her good intentions. "And it wasn't at all necessary," she said. Susan, who was a conscientious environmentalist, had brought home one of those fashionable plastic Teenage Mutant Ninja Turtles that the kids were so crazy about, a disconcerting creature with a human body, six insect limbs, and a startling hippopotamus-like grimace for a face. She had told Sharon the heart-rending story of how some perfectly nice, peaceful little turtles were overtaken by a nuclear accident, and how their DNA had been damaged and began to mutate. "This is why they have become so ugly," she explained, knowing full well that her explanation was in the nature of a shortcut leading things *ad absurdum* from a scientist's point of view though it was undoubtedly more tailored to fit the mind of a little girl of Sharon's age.

"And we must love them specially," she said, "just because they are so ugly, and because they are the victims of very bad men who use nuclear reactors to produce electricity, which in itself isn't very healthful, either.... So we must try and develop solar energy as soon as we possibly can...." She exhorted Sharon to embrace the unfortunate critter. And Sharon pressed it dutifully to her chest; and then put it aside and hugged her favourite, silky teddy bear, the one with the cute smile. Susan scrutinized her daughter with deep furrows in her brow. "I am raising a shallow, callous little no-goodnik."

"She hasn't a clue what you are talking about," said Eve.

"I know," Susan admitted. "But you can't start too early with an awareness program."

"Let her be a child! For goodness sake, let her be a child!" Eve called out, drawing Sharon to herself, teddy bear and all. They had quite a debate concerning this. "Your father and I protected you when you were little, and you've grown to be a compassionate woman," Eve remonstrated, trying to mix in a little honey. But Susan came up with her usual irritating trump: "Today things are different...."

*   *   *

Eve was intent on making amends. "I'd like to say something to her that will please her. I've been thinking...." she said. "She keeps on talking of how religion discriminates against women. I suppose it's true in some places.... But why she objects so much when God is referred to as He, I'll never quite understand. When people were surrounded by hostile tribes, didn't they need a protector who was strong and able to fight for them? It wasn't a woman they could look to in times of stress. She loves you. Why can't she think of a loving father? Anyhow, I've been thinking, couldn't we—when we refer to God, instead of using the pronoun "He" that upsets her so—use the word 'Infinite'? What do you think?"

Jacob turned this over in his mind for a moment. "Why not? Or maybe we should use other substitutions I have heard. Some make for beautiful language: *Blessed is the Lord; blessed is His glorious kingdom for ever and ever* can become *Blessed is the Ruling Spirit; blessed is the Eternal's glorious realm for ever and ever.*"

"That's great, then," Eve said, relieved she didn't have to deal with any opposition. "I'll tell Susan tomorrow. I'll tell her we'll try to use the substitutions ourselves and maybe try to persuade other people to use them also. Even in private conversation. She'll be happy we're taking her side for once."

Jacob looked at his wife with a kind of grim admiration. He didn't tell her that Alice Lombard wouldn't accept this as a compromise. If Susan was to please her friend, she'd most certainly have to substitute "She" for "He." And Alice would probably insist on keeping the use of "She" for the next four thousand years or more; after which, maybe, she'd agree that equality was achieved and that we could get away from pronouns with gender connotation. He liked to share humour and had some difficulty holding back, but he refrained from saying anything. Why grease that wheel? Only last night Susan had scandalized her mother, declaring that a woman had to be on guard constantly if she didn't want to lose her identity in marriage, and that from the outset it must be made clear that people didn't own each other.

"Poor thing . . . so much insecurity . . . ," Eve said later in the privacy of their apartment, wavering between maternal care and blunted antagonism.

"You own me." Jacob smiled with satisfaction as he said it. "And I own you."

Eve was sitting in front of the mirror in their bedroom. She let her loose hair fall over her shoulders for him to touch. "I feel free," she said. "Being one with you, I feel free. Belonging to you gives me the freedom of a tree in the sun. It's rooted where it wants to be. And it can spread itself in all directions, to its full capacity."

Her caressing visions always touched him. They appeared like wildflowers along the way. He thought she had got over her vexation, but she came back to what had preoccupied her all evening.

"This anxiety . . . this misunderstanding of independence. She thinks we haven't any stake in it. She writes us off. . . ."

"No. Just a bit overwrought," he said. "But she isn't stupid. She won't do anything to wreck her marriage, I don't think." Jacob spoke as much to convince himself as to scatter Eve's misgivings.

"I don't know. I hope you're right."

"Don't you know your own Susan?"

"I'm no longer sure." Eve was watching her husband in the mirror. "All that greedy monitoring of what she calls 'conjugal equality.' I can imagine where she got that word. . . . Sooner or later it will dry out the marriage. Eventually it will crack it open . . . ."

Jacob couldn't bear imagining his little girl in trouble. He started walking to and fro. "Maybe she can't help it. Maybe there've been too many miserable marriages around, and that brashness in her generation will cleanse something that's been going moldy."

"Can't help it. . . . !" echoed Eve, annoyed and weary.

"Maybe the thing will mellow, preserve a little of what's

been good all along and evolve." Jacob was fighting for tranquillity of mind. "Maybe it will transform itself slowly into something altogether admirable."

"And so, meanwhile, to help marriage evolve, my baby may have to pay . . . ," said Eve with asperity.

He had no words to dispel her fears and only with his body was he able to reassure her.

* * *

He remembered it with great pleasure now as he was walking down to the beach. Eve had gone out. She was driving Susan downtown for a visit to the prenatal clinic and some shopping, and while Susan was having lunch with a friend, she would take Sharon to a birthday party. So he was alone this morning. He walked along Point Grey Road. The older homes with their elevated porches were giving way to luxurious, modern villas with evidence, at times, of solar heating and hints of oriental taste. They were partly screened from passersby with healthy-looking specimens of birch and cedar and pine, Japanese maple and bamboo. Reddish buds were opening on clusters of rhodo-dendron. In the rich, dark soil of tubs and foundation beds, annuals were in strong bloom. When he came to the small, open lawn at the foot of Waterloo Street, their favourite bench at the shrubby cliff was occupied. A thin young man with intense con-centration on his face sat there writing rapidly in his ring-folder. So Jacob climbed down the stone steps to the rocks and pebbles of the beach and took off his sandals. Along the water's edge, he picked up the occasional fragment of a shell or a bit of kelp and the soft, bright green filaments of "mermaid's hair." He looked at them briefly and threw them back, not finding anything remarkable to interest him. Large rocks were piled high in places to prevent the tide from hollowing the steep shoreline. He examined the white encrustations of barnacles on a boulder, but no tight little skeleton fortress yielded to his gentle curiosity. "Don't be scared," he said. "I've had my breakfast."

Eve had been gorgeous last night. Thinking about it made him feel good everywhere in his body.

It was a warm and sunny day, but the mist of late spring hung over the water, and the mountains on the north shore of the inlet were invisible. Jacob suddenly became aware of something: it seemed intangible, like a faint condensation from the surrounding vapour. Pale and grey, barely the outline of a shape, a heron stood in the calm water. Motionless it stood there in the mist. A mere suggestion. Almost transparent. Jacob sat down on a log not to disturb it.

The comprehension how. . . . I wish I could bring it to Susan like a present. But that is not possible, unfortunately. Jacob was telling himself Tolstoy was wrong in that famous gambit when he said, *All happy marriages resemble one another.* He had always revered the old master, but this was quite simply false. No blueprint was possible. Sure, you can teach people how to paint, but ultimately, you can't teach people how to paint. . . . It was exasperating, humiliating not to be able to give this to one's own daughter. There's nothing we can do for her except stand there—like a pair of old boots. Painful sarcasm was arching his mouth.

Rector Universitatis Artium Amatoriarum Eve had once jokingly called him—my president of the University of the Arts of Love! (And wasn't it just like her to turn the poor crumbs left over from two years of high school Latin into a heartwarming dish?) He remembered it with a shadow of a laugh; touched, flattered, but quite humble, too. He hoped she said it to compliment him for being a forceful and gentle lover, and maybe it was gratitude for the manner in which they lived together, neither with a penchant to be a martyr, and yet, each placing the other ahead unstintingly, as a matter of course. How could one tell anyone how this was to be done?! It consisted of day-to-day decisions, of a fine perception of the other's nerves, idiosyncrasies, emotions. . . . But had Susan not been there to *see?* What was it with her that she was sold on such a simplistic notion of equality? Hadn't Eve always made it clear that she considered him the head of the household; and yet, could anyone have doubted that Eve was his equal, his best council, his guardian angel, possessed sometimes of a fineness of foresight more acute than his own? Had he, when all was said and done, ever made an important decision against her will? He was proud whenever he could acknowledge her superiority in this or that area. . . . Slowly he came to see the difficulty. With all this, how could he explain to Susan that in the totality of their marriage, in some fundamental, permeating sense, he had to be at the helm. There had to be in him something that Eve could look up to. He was more than Eve's buddy.

His gut knowledge in this respect was undoubtedly more enduring than contemporary politics would allow. Even public policy was taking note of the radical feminist battle cry, "Men must be re-educated and social values changed." Well, thought Jacob, I'm sure you're going to succeed in many ways. Only a man who is secretly weak and afraid to be shown up would prevent a woman from doing whatever work she is qualified to do or pay her lower wages just because of her sex. A man at peace with himself doesn't need to bolster his pride by keeping someone else down. But with this one thing you will have trouble, he thought, a lot of trouble. Annie of the musical, who abandoned her unfailing skill and let her man be champion in their sharp-shooting match so that he should love her, may be déclassé nowadays, and the noble knight on his charger who comes to rescue his damsel you may call a rusty literary cliché, but it can't really change this vital thing as far as men are concerned. It's too deep in us. Genesis has the archetype all right: when Jacob the patriarch meets Rachel at the well, he rolls away the big, heavy stone from the mouth of the well and waters her flock. In their shepherd world, he has made himself a hero in her eyes. It's an expression of his love. He never tries to impress Leah because he doesn't love her. He's an obedient husband to her. Maybe a friend. When Leah says: "You are to sleep with me," he sleeps with her. But Eros does not thrive on the plains of buddydom. Leah will never have what Rachel has: something of which the symbol is the favourite son, the handsome, wise, mysterious being in the many-coloured coat. A man will always want to be a hero for the one he loves, and conversely, most probably, he can't ever be in love where he is not allowed to be heroic. "In sex," yes; "in friendship," yes; but not happily *in love*. It's not a matter of looks, or talents, or spectacular doings: it's what a man finds he can be in his woman's eyes. . . . And you can't educate this out of existence.

They were clumsy words, quite inadequate. If he told Susan, she wouldn't receive the true message, supposing even that she were willing to listen, which she probably wasn't. I can't explain it, Jacob thought, because I lack the essential words; I who all my life have been a teacher of words.

* * *

And strangely, something that he thought was over and done with was presenting itself with new insistence. He could see Pierre's face with unaccustomed accuracy and that expression in his eyes, the earnest stillness that had so powerfully risen to the surface of his personality so many years ago—in their living room—the night Susan had clobbered him with her merciless question, "Why don't you marry Micky Boudreau?" Jacob thought he understood it now. He was certain he did.

Most probably, the only women that had ever been attracted to Pierre were like Miss Boudreau, strong, independent, efficient women, women who liked to mother their men. It probably needed a stronger man than Pierre, a man secure in his position, to accept such mothering with joy. And though Jacob rationally had to admit that he would never know what he had seen, in his guts he knew he had the truth: After Pierre had rebuked Susan's forwardness with such excessive vehemence, when he looked at her and truly saw her—it was in an elementary manly way that he longed to enfold this vulnerable bit of disheveled humanity in his arms and hold it protectively. Better than her parents, he had sensed her softness and her struggle behind the unabating, grinding show of militancy.

We've never really acknowledged it, Jacob thought, the extent to which Susan struggles to be what her friends prescribe. Quite a distance to go before an Alice Lombard would consider her life-style politically correct. The only jobs Susan had ever held were waiting at tables at the Banff Springs Hotel during summer vacations and a cushy part-time job in the interior decorating business of family friends. Fact was, she really liked looking after her kid and her beautiful house. She was impressively good at this important work. Bitterness and pity mingled in Jacob's mind. What could they do for her?

Susan was being swept away from them and their ways, carried off on the crest of an evolutionary flood. He had no illusions. He thought, if the battle cry is loud and persistent enough, the only marriage left will be Leah's kind. And is evolution going to discard then what Rachel had—what Eve and I have? he wondered with the anxiety of a man who felt he knew perfection. And is it ever possible for evolution to circumflow islands of perfection? Can it preserve what is best? Or is it all shifting in the broad, evolutionary stream?

The night was vivid again and he . . . saying, . . . Like the moon . . . when I have you like this . . . I make the sea obey me . . . and then the tidal progress storming into the soaring simultaneous moment—and he in his exhaustion too tired to move away from her . . . and Eve smiling up at him with half-closed eyes answering sleepily, Yes, I am all sea. . . . Your light suffuses me . . . and under him her body in slight motion like a wave on calmed waters.

"Evolution, you're not going to discard it," he murmured, "because it's in your nature to let the fittest survive, and of all the different kinds of union on this earth, the relationship of which Rachel's and Jacob's is the archetype must surely be the most happy, the most alive, the most fit." He was spinning out the metaphor: in time of need, it's *their* son who protects the whole tribe. In a crisis, it's what their kind of union creates that is able to rescue and preserve. . . . No, evolution won't do without this. Its direction is toward more and more life, greater intensity of life. . . .

The heron stood in patient repose: misty, graceful, slender, and entirely without motion.

Only I can't be sure, Jacob thought. Is there really a strengthening of consciousness, a lengthening of life . . .? He had to confess it: even at the point of greatest efflorescence, consciousness remains quite precarious, sustained only for a few-hours, and then sleep has to fuel it. But mankind is still young, Jacob said to himself, and he stretched his limbs in the pleasant morning air. He did it cautiously so as not to disturb the heron. A baby sleeps most of the time. Old people, by and large, don't need so much sleep. So if the ontogenesis is a short repetition of the phylogenesis, then maybe sleep will be less important in the future when humanity as a species matures. Maybe sleep will become superfluous. Maybe conscious life will become extended in this way
. . . .

But otherwise? Can nature overcome—actually overcome disintegration altogether, conquer that devilish old obstacle they call The Second Law of Thermodynamics, according to which everything there is runs down eventually and order is transformed into chaos? He remembered that he had asked some such question a long time ago, one autumn night at the lake. Neither Eve nor Pierre wanted to talk about it then, and he himself had not much to say. Today he felt better equipped to deal with it. I've gone a long way for Pierre, he thought, and all the while I was really travelling home. I have seen islands of clarity. Maybe that's as much as I can ask for. At least, now I am convinced that nature tries to overcome death.

* * *

I know it does, Jacob thought. I know it does. The very fact that I long for immortality is proof of this. Not everybody wants to live forever, but those who don't are impaired—through illness or want or weakness of some kind. Living things who are in good health and whose normal needs are met can't help wanting to continue. And where does this craving for immortality come from? As colouration of a flower is essentially present already in the genes and begins to appear when the plant comes to full bloom, so the great longing in me rises from the depth of nature—from the constructive reachings of matter, the forming tendencies of space-time, of nothingness. Yes, the Originating Existence does work toward immortality. With every stirring in the subatomic web, it is YES and YES.

A surging joy made him scoop up a handful of sand. Each grain was precious. But let's be reasonable for a moment, he admonished himself. Wanting and achieving aren't always the same thing. What hope that it will ever come to pass? Possibilities flashed by: a deathless world populated by a limited number of conscious beings who lived on plants and inorganic matter alone, evolving, changing, becoming more intelligent, sustained by an ever-rejuvenating metabolism. Perhaps somewhere in the galaxies a world like this existed even now. . . . The reverie made his lungs expand in well-being. . . . But given nature as we know it here on our planet? Is there a path we can take to escape destruction? "Let's see," Jacob said in a low voice.

* * *

Our cellular vigour may eventually increase, perhaps with the help of human ingenuity. This would prolong life. With our buoyant technology, it's no longer unreasonable to expect that science may one day protect life indefinitely. If there are too many of us, there is a real hope that we shall be able to colonize other worlds; and if overpopulation even there becomes intolerable, then conception could be discouraged. A sad future, Jacob conceded, a civilization without children. Would this not bring about a stagnation in which the very springs of human energy might wither? Not necessarily, not if our entire psychological makeup changed, he argued. The human mind has gigantic resources, an entire spectrum still unexplored.

Yet even if we colonized worlds in distant space and lived there a fulfilled life completely liberated from disease and death, could we then say we had true immortality? Would our ambitions not be frustrated in the end by changes in the universe where even the most sophisticated technology would no longer be applicable?

Maybe this is madness. Given billions of years, why should this concern me? And yet, thought Jacob, there is something in me that does care when I am presented with a cauldron full of macabre possibilities. There is something in me that cries out when I find that space may expand in all eternity and within it—an assembly of spent stars and black holes, disintegrating, drifting into irreversible desolation. Why should I weep for them? Or why should it affect me, Jacob Harald, if the material universe and space-time itself disappeared altogether, as some cosmologists say they will, crushed out of being in a cataclysmic event —billions of years from now? And yet, even in this I seek immortality, he thought. Even in this.

*   *   *

If it is true that space-time has always existed without beginning and will always exist without end and will go on in an eternal cycle expanding and contracting, driving the stars and galaxies apart, as it does at present, for untold billions of years and drawing them together again until they are crushed into one fiery explosive point whence a new expanding universe will be formed—if *this* is true, is this not immortality? Shall we not forever be part of it, of this life, of this great, luminous, pulsating Heart?

But what if it is true (as most cosmologists believe) that our universe emerged from nothingness in one spontaneous explosion and must go on forever expanding because it does not seem to hold the quantity of matter necessary for its renewal? What if it must balloon without respite, slowly unwinding, running down, turning into a vessel that contains nothing but lone particles in ever-increasing isolation; ghostly remains of burned-out stars too far apart to act upon each other, dead matter and faint energy, the vast and final dying where the glow of heat itself is inexorably extinguished and cold, unassailable night will stretch to infinity?

What if *this* is true? The ultimate spectre that looms at the end of all those clever speculations, calculations, predictions, and mathematical prognostications dripping from the mouth of computers. What if they are right? You can pack in your little optimistic dreams! Hadn't you better take a lesson and study the art of resignation after all? There are many experts eager to teach you.

"I think not," Jacob murmured to himself. If nothingness has the capacity to create a universe, is it at all probable that out of an *eternal* past, this capacity became active only once and that only this one, present universe has come into being? And if other universes were created and will be created in the future, is there not logic in the assumption that an eternally expanding universe may eventually collide with another, and that from this fusion and chaos, fresh energy may spark and new beginnings? Possibilities of salvation beckoning from the depth of ruin are probably myriad. Nature will always have solutions at the heart of its mysteries.

And even if our universe were a single phenomenon, the product of a unique birth from nothing, its matter condemned at last to perish either in an imploding conflagration, where every particle is scorched out of existence, or to linger irrevocably in a growing void until it disintegrates and vanishes forever, even then, even then we shall continue to be. For in becoming nothing, matter would dissolve into the "No-Thingness" whence it was born. Stardust returning to the womb. And what can be more alive than that from which all being originates, that which is harbour of the great Potential? And in this case, how can we ever die when we shall always be part of this eternal vitality, and united within it, at one with all we love? Reverberating in Jacob's mind were the ancient Hebrew words of liturgy and sacred hymn: *Adon Olam . . . He was, He is, He shall remain. . . .* And the questions rose in Jacob like music. Even to be able to ask them was infinite happiness.

*   *   *

And is there not also this personal kind of immortality? He remembered what he had told Eve: An evil deed is forever a non-erasable component of reality. Surely, then, we must say the same for all that is good in the world. Our good moments can never be annulled. And perhaps, because of our love, there will for ever be in the cosmos an essential contentment. Whatever supports life will always remain—part of a cosmic joy.

There will be for us, always, an immortality.

But not a conscious one! It struck him with unexpected force. Have I given up hope then, after all? Consciousness! Isn't this what we crave? Isn't it for this that we labour like mountaineers on our long evolutionary journey: We have climbed the foothills; we have traversed many perilous mountain ranges; we have descended many times after having reached a summit, falling even into the darkest abyss; but we have climbed upward again and again, reaching higher and higher peaks. . . . Is the prize nonattainable after all?

*   *   *

And still I believe, Jacob thought with all the stubbornness of his ancient heritage. On this planet, the potential of consciousness has been realized through a form of electric activity in the biological apparatus. Is it not conceivable that another way may be found to produce consciousness? Given eons of time, could mankind not discover how to organize energetic currents and matter so that a consciousness might emerge that would have no need of the biological apparatus for its articulation and maintenance? Faced with changes in the universe that make extinction of material existence inevitable, mankind may at last turn itself into a condition insubstantial but conscious. The ubiquitous, ever-present potential of consciousness would be realized in a new way where the physical limitations of matter are no longer relevant.

Jacob smiled. I am thinking science fiction. This is the unattainable. This is impossible—like the dream of Icarus . . . !

Impossible? What confounded arrogance! He looked at splinters of granite that lay scattered on the ground. Can they imagine what it is to have an orgasm? A school of little fishes, each not much longer than his thumbnail, were playing in the shallow water. Can they imagine quantum mechanics? How can I maintain that nature cannot evolve a new mode of being whose workings and joys and ecstasies are beyond my grasp?

Jacob was surprised, even amused at himself, for when he contemplated that the last generation of mankind might have the power to return to its Source redeemed, insubstantial, in a state of permanent consciousness, there was in him something like envy. That generation may attain a conscious immortality. But what about us? What about us, the countless generations on the way?

And still I believe, it said in Jacob. Throughout the cosmos, a force is at work, throbbing inside my brain, inside my heart, inside my desire—it *is* my brain, my heart, my desire and longing, the will and vigour that seek continuation of the conscious self. The thrust toward life is transcending the self. I am merely a realization of the potential. So the longing must include the wide reaches of the sky; the longing at last will be for an all-embracing consciousness. . . . Is *this* within the realm of the possible?

It was as if an echo were coming to him from very far away. It came from Tsefat in the mountains of the Galil, where the mystics had spoken of a primordial event that separated part of the light of Godhood from its Source. In this they envisaged the beginning of our world. And the sages dreamed of a process of cosmic healing, of a returning to God. It is humanity's task, they said, with good deeds to help gather the splinters of light.

*   *   *

Jacob nodded as if he had received and understood a message. "Yes," he murmured. We must help to bring about a return to the Godhood, *Tikkun olam,* the final integration of *all* the scattered lights. It is possible—YES. Even we—we of the countless generations on the way—can hope to share in the final redemption, but only if we can make our science and our technology blossom beyond the mist of our imagination's furthest borders; and if, at the same time, we use our strength to help compassion emerge as a dominant characteristic of humanity, so that it will take pity even on the soil and the grass and the very air:

In Jacob's vision, the last generation of humanity was preparing to turn itself into a mode of conscious existence unfettered by the limitations of matter. And in its final act, the act of compassion, *to keep faith with those who sleep in the dust,* as in a giant chain reaction, humanity was taking into that free and energetic state all matter within its reach, the surface of the earth and colonized planets, which comprised all its ancestry, and all the energetic currents that envelop and nourish us and pulsate through our being.

*　　*　　*

The air was getting warmer, and it felt soft and soothing against the skin. From the gardens on the cliff came the scent of early June, and it mingled with warm, soporific smells from the sand and the sea. Jacob filled his lungs with it.

He was thinking of Eve. A thousand years with you would not be enough. Not all eternity that ever was or can be.

On the opposite shore of the Inlet, floating above the mist in the morning sun, the snow-covered summit of Crown Mountain appeared. It had no substance, only a faint luminosity, a rosy glow, like the inside of a seashell.

Jacob was moving towards it. He could feel sand and the muddy silt and seaweed and small pieces of rock under his feet and cool saltwater rising about his ankles. Before him, the lithe, grey silhouette of the heron opened wings wide and strong and disappeared in the sunny haze.

At The Lake

IX

The old cottage had become one of their greatest plea-
sures. An architect, who was a friend and neighbour,
helped them add a glassed-in porch with a view of the lake and
the hills; and he saw to it that the extension did not violate the
simplicity of the modest old homestead. The Haralds were
almost as proud of this achievement as if it had been entirely
their own.

They came as often as they could, sometimes with friends,
especially in the winter. Snowploughs working their way along
the main thoroughfares ignored the winding lanes which led
through timber and farmlands down to the immaculate white
expanse of the frozen lake. So they had to leave the car in a
clearing off the highway and snowshoe in. It was a strenuous
effort, and it made every wrinkle on their faces disappear in the
glow, vanish into insignificance.

Now and then they would stop and breathe deeply and seek
the wonder and elation in each other's eyes. They were children
who cast their own enchantment over the surrounding world.
Pine and cedar and spruce and graceful junipers extending their
low branches above outcrops of rock had become exquisitely
strange under an abundance of snow that undulated softly
among the trees, was piled high in fluffy drifts clogging bushes
and underbrush, in unmeasured depth covered rivulets, trails and
stumps, and was weighing down the dark, prickly greenery like
a silent spell that kept them from knowing the secrets of the
forest. The sharp air made them glad and hungry for more.
Always for more.

And they had their great private celebration one dazzling silvery morning. All around their cottage a lacework of motionless branches and bare twigs encrusted with clear ice, bright sun rousing from each twiglet sparkling purity of crystal; and small explosions of brilliance—as if stars had settled in the glassy trees defying the sun at noon in their orange, gold, and white fire and unexpectedly, here and there, sending fierce fiery shafts of red or a piercing light—blue or violet or green— against an azure transparence above. And they felt happy in the wintery stillness of the forest, and there was in them a contained excitement. Something festive inhabited these woods in the deep, loose, untouched snow.

They built a magnificent log fire and listened to Mozart and Beethoven and Bruch and Schubert and Mendelssohn. And friends gathered around a large bowl of nuts, and flinging the shells into the hearth, watched how the sparks disintegrated crackling among the flames. They did not dream about their youth, for the present was invigorated with all the energy of bright Canadian winter days, and their conversation was to them an unending voyage of discovery and adventure.

*   *   *

In the spring they returned when the boggy lanes became passable and catkins appeared on the willows in the forest. They always came long before their neighbours opened up their cottages and started their big yearly cleaning sprees. But the spring floods made them uneasy. They wondered whether next summer the lake water would still be wholesome for swimming, and whether the sourness from the smokestacks farther west was infecting the water table that supplied their cottage. One of the beautifully crystalled maple branches, which the sun had sparked into a crescendo of glitter—the branch they had photographed in a vain attempt to catch for ever this fantastic frolic of colour and fire—had crashed under the weight of ice and landed on the roof that had been freshly shingled not so long ago, and there was much damage. Eve contemplated getting help in the house, maybe once or twice a month—she tired more easily now, even though Jacob gave her a hand with most of the chores—but the money had to go toward the repairs, and she knew she had to wait.

*　　*　　*

The telephone calls from Vancouver filled them with disquiet. Shortly after their visit, Susan had suffered a miscarriage, and there had been no other pregnancy. For a while she didn't seem to want to talk to them, but lately her calls came with greater frequency. There were hints of something about a girl in Ronny's office and the possibility of a temporary separation.

"With so much AIDS around, an adulterer is a murderer!" Eve screamed. "Go at once and have your blood tested!" She wanted to shout and shriek into the telephone, turn herself inside out.

"He didn't commit adultery. He just wants to sort things out for a while," said Susan. Calm. In a studied way. Because they knew Ron, they believed her. "If you separate, you'll make things worse," they told her; but it was no use. "Anyway, she trusts him; that's a good thing," Eve said to Jacob afterwards. But after a few minutes, she was close to tears. "Susan tells me she is quite sure Sharon will be OK because so many kids are in the same boat nowadays," she said with an angry laugh. "Poor child! That poor darling! I know she won't be. I wasn't. I remember. Susan says today things are different. But some things aren't. I remember. I know. . . ."

As best they knew, they tried to be supportive. They did not reproach. They wanted to believe that it wasn't Susan's fault, after all. When Ron was present, she had always kept her gender politics under control. But then again, Ron had fine sensibilities, and somehow, perhaps, he had become aware of the social force that was tugging Susan away from him. And yet, again, maybe Susan's mind-set had resulted from some dim perception that Ronny, for all his devotion, had never been fully hers. But it was impossible to tell. Inwardly they wept because they loved them both. "To think of the banality!" said Eve. The situation infuriated her and left Jacob vaguely disgusted and unutterably sad. "Sometimes when I think of it, my stomach feels exactly the way it did in school when I thought I had screwed up on an exam," he said.

*   *   *

The rich, pleasant voice of the radio poured endless misery into the room. It kindled outrage. It left one hanging in midair. People in faraway places taken from their homes and vanishing in the night. Refugees clamouring for respite. Floods and droughts and earthquakes. Unrepentant murderers wheeling and dealing with men in high places. Unmentionable tortures inflicted on political internees. People sold into slavery—even now, even today. And wars—mad, senseless, rabid murder polluting the earth, even as the products of stupidity and greed were polluting the water and the soil and the air and all that depended on them.

And the Haralds wrote concerned letters of protest and entreaty about this and that, and they sent them all over the world: to editors, to politicians. And they sent their absurd little contributions to a vast number of charitable organizations . . . and they felt small; a tiny island of selfhood among torrents of confusion washing over spongy, treacherous ground.

The rains kept falling. Could this be acid rain? The mice had made their nest in a kitchen drawer; and something had gnawed at the garden gate and had badly scratched the front door. But they kept going. "We sing in the dark," said Eve, "because we know there is plenty of flint around. Maybe sooner or later someone will find it and strike fire." Jacob liked that. "Thank you for putting it this way," he said. And within them glowed the knowing of a Strength that beckoned with immeasurable possibility of life. And so they continued.

* * *

They were alone after lunch, and they settled down in the comfortable chairs where they had a view from the glassed-in porch. Eve was knitting a sweater of Cowichan wool. She was hurting because Berni's contract had not been renewed. The government was reducing grants. Programs had to be slashed. Those who had come last were the first to go. Berni said he wanted to stay in the North. He dreamed of teaching children with learning disabilities and of trying out new ways to teach the handicapped, or of getting a job, any kind of job, around the outports of Newfoundland or in Labrador. But the prospects were fuzzy, to put it in the gentlest terms possible, and she was hurting. Something was deeply, deeply wrong with a system that had no use for young men like Berni, and she was hurting so badly because all she could do for him was knit a sweater of heavy Cowichan wool. Her fingers lovingly plied the coarse, undyed yarn that was naturally waterproof because the Indian people of the Northwest had never subjected it to relentless processing.

She did not speak. They were silent sometimes, happy to be together in the same room. And today she knew Jacob needed the silence. He had to think it through once more.

* * *

A few days ago he had gone to the soup kitchen as usual to help with the morning's chores. The task done, he was on his way home, and he traversed the dining room to go to the parking lot.

It was here that a pain constricted his breast, a pain that brought with it a fear; and the fear was even worse than the pain, and for a moment he turned back, as if Mrs. Weymouth could have known what to do with a heart attack, that stout figure behind the counter against the violence of his pounding heart and the weakness in his knees.

At one of the long tables—he recognized the unruly hair, the sharp features and their habitually ironic expression. . . . He hurried over to him.

"Pierre! We have been worrying about you!"

The man looked up. A stranger. A man in faintly thread-bare clothes who smiled at him sourly.

"I am sorry, Jacob, I should have written. But you know. . . ." His plate was half cleared, and he seemed anxious not to let the remaining food get cold.

There was no space left at the table and no extra chair he could have pulled close. People were eating silently. Some were measuring Jacob with curiosity and made him feel uncomfortable.

"Please, do finish in peace. Don't let me hurry you. I'll wait over there near the counter. I'm so glad to see you. We have to talk. . . ."

Pierre continued his meal. He ate slowly, steadily, conscientiously. Jacob watched him from a distance. He saw Pierre's profile. It was sharper than he remembered it. He had grown thinner, narrower, more angular. Quite seedy-looking.

Jacob didn't know what to do with himself. He walked around aimlessly between the counter where the food was being served and one of the tables, where a big woman in dungarees tried to calm her hyperactive toddler so that the fellow diners might eat their shepherd's pie undisturbed. He got into the path of people who were carrying their trays. At one point, he became aware of subdued, hostile murmur. People thought he was trying to get ahead of them in the line-up at the food counter. He did not dare leave the room in case Pierre escaped him, and at last he stepped behind the counter and busied himself, pretending he was one of the people who were serving the food. When Pierre got up and put his dishes on a trolley, Jacob rushed over to him. The embarrassment on Pierre's face was obvious and painful. Jacob thought, I should have let him leave the building. I should have pretended we ran into each other by chance. . . . But it was too late. With a rigid smile, Pierre was meeting him head-on.

"Jacob—what are *you* doing in a place like this?"

"I work here."

"Ah. A volunteer."

"Come, let's go and have coffee somewhere."

"I just finished my dinner."

"So come home with me. You must come. Eve has been worrying about you, too. She'll be so glad to see you."

"Please, give her my regards. I apologize, but I came here just for a job interview."

"And did you have it?" Pierre nodded. "How did it go?"

Pierre answered with a skeptical smile.

"I suppose you won't know for a few days. . . ."

"I think I know very well. They didn't ask me a lot of questions. I was in there for just about ten minutes, if that. The fellow ahead of me, they talked to him for almost half an hour."

Jacob said, "I'm sorry," not quite sure whether this was an appropriate reaction.

"Also, I left some things with my former landlady."

"Your books! Your violin! Your landlady told us. Eve and I came to look for you. . . ."

"I went there today. They tell me their basement was flooded last year. So. . . . Anyway. I have to get back to Toronto. Tomorrow they are going to start hiring at a plant. People will be lining up early. . . . I want to be there first thing in the morning. Maybe five in the morning or earlier."

"You've been out of work for a long time. . . .? What happened? It's so long. We really worried about you. . . ."

They were slowly walking down the street. It seemed to suit Pierre because he didn't have to look Jacob in the face. "I lost my job here, but . . . I thought I'd get on my feet soon enough. I put all I had—almost all I had—into a little doughnut and pizza place. Outside Montreal. Together with a young fellow, a graduate from a community college. He'd taken a chef's course. Everything seemed to work out fine. Slowly, of course. But fine. It was so good to have no boss. I can't tell you. I was independent for the first time. We renovated an old gas station, put in a kitchen and a bit of furniture. It wasn't a bad place. We were opposite a shopping centre. People came over to have a bite at the counter or take things home. We thought one day maybe *Chez DO-ZA* will be known all over town. . . . We even had a big sign put up: a smiling doughnut over a body that was a pizza wedge standing on its tip. It was made from glass and at night it was lit from the inside. I suppose you think that's a bit . . . tacky; but it was . . . bright, you know."

Jacob hurried in: "Oh, no. It sounds like a very attractive sign. Jolly."

"One could see it a long way off. The kids liked it. . . ."

The wistful expression on those haggard features was unbearable. Thrashing about for something reassuring, Jacob said, "Chez DO-ZA must have been a good place. A very good place.—What happened. . .?"

"The supermarket in the shopping centre took over some adjoining premises—from a store that had gone bankrupt—and they turned it into a restaurant. They had everything. Pizzas, doughnuts, full meals. And the place looked much nicer than ours. If anything, the prices were even a bit lower. Why would people cross the highway to come to us when they could. . . . Anyway, within six months we were out of business."

"And you lost the money you had invested."

"You can say that. The young fellow, my partner, he went to Edmonton. He's got a brother there who runs a little place. He's all right. But me. . . . I was working for a while in a small plant; they were making men's shoes, a very cheap line, you know, but nice. . . . They were nice shoes. . . . I was in the shipping room until we were laid off. It didn't pay them to keep the plant open. . . . I haven't been able to find a job since then."

Jacob searched his mind frantically. His friends and acquaintances were mostly academics; many of them were retired. They had no jobs to give. "I know a surgeon. Maybe he would use his influence with the hospital administration. They always need. . . ."

But Pierre interrupted him: "Save yourself the trouble. I always check out all the hospitals when I get to a place."

"But maybe with some influence. . . . I could phone the man right away."

Pierre shook his head emphatically. "Never. They are letting people go. They had to lay off staff everywhere. Lack of funds. When they hire again, these people will be their first choice. Believe me, I know."

I have to do something for him! But what? But what? If I had more time, Jacob thought, surely I can find a solution for this. "Come spend the weekend with us," he said. "We are going to the cottage. Remember? Maybe we can work out some strategy for you."

"I told you, I have to be back in Toronto."

"Then afterwards. Come and visit with us—for a few days." Jacob was distraught. He knew he should discuss such a thing with Eve, but he couldn't help himself. And at the same time, there was panic in him. How could they ever ask a man in this situation to leave their house? What if he stayed—stayed—stayed—? Aloud he said, "Eve would be delighted."

"My dear Jacob—I can't afford to take pleasure trips. When I see an ad in the paper and I think it looks promising, I just go by one means or another, regardless, but otherwise. . . ."

"We would send you the ticket . . . of course. Or we might come and drive you. . . ."

Pierre's head gave an impatient twitch. "Please . . . Jacob!"

"Forgive me. It's just that I really want you to come and visit. There is something I have been wanting to tell you for a long time. You remember that last weekend you spent with us at the cottage? You asked us a terrible question, then. You remember? Up on the bluff? It was about—about religion. You wondered how . . . why. . . . Now I believe I have an answer. I've gone such a long way to get it for you. . . . I thought maybe—it could solve. . . . It has for me."

He could not tell whether Pierre remembered. His face was impenetrable, as usual. But then, something like pain appeared as he said, "Jacob, I really do need a job. I do need a job." And for a moment Jacob thought he saw in his eyes both fear and despair. The comparison was ludicrous, of course, and yet, Jacob could not help remembering the eyes of starving Africans he had seen on the TV screen. There was a reproach, a sadness, a longing in those eyes, an overwhelming dread that life might end without having dispensed some of its immense beauty and sweetness. After a moment, Pierre seemed completely in control.

"Do you know what that arsehole of a scoundrel at one of those employment agencies said to me? He told me I should make peace with the idea that I might never work again!" Pierre gave a contemptuous, angry chuckle. For a second his nostrils extended in fury. "And I'm not sixty yet."

Jacob thought, if I had written the *Inferno*, there would have been a special punishment in it for people who destroy hope; for they create hell on earth. Usually the excuse is that they want to spare someone a disappointment. Aloud he said, "No . . . no . . . you'll be like the third little frog—You remember the story of the three little frogs?" He placed his hand on Pierre's shoulder but removed it at once.

Pierre's head twitched nervously. Impatience afflicted him like a disease. "I don't know that story." He gave no sign that he wanted to know it.

But Jacob was occupied searching his mind. "I forget where it comes from. I wish I knew. But I remember it: One dreadful night, three little frogs fell into the buttermilk, and they jumped and they jumped, and they couldn't get out. After a while the first little frog said, 'I can no more.' And he stopped jumping, and he sank to the bottom, and he drowned. The other two kept on jumping and jumping, and after a while, the second little frog said, 'I can't any more.' And he too was drowned. But the third little frog said, 'I must get out! I must get out!' And he jumped, and he jumped, and he jumped, and in the morning—the buttermilk was turned into butter, and he jumped out."

Jacob took Pierre by the arm: "You will be like that third little frog."

Pierre said, "Yes." He gave a barely audible derisive little laugh and turned away.

"How are you travelling?" asked Jacob. "Can't you come at least for tea or supper, and I'll drive you to the station or the airport."

"I can't," said Pierre. "Thanks all the same. Give my regards to Eve. I'm meeting a fellow. He's giving me a ride back to Toronto. I'll see you."

"But I have an answer—an answer to your question—that time—on the bluff. I could write it down for you. Give me your address."

Pierre's head twitched nervously: "Look, all I can do is try to live. I can't concentrate on literature—or philosophy. Maybe I should say, I can't concentrate. Period."

A bus had pulled up at the curbside. The door swung open, and Pierre jumped in before Jacob could prevent him or even say anything in reply. He stood there gazing after the clumsy bulk of the vehicle until it turned around a corner and was gone.

*   *   *

There were tears in Jacob's eyes.

Eve put aside her knitting. She got up and walked across to her husband and sat down on the rug by his chair.

In the bright silence of the room, the fire of their bodies mingled at their touch. They were looking at the sunny trees and the lake and the blue sky.

Epilogue

Letter from Eve Harald to her son, Baruch

My Dearest Son,

Your letter has given us great joy. It shows us that the good discussions we had during your all-too-short visit were important to you, and that you are formulating your views with much that we said here in mind. Your father will write to you as soon as we are back in town. He is in the garden right now, tending his beloved and, I am happy to report, quite prolific raspberry canes.

Meanwhile, I want to tell you this: your decision to call yourself Baruch pleases us immensely; and we are happily surprised also to know that during your long, dark northern winter you will, in addition to practising your fluency in Inuktitut with your old friend Joe Igutak, embark on a study of Hebrew and Jewish literature. These are vigorous signs that you want to strengthen the link that binds you to your ancestry. It seems that the recently arrived young lady doctor, with whom you plan to study, has brought with her only a lot of books for the purpose; so we sent off a set of tapes with Hebrew lessons to help you with the pronunciation.

We also realize that your new awareness makes you concerned because you wonder how you can reconcile our science-based philosophy with the Jewish tradition, which so evidently is becoming very important to you. I find your main question particularly intriguing. You ask whether the ideas which your father and I placed before you did not make all creeds superfluous; whether in adopting those ideas, one did not become simply a universalist; and was there, then, any philosophical reason left why one should profess to be a Jew.

213

I shall tell you what my own perspective is: I find it easy to reconcile our science-based philosophy with our Judaism. For what, essentially, does Judaism ask of me? To believe in the one God, who created everything; to act in favour of life, to alleviate suffering to the best of my ability; to honour The Torah, in which is enshrined the central element of our faith, *You shall love your neighbour as yourself,* the signpost leading toward a betterment of life. Everything here is in harmony with the promptings of Originating Existence. My philosophy even strengthens my Judaism because it gives me confidence that the essence of my belief in the Creator, from whom flows the life-affirming imperative, is not a myth but actuality.

Yes, when you stand in awe before the Originating Existence, when you understand the Creator's inherent thrust toward life and inherent revulsion at its degradation and destruction, then your values *are* universal, no matter what your creed, because you are standing shoulder to shoulder with all who seek to harness everywhere the powers of healing. But this does not mean that you should not express your awe and your understanding in your own family's traditional ways. Even if all the people on this earth were to share the same faith, there would, I think, still be room for a diversity in how they express it because human beings have so many different needs, so many differing talents. Many potent reasons make us want to remain what we are.

Would you, for instance, be willing to change your personality, including all the good traits of your individuality and, knowing full well that this would please an enemy, eliminate the unique you? Surely not! Nobody's self-respect would allow this. In the same way, can we abandon our collective self, when so often in our history attempts have been made to destroy us?

Of course, resistance to enemies cannot be a main reason for one's decision to remain true to oneself. Such a decision can only be based on what is best in one's tradition. I feel in mine the joyous affirmation of this life, an insistence on compassion and the glow of its inexhaustible imagination. But most importantly, beyond it all, I am proud to be allied with our ancestors who enshrined and have nurtured for millennia the great spiritual truth. Their achievement is not diminished because others, too, have found this truth. That there is goodness and beauty in other traditions is a cause for rejoicing, for our fervent salute.

My dearest son, you have spoken to us so eloquently of the issues that you feel demand your action. Tell me, then, as one who is passionately committed to the protection of our environment. Would you not go out of your way to preserve even the most inconspicuous little bird in the forest if its species were threatened with extinction? And what if it were a beautiful bird and of sweet voice? Knowing you as I do, I am certain you would, if necessary, man the barricades to preserve its habitat. And is a precious culture not deserving to remain a vital force? When I look within, my tradition offers me peace. When I look without, it beckons with infinite purpose. I know of no better means to contribute to its survival than to participate in its being and to give it of my strength and creativity.

My dear, I can sense that you feel the great fragmentation in this world, the ferment that leaves millions of people in constant flux and uncertainty. So many reaching out and so often reaching past each other.

As for us, let us attend to our way—for this we can do now and this we can give to the future—to be counted among the keepers of God's fire.

Take care of yourself, my dearest Baruch. Be well.

We embrace you with love.

Your mother,

Eve

28 September 1993

AGMV
MARQUIS
Québec, Canada
1999